VETERANS PARK

DON J. SNYDER

VETERANS PARK

A Novel

Franklin Watts
New York / Toronto / 1987

Library of Congress Cataloging-in-Publication Data
Snyder, Don J.
Veterans Park.
I. Title.
PS3569.N86V48   1987   813'.54   86-28271
ISBN 0-531-15049-6

Copyright © 1987 Don J. Snyder
All rights reserved
Printed in the United States of America
6 5 4 3 2

*The author wishes to thank
James Michener and the
Copernicus Society of America
for a fellowship that enabled
him to complete this novel*

For Erin Colleen

VETERANS PARK

PROLOGUE

At a distance, young men in uniform satisfy all our vague longings for grace and order.

Bobbi Ann Mullens watched these young men from the time she was a little girl riding on her father's tractor, wedged between his knees when he sang his song to her, the song he sang when he took her to town perched like a parrot on his arm, the song he sang like a lullaby at night in her bedroom when the windmill in the backyard sliced the moon into narrow white bars of light that fell across her blankets,

> *Take me out to the ball game,*
> *Take me out with the crowd.*
> *Buy me some peanuts and Crackerjacks,*
> *I don't care if I ever get back....*

He sang with a lost look in his eyes, and the years went by faster than anyone could believe, and then suddenly Bobbi Ann was singing it to her own child in the vastness of summer days on the outskirts of a small farming town in northern Maine where people gathered to watch baseball games at Veterans Park.

This was a fine wooden relic of a ballpark where the Cleveland Indians ran a minor league team for twenty years before baseball died in this town during World War II. Henry Sockabasin, a real Penobscot Indian from Perry, Maine, got his start here and then went on to become one of the big leagues' great stars. Babe Ruth hit five home runs once in this park in an exhibition game, and one of the Dean brothers struck out nineteen men in nine innings on a Sunday afternoon.

But then, when the Japanese attacked Pearl Harbor, the Northern League was suspended and Veterans Park was closed, its entrance boarded up and festooned with posters urging the purchase of war bonds.

During the years while Veterans Park was closed, the Department of Defense began buying up thousands of acres of farmland for the construction of an Air Force base. By 1961, Loring Air Base, the second largest Strategic Air Command unit in the country, was completed and 11,000 officers and enlisted men were assigned there.

With this activity Waterboro, Maine, became a boomtown and soon the Cleveland Indians dispatched a new minor league team. Wooden billboards along the outfield fence at Veterans Park began advertising the virtues of fertilizers and credit unions and announcing that Waterboro was the HOME OF THE 79TH BOMBER SQUADRON. Out beyond the scoreboard there were barns and silos and an elaborate network of radar towers.

Waterboro became a small city of soldiers and farmers.

As in baseball, there have been good and bad seasons for the potato farmers here, seasons of profit and loss, seasons of lean and fat. Over the years the farmers have come to Veterans Park to escape the worries and the tedium of their work. They have taken their places at the ballpark and fretted about batting averages and watched the shirtless school kids chasing down foul balls in the seats, their backs as smooth as glass, as brown as the infield dirt.

But as this summer of 1969 began, the farmers didn't know what to expect. A spring drought turned their ground as hard as iron, and many of the farm boys had left home and were dying like mad in Vietnam for a reason that was hard to understand. Though they couldn't know it, the farmers were facing the strangest summer of their lives, this last summer of the 1960s, the summer when men would walk on the moon and Senator Kennedy would drive his car off the bridge, and there would be great anger and deafening music on another farm a few hundred miles south of here in Woodstock, New York.

Bobbi Ann Mullens sat among the farmers at Veterans Park as another season began. She was the girl with long cinnamon hair and dark eyes sitting in the fifty-cent seats along the third-base line, two rows back from the roof of the home team's dugout. She was twenty-three years old this summer and not really a girl anymore, though she resisted being called anything else. "Ladies carry pocketbooks," she has proclaimed. "And women don't wear sensible shoes." Bobbi has been coming to the ballpark since she was a child because Page Mullens had an immoderate love for the game. He was the one singing to her at night in her room while the hot breeze smelling of dirt blew the curtains full at every window. He sang the tune with reverence, as if it were a hymn. He stood there in his yellowed undershirt, singing away, and the song seemed to transport him. And it was this song that ran through Bobbi Ann's head, this song and the picture of her father singing it at the foot of her bed, that summer night three years ago when a shortstop named Roy Swift undressed her in the sand pit beyond the right-field fence and made some kind of love to her there. It was Roy's last night in town, and by the time his daughter was born he was long gone.

All the young men who have ever played baseball in Waterboro, Maine, have dreamed only of leaving here, of moving up higher on the baseball ladder, closer to the big leagues.

Bobbi Ann Mullens had a life that the boys of summer only passed through.

She named her daughter Zoey in hopes of pleasing her mother, who was very fond of a book with that name in the title. Gwen Mullens was a woman with a knowledge of literature and history, a knowledge that was often reproachful of life on the potato farm. Seeking what she called "some new oxygen in my life," she enrolled in the spring of 1966 in a correspondence course in creative writing offered through the University of Maine, 150 miles to the south in Orono. She wrote her instructor long letters accompanying her lessons; she poured out her soul to him and composed poems and prose pieces telling of the horrible inertia of her life and disparaging the romantic myth of family life on a farm. The instructor took an interest in her, and in June when Gwen went to Orono to take part in a fiction writing symposium, the two of them left the university together and never came back. While Gwen was driving to Orono with her spiral notebooks next to her on the front seat of the Ford station wagon, Page was at the oak table in the kitchen talking on the telephone with the manager of the University Motor Inn where Gwen was registered to stay. Finally Page turned to Bobbi Ann and smiled. "We can write anything we want for twenty dollars," he announced. Together they quickly decided on the following greeting, which appeared in huge block letters on the neon sign of the motor inn:

**WELCOME GWEN MULLENS
THE NEXT VIRGINIA WOLFE!**

Gwen was not alone when she saw this. That evening she called home. "You made me feel like an absolute fool," she said.

For two years she sent birthday cards and cards for Christmas and Easter, cards signed, "With love, Gwen," postmarked in California, Oregon, and Pennsylvania. Then, in the autumn of 1968, she sent a long essay published in the *Pottstown Mercury* in Pottstown, Pennsylvania. Along the left-hand margin she wrote, "I hope you enjoy this. Each time I return to Maine I think of you all."

The newspaper piece was printed in italics and surrounded by a black border and entitled "The Rituals of Summer":

> *Each year from June to September we return to a small seaside colony on Frenchman Bay in Maine and content ourselves with the rituals of summer, unremarkable events in and of themselves, yet they possess a resonance and clarity for us. We forage for*

the season's wild berries, first the strawberries growing along the damp lanes, then blueberries on the hilltops and by late August blackberries out beyond the abandoned baseball field whose red picket fence leans closer to the ground each year. Along the shore we search for seaglass under a high sun, our voices calling now and then, "Green, here's green!" Or "Blue, I found blue." More seldom the call of "Red!" can be heard, and this is an occasion of considerable note, for red seaglass is extremely rare in these parts. From one spot on the shore we watch the headlights of automobiles spiraling up and down Cadillac Mountain like stars in an ever-changing constellation. There are music students in our midst studying at a summer academy and boarding at various cottages on the Point, and often we hear through the cedar trees a French horn warming up or the exasperated screech of a flute. Once we heard a violin playing to perfection "Winter" by Vivaldi; that was several summers ago and yet we seem always to expect it to happen once more at any moment. The sailboat races and the tennis matches played on fine green clay remind us of the fitness and energy of youth. Watching the teenagers as they arrive in June, we try to forecast the caprices of seasonal romance. Our first morning back this summer we saw Doctor Pike at the one-room post office. He had grown nearly blind over his 86th winter, and he had to pull me close to recognize me. Every day since that first morning we have seen him walking to the post office in half-darkness to pick up his New York Times *and*

> *to say hello to friends. He has already said to us twice, "Isn't it wonderful to be back!"*
>
> *We all draw repose and consolation from these summer rituals, for they reassure us that good things do happen in this world. And in their continuity the passage of time seems almost as effortless as memory. Here with our summer rituals we do not look ahead for something better to happen in our lives. What we have is enough.*

Page read this. "She's been here," he said with a stunned expression. "Here, in Maine."

"She's become one of the summer people," Bobbi Ann said. There was a certain derision implicit in that term. Among farmers the summer people were known to lead lives more prodigal than theirs, lives of migration and leisure.

"She's still with him," Page said.

"It could be anyone, you can't tell."

"No, but I mean by the way she writes, it's beautiful, she must have learned it from somebody." He set the page of newsprint aside and said, "She must be happy, doesn't she sound happy to you?"

A moment later Bobbi Ann said, "It was me and my baby, we scared her away from here."

Page looked up at her. He walked across the kitchen floor with an expression on his face both smile and frown. "No, no," he said taking her hand. "It wasn't you and it wasn't your baby. It was me. Next to her I was never nothing more than a scuffed boot left behind at a barn dance." Saying this he took a half-step backward and looked out through the window, out across the three hundred acres of land he was struggling to hold on to. "She was here," he said to himself. "She should have come to see us."

Bobbi Ann remembered her father in better days, summer days he shared with her when she was a girl. He would fly a homemade kite with her. They cut the kite from an old pillowcase and would sail it up on Dutton's Ridge, her father running ahead with it and Bobbi hearing the spool of string whisper between her palms. Then as the kite caught the wind she would feel it tugging at the other end of the string like something alive in her hands.

Other times he took her fishing with a pole he seemed to make out of thin air, and she felt the same sensation of life being transmitted through her hands. He taught her to hold on gently but firmly. Eventually she saw that he had tried to do the same thing for many years in his marriage to her mother. Her mother pulled hard against the margins of his influence.

After Gwen left, Page became a man who needed to be alone a great deal. He would disappear for hours at a time, vanishing from a room he had been in just a moment before. Sometimes Bobbi Ann would follow him out the back door of the kitchen, behind the house, past the wood shed and way down beyond the barn to a back field of rocks and potholes and arthritic apple trees. She would watch him take an old, tin bread box from the hollowed trunk of one tree. With the box under his arm he would turn and march in a straight line from the tree, counting out loud with each step until he reached sixty and one-half steps.

Here he would place the tin box on the ground. The box was filled with old baseballs. Bobbi Ann would follow him here and watch him take one ball at a time, gripping each carefully with two fingers across the threaded seams.

He would throw each ball and then wait until its flight had ended, waiting as if enchanted by the flight.

Almost sixty-six years old, a cap cocked on his head and a pipe in his mouth, Page Mullens was trying to teach himself how to pitch baseballs.

"I'm trying to throw curves," he said to her once. And gradually she came to see that he had this picture of himself in mind, a picture of himself arching his back, majestically sweeping his right arm high overhead and doing that little snap of the wrist and pirouette of the hips that would make the ball spin and hop.

Bobbi Ann learned that her father was a man who had a picture of himself that was a little better than the man he knew he was. It was his dream.

And it was something very much like the dream of Brad Schaffer, the tall, black-haired boy who came to town with the baseball team this spring of 1969.

Brad had dreamed all his youth of one day pitching in the big leagues, of grabbing hold of baseball to make something of his life. Now he was twenty-one years old and had just graduated from Princeton and, to his father's consternation, had passed up law school for baseball. Lanky, good looking, Brad came to Maine fighting out many big ideas in his head. All spring his mother wrote him letters from their mansion on Long Island, pleading with him to come home. "Your father forbids me to mention your name at the table," she wrote. Her letters all started out vividly and then trailed off into abstractions.

Brad's brother, Michael, had been fighting in Vietnam with the Marines since February, trying to prove something about manhood to his father, something Brad wondered about a great deal.

Brad's father was a man who believed life should be

lived only one way. He was a man who raised the flag each morning in his boxer shorts and by dusk had usually prevailed at something.

Before Brad left home, his father took him to his office in midtown Manhattan. They stood at the big glass windows looking out over the city.

"Sometimes I stand here," Mr. Schaffer said, "and I imagine that the war is over and your brother's come back home. That he's coming up the elevator in his uniform, and in a few minutes we'll be drinking Scotch and making plans."

"What kind of plans?" Brad asked.

He didn't hear or just didn't answer. He lifted his chin and gestured toward the Hudson River. "During the Revolutionary War, Washington was determined to protect this city. He had his troops hook up this elaborate system of chains, heavy iron chains draped across the river to keep the British ships out." He paused and turned away from the window.

"It's amazing," he went on. "Isn't it incredible what people will do to preserve freedom?"

Brad asked him what he wanted *him* to do.

His father looked puzzled. "Well, you'll do whatever you want to do, I guess. But I pulled some important strings to get you out of the draft and into law school, strings you only pull once."

He walked slowly from the window to his big desk. "Well, it would be pretty hard for me to swallow, Brad. I mean the whole idea that it wasn't just some colored kid from Tennessee who was getting shot at over there, but my own *brother*, while I was playing hick-town baseball."

All this spring in Maine, lying on his back at night in the Blue Top Motel, waiting for sleep to come, Brad heard voices. His father's angry voice, his brother's voice full of apprehension, his mother's lost and aimless.

From these voices Brad recoiled into himself, deep into himself. And his self-containment made him nearly untouchable on the pitcher's mound. Pitching became his nourishment, his revenge, his life.

And now, on Opening Day at Veterans Park, Brad was aware that his dream was at hand. If he pitched his heart out, he would go up, as they say in baseball. Up one step higher, maybe even up to the big leagues.

He could almost see himself boarding a train in Brownville Junction bound for Montreal, then south to Cleveland. But for now Brad Schaffer belonged to Waterboro, Maine. And he was the center of attention as he walked toward the pitcher's mound to pitch the first game of the season.

Bobbi Ann sat down the third-base line watching the new pitcher and thinking about her father, a man for whom the scent of apples or the sound of rain ticking on the tin roof of the barn was enough to redeem the world from loss and anguish. She pictured him in the apple orchard, marching off his steps, throwing his baseballs and trying to make them curve. She wondered if there was anyone else on earth who would believe that this was more than something fanciful and pointless for a sixty-five-year-old man to be doing with his time.

Soon the Eldredge boy began raising the flag in center field. The ballplayers were waiting in their dugouts, and Bobbi Ann was thinking about love, how finding love is one thing and keeping it is another. The umpire appeared from a narrow door behind home plate. He wore a policeman-blue uniform and a big chest protector that resembled a turtle shell. Bobbi's little girl crawled up on her lap. One of her shoes had come off and fallen down under the stands.

"We'll get it after the inning is over," Bobbi said. "Don't worry about it, sweetie."

Looking out to the mound, Bobbi watched the tall, black-haired pitcher take loping steps across the grass. She pulled her daughter tight against her chest and kissed the crown of her head. "We're going to have to wash your hair tonight when we get home," she said gently. And then she started singing to her as if she were singing a lullaby, "Take me out to the ball game, take me out with the crowd."

1

Late spring, early summer is a restless time for people to whom the world is revealed through desires. Bobbi sat in the bleachers holding Zoey and thinking that all her life, from as far back as she could remember, the world's impulses and her deepest responses to those impulses had registered in her body, along her skin, before traveling to her brain. Her mother had called her a sensual girl, attributing this condition to an overactive imagination. "You'll have this urge to be impulsive," Gwen had cautioned her. "You'll have to fight against it all your life."

"Me?" Bobbi said to herself today. "And what about you?" She had this picture of her mother driving away with her professor that hot day in June three years ago, driving away under the influence of similar impulses, her bare thighs sticking to his front seat.

Perhaps it was only the excitement of a new season, but today at Veterans Park Bobbi started to believe once again that she was different from the rest of the world and that providence or coincidence or something as inexplicable as God himself was taking hold of the circumstances of her life and turning her to face an extraordinary chance. She had believed this as a child; she had waited for something special to happen to her. Then, after the turmoil of adolescence and a fair share of mistakes made innocently enough under the influence of moral uncertainty, physical hungers, or hormonal chaos, Bobbi Ann lost the peculiar individuality of her youth, or so it seemed to her. Her life began to blend in with the lives lived around her. She became like everyone else in Waterboro, Maine.

"There's not a thing wrong with being average," her father said many times. "The world's held together day in and day out by mainly average people who believe in something bigger than themselves."

Bobbi Ann had only smiled back at him, a man of such unreasonable hope and goodwill and optimism that his perception of the world could not be relied upon. "Well," she went on, "I always believed that I would turn out different."

"Pepsi," he said, "it's too soon, isn't it, to know how you'll turn out?"

It was not too soon this spring afternoon to see how her father would turn out. Bobbi sat down the third-base line on Opening Day watching him drive a bright red, three-wheeled tractor around the infield with an attachment dragging along behind to smooth out the dirt in preparation for the day's game. She imagined his secret thoughts as he rode high on the tractor seat below the gazes of practically the entire citizenry of Waterboro, Maine—I'm going to get every lump out of this infield, and there won't be any surprise hops today, no balls shooting up in some kid's fresh face, causing him to look bad in front of these folks. I'm going to make it as smooth as the palm of your hand. Smooth and true. Nothing but true hops off Page Mullen's infield. Yes sir, they'd be talking soon enough, talking all through the Northern League from Burlington to Portland about how Veterans Park was the best place north of Boston to play a ball game, and when they got to discussing the conditions of the field they'd agree that the infield was a work of art. Yeah, the infield up there is truer than the New Testament. True. That's what there was to love about this game, the absolute truth of it.

Page Mullen's work was judged by how true the balls skimmed across the infield dirt and how they rolled through the grass. He was the creator of the true hops, the steady rolls. When he finished dragging the infield he lined the batter's box with white lime. Then he tied the canvas bases in place.

Baseball is a game of inches, isn't it, Pop? Nothing can be out of place. How many times have you told me, Pop? "A ball field is a living thing, like a garden or a boat in the water. And just like a boat, it's one of the things that man created and pretty much got it just right the first time, so it hasn't had to change much over the years. It was true, and it stayed true." And you care about this truth, Pop, not for yourself but for the boys. It's always the boys you're thinking of. You want them to play their best. You want to have a hand in their destiny. The kid who played second base a few seasons back, the one who could turn the double play with the quickness of a magician, he's playing on the radio now and you had something to do with his making the bigs; he used to tell you it was your infield that made him look so good. When that boy put down his glove to stop a ball that was moving like it was shot from a gun, the ball rolled true, straight as an arrow. When there weren't surprises in the way the ball rolled, then a boy could rely on instinct alone to make the play. Instinct and reflex. Something you call the "mix." "When the mix is right, the mix is right." That's your line. That's how you explain perfection in ball players.

And what about your own life, Pop? What about the mix in your life? It's been three years since Mom left, and you're still waiting for her to come back. Put your glove down in front of that assumption, Pop, and it would jump right up and hit you in the face. The truth, Pop. You can't see the truth in your own life.

But it's true, no one can drive a tractor the way Page Mullens can. Years of experience, countless hours under empty summer skies. The neat, invariable rows of potatoes running out ahead as far as you can see. Days of planting, days of harvest. But so little money, never enough money. The debt accumulating silently, the walls closing in. He is a man who always sees a way out. He always believes there is a better season coming. He has always known what to tell himself: "I just have to ride it out, wait for the darkness to pass. It's like a slump, that's all. A fellow goes for twelve games without a hit and he gets to believing that he never was able to hit the ball. You get down by two strikes in the count, and that's when you have to hold on, dig in, and wait for your pitch. Wait, wait, then slam! Out of the park. It only takes one pitch. Turn the whole game around on one swing of the bat!"

He is dreaming. The slump doesn't subside. His pitch never comes. Now he makes twelve dollars a game for taking care of the field at Veterans Park, and everybody who watches him riding around the infield on the miniature red tractor knows he's a man in debt to his eyeballs. These few dollars plus the money his daughter earns waitressing at the Blue Top Motel and Coffee Shop aren't enough to diminish the debt. Time passes. The slump goes on. The bank wants the farm. Page could sell it himself, sell it to the U.S. Air Force and maybe walk away from the deal with the shirt still on his back. But he won't sell. It's the principle of the thing. It would mean he'd given up.

Page Mullens steers the tractor over the infield with two fingers. He has the look of a man who believes this season will be a different story. My God, you can see the hope in his eyes, eyes brimming with hope. Everything is possible again at the beginning of a new season. He waved to Bobbi Ann and she waved back. Then she waved the small hand of her three-year-old daughter. Zoey was dressed like a pirate from *Peter Pan*, a red bandanna around her head. She smiled at her grandfather, and had it not been for a B-52 exploding across the sky, they would have heard Page Mullens coughing up sixty-five years of dust and fertilizer from his lungs, spitting it into a gray handkerchief.

So we believe what we need to believe, Bobbi thought.

But she had told herself that she wouldn't be fooled again, not a third time. All those years she had believed that she was different, that her life was going somewhere. Then she got herself pregnant by Roy, and then her mother left. Tricked twice.

Her mother had told her that her life *would* be special. Like the celebrated lives of the people in the books she used to read to her. People riding on unbelievable trains, people ordering whatever pleased them from the menus in fancy hotel dining rooms. This world Gwen Mullens had described as if she had once inhabited it herself, in another life, and she spoke to Bobbi Ann with rapture. She had hungered for a different life, and then she had run away perhaps to find it. And Bobbi blamed herself for the loss of her mother.

"My baby was just another bar on the windows of this house," she once told her father.

He said she was wrong. He smiled wistfully and tried to make her see otherwise. "No, no. It's you and that beautiful child that's going to bring your mother back here. One morning she's going to wake up, and all around her everything's going to be real still and quiet. And just plain empty, sweetie. And your mother's going to wish to God that her life was filled with something she can't find in any of her books.

"I know how it's going to be because I can tell you, a person lives her life and dies, and that's all there is unless she has children left behind to remember something good about her. And by the time your mother decides to come back to us I'll have a way figured out to get us out from under all this debt so we can say to her, 'You see, we did okay.' "

When her father talked this way Bobbi thought of him as an old man, a foolish old man. But watching him sitting high on the red tractor this spring afternoon she held her daughter close to her chest and, for a moment, was filled with hope, the kind of hope that stands up against the most dismal and unassailable facts of life, hope that says that despite all the bad in this world, despite the runs that have been scored against you, you are going to have some good innings before everything is said and done.

Opening day at Veterans Park. A new season. A whole new story beginning. It was enough to bring a smile to her lips. It was enough to make her think once again that her life might be special after all. After all the mistakes, after all the bad luck, after all the sin.

I am like you, Pop, she thought to herself. She looked out at him once more. But only a little like you. I won't be fooled again.

She rocked her baby back and forth and kissed the top of her head, which was as soft as corn silk. She thought, Zoey, when you grow up you must see things as they really are. You must not fool yourself.

Across the bleachers she spotted Noel Libby. Countless Sunday mornings, from the beginning of time, Bobbi had seen him in church when she was a girl, before she and her father stopped going to church. She had seen Noel Libby grow fatter in his pew, his bald spot enlarging from Sunday to Sunday, from year to year. He had often patted the top of her head while reaching to shake her father's hand. "Page," he would say, nodding, and then he would say something about the weather and finally something about her, something like, "She's shooting up like a weed, isn't she?"

Last month she sat in Noel Libby's office at the Pine Tree Credit Bureau while he told her about her father's financial situation. He had called her in. He sat in a swivel chair, rocking from side to side. He looked over a glass-topped desk on which stood only a small calendar and two long, black pens stuck headfirst in a rectangular block of polished marble.

First he spoke of historical matters. "I could have got your father a fair price for the place. Then, when he refused to sell it to the Air Force, I went to bat for him. Do you know *why* I went to the effort of persuading my board of directors? Well, for *you*, as a matter of fact, Bobbi."

He seemed to want to let this fact sink in. Then he leaned back in his chair. It creaked under his weight. And for an instant, from Bobbi's perspective, his head was perfectly centered between the two black pens so that they looked like antenna or horns protruding from his skull. "Oh, not just for you. I mean, I know what it means to him to hold on to his farm. But when I made my pitch to the board I had you in mind."

Bobbi thought, First he goes to bat, then he makes a pitch. He knows nothing about the game of baseball but he uses the language in order to sound like one of the boys.

"You know we're grateful," she said.

He cut her off, raising his right hand. "No, please. I already know that. I don't want you to thank me, I only want you to know that I don't treat your"—he opened a drawer and took out a manila folder—"your *case* as just some run-of-the-mill case. I mean a man like me doesn't have the chance to save too many people, you see? So here I am wanting to save your farm." He waited for a moment, then opened the folder and said, "Well, here it is. It comes down to four hundred and eighty-four dollars and twenty-seven cents a month above what you're paying already. We have to come up with four hundred and eighty-five dollars or—"

"Eighty-four." She said.

"What?"

"Eighty-four, you said eighty-four."

He looked down. "You're right, I'm wrong. But the point is there's no way I'm going to get this past my board again. I can tell you the scenario: They'll recommend foreclosure, immediate foreclosure, put the property up for sale, and that's that. I'll strike out."

She asked, "Who's going to buy the farm? Who's the bank going to sell it to? Nobody wants a farm up here anymore."

"Well," he said, "as a matter of fact we've got a group of doctors in Bangor interested in farms in the County."

"What's a doctor going to do with our farm?"

"It gets a little complicated. But these doctors make a lot of money, taxable money, and they can use a losing proposition."

"Losing proposition?"

"For tax purposes." He closed the file.

"You're saying nobody cares if the farm loses money, it just depends whose money it is?"

He put the folder back into the desk and said, "Look, could we maybe go for a walk, talk about this outside, maybe?"

Outside they walked through the parking lot of the A&P, and in front of the red Salvation Army bin he told her there was a way out. "I can't save your father's farm." He said solemnly. "But we can buy him some time. I mean *you* can buy him some time if you want to."

He stopped to blow his nose into a white linen handkerchief that he rolled into a ball and stuffed into a rear pocket of his pants.

"What is it you want me to do?" She asked.

"No, no, I don't want you to do anything. I'm just suggesting there is something you can do, is all. I'm going out on a limb for your father, way out on a limb. I know a man, a colonel at the base who's looking to hire someone to help him in some business enterprise. He's involved in all kinds of projects. You understand."

"How do I meet him?"

"I want you to know I'm not condoning anything. I mean, we're strictly business associates. I have nothing to say about what he spends his money on. And this would have to be kept confidential, especially from your father."

"Why don't you tell me how much I could make?"

"Well, the amount I told you in the office. Enough to keep the wolves from your door."

"Four hundred and eighty-four dollars and twenty-seven cents a month?" she asked.

"You have a head for numbers, Bobbi. You should have gone off to school."

"I despise your numbers, Mr. Libby," she said. "But how do I meet this colonel friend of yours?"

She met him the next morning in his room at the Blue Top Motel. She knocked, he swung open the door. "Hello," he said. He stood without his shirt on, then turned to a large TV and said, "I'm just watching Andy Griffith, have a seat a minute, it's almost over." He roared with laughter when Barney Fife tripped and fell down the steps in front of the sheriff's office in Mayberry. He took a swig of bourbon from a bottle. "Jesus," he said, "Isn't Barney the funniest character to come out of Hollywood in the last half of the century?"

When the show was over and an advertisement began for Ivory soap, he called Bobbi closer to the bed where he sat and said, "Twirl around, will you? Twirl around a couple of times for me, why don't you?"

The world of make-believe, Bobbi thought as she watched Darcy Maynard make her way toward the third-base seats.

Darcy smiled at Zoey. "How old's your girl now?" she asked.

Bobbi looked up at her, squinting into the sunlight that poured over Darcy's shoulders. "Three and two months," she said.

"Heard nothing from her Daddy, have you?"

She didn't wait for a reply and Bobbi was grateful for this. Darcy had turned her attention to the bull pen down the left-field line, where the pitchers for the Waterboro Indians were taking their warm-up throws. "Holy cow!" she cried, and when she turned, the considerable weight of her bosom shifted in the front of her halter top. She waved Bobbi off and marched purposefully down the row of bleachers. A mob of kids straggled behind her, all crazily dressed, all looking something like Darcy but nothing like each other, really. Bobbi Ann watched as Darcy leaned out over the railing, lowering her top half and the royal blue halter top into the bull pen.

Up in the stands people began egging her on. "Show your stuff!" someone yelled. She turned and smiled a happy, toothless grin, then put her hands on her hips and did a gyration with her stomach. She looked like a belly dancer who hadn't quite recovered from abdominal surgery.

After a few minutes when the pitchers didn't respond, Darcy waved her hand deprecatingly and turned to walk back to her seat. All the children followed her haphazardly and when she sat down they clustered around her. Darcy seemed to be thinking things over. Suddenly she jumped back up and marched down the row, and this time she started yelling out at the pitchers. The fans cheered and applauded with delight as she thrust her hips to one side. She waved and smiled again at the crowd.

Bobbi Ann watched all this. Darcy was her contemporary, a girl she had known forever, a schoolmate, someone she'd shared cigarettes with behind the water tower, an encyclopedia of knowledge about boys. Now she strutted and gestured grandly to the jeering fans who knew her to be a floozy, someone whose girlhood dreams had turned to garbage. She marched the length of the bleacher seats once more, waving, flouncing. She yanked at the straps of her halter top, smiling merrily, showing her toothless gums. She was as unselfconscious as a circus clown. Spirited, hopeful, unperturbed, indomitable. People were standing. Teenage boys called out obscenities as she rotated her hips. She ignored the boys in the stands. Her eyes were on the boys in uniform, the ball players lining up in the green grass to hold their caps over their hearts while the national anthem was played over the loudspeaker. She scooped up two children, and soon there was a flock of them at her feet. Like pigeons they pestered her for food. She fed them sandwiches made of white bread and sugar.

After she had fed her children and performed her wild mating dance to no avail, she started to think of better days. She turned to Bobbi and said defiantly, "There isn't a one of them that looks good to me. They all look underfed, if you ask me. Hey, did I tell you Eddie's sending postcards to me from Nashville, Tennessee? He's writing a lot of songs in Nashville. Some of them will probably make him lots of money."

"That's great," Bobbi said.

Darcy smiled at the prospect of this prosperity, but the smile quickly slid from her lips, and she confessed that Eddie's music wasn't doing so well in Tennessee. "Oh, he just don't write nothin' people can dance to, that's all. He's got good words and all, but today you got to have a beat to make people want to get up and dance." She told one of her kids to hush up and then went on to explain the economic imperatives facing contemporary songwriters. "These records get played in bars, and when people dance they sweat, and when they sweat they get thirsty and spend more money drinking. The bars and the record companies are all in cahoots anyways. But Eddie writes sweet words in his songs. You ought to hear his songs. And anyhow, Bobbi Ann, after all these years, how is it you kept your figure so nice?"

Bobbi felt her face flushing. She slid along the wooden bench closer to Darcy so that their conversation would be less a matter for public consumption. She told Darcy that she'd just been lucky about her figure. But in Darcy's eyes there was some fleeting sign of recognition. And Bobbi was pleased to see it, for it seemed to say, "It's a lot more than luck that separates us, that makes you look good and me look like a slob, and sooner or later you're going to go on to a much bigger life than this."

And why is this so? Because Bobbi was raised by a woman from another world, a woman who read to her words much sweeter than any of the songs Eddie Turbot ever concocted, words of Flaubert and Durrell and Tolstoy.

Bobbi is meant for better things. Darcy knows this. Roy Swift knew this. Roy straddling her in the sand pit, both of them shining with sweat under the moonlight. Roy not even taking the time to get undressed and Bobbi Ann with her dress pulled up to her chin for him. Don't get me pregnant, Roy. Let's just come close, see what it's like. There is Roy not even taking the time to take off his ball cap, thinking to himself that he should be careful with this girl because she's different. But there is something he wants, and every time he looks down at Bobbi he wants it more.

"You tricked me, Roy. You said you weren't going to make love to me."

"I tried, honest."

"I won't be tricked again. Not by you or anybody else."

Bobbi folded her arms around Zoey and thought there must be some kind of God in this world, because out of that came her daughter, perfect in every way, every fingernail, every toenail completely formed. But it was the baby who made Gwen Mullens see that her daughter was destined for the same small world everyone else inhabited in Waterboro. And this was not at all the world she had prepared for her only child. She must have dreamed that the two of them would live a bigger, better, more uncommon life.

Odd, that now Bobbi Ann dreams of a better world for Zoey.

"Do you remember Lenny?" Darcy asked out of the blue.

"Sure," Bobbi said. "I remember him."

"Wasn't he somethin', the way he played third base?"

The players were on the field now. The crimson numbers on their shirts glistened in the sunlight. Their caps and shoes were right out of the boxes, no creases, not a scuff. In the stands the farmers rose to their feet, applauding. They clapped for these young princes, the boys who because of some God-given talent would go on to become different kinds of men. To lead exalted lives. They would stay at Veterans Park only long enough to prove themselves ready to move up one step higher, one step nearer the glory and honor of the big leagues.

"I'd like to get me a nice pitcher this summer," Darcy said dreamily. "One of them boys who laughs a lot." She picked a crust of bread off the bench, put it in her mouth, and chewed it with her violet gums. "Laughing is the best thing of all."

Bobbi Ann was listening to everything, the jets overhead, the applause behind her. She thought again about dreams. That dreams are only part of the trick we play on ourselves and on each other. One of the self-deceptions. A fat girl with no teeth dreams of having a pitcher who will make her laugh again. A mother with one child dreams that this child will grow up to discover a better world. A man dreams that the wife he has lost will somehow find a way back to him.

Bobbi felt Zoey's hand reach into the pocket of her blouse for a licorice square. It was just then that Bobbi looked up from her daughter's brown eyes and saw him staring at her from one end of the dugout. He looked at her from under the crimson beak of his cap, then reached slowly and adjusted the cap on his head. It was almost as if he were tipping his cap to her.

She turned away, and when she looked back, he was striding to the pitcher's mound, his glove tucked under one arm. He was rubbing a new white baseball between the palms of his hands.

When he reached the mound he paused and looked up into the sky. Bobbi could tell he was under the influence of a dream. His lips moved silently, and this, for some reason, was enough to cause Bobbi Ann, who had dug in her heels against hoping for much of anything, to pause and wonder if in a world like this things did come true, in a world where the giving and taking of love and the passage of time itself were made to feel as effortless as memory.

A wistful expression fell across Darcy Maynard's face as she stared out at the infield.

"What's the matter?" Bobbi asked her.

"Oh," she replied, "it just don't look the same no more without Lenny on third base."

2

A week passed. Each new day for the ball players was like the day before. There was another game to wait for all morning and to play all afternoon, and then the next game to think about all night.

Today's game had just ended, the home team had won, and four boys lingered in the humidity and easy pleasure of a hot shower room, one of the pleasures of early manhood. Their necks and forearms were browned from the sun. There was an echo resonating within the concrete room.

"Well, I don't know about you," a red-faced boy named Grady was saying, "but I've been walking around this town for thirty days now trying to figure out where the hell I am."

"You're in Maine," the right fielder, Woody Blake, informed him. "Vacationland."

"My ass," sneered Grady. "I've been exiled."

"You're paying your dues, mon," said Josh Duncan. He had a gash on his right hand, and when he stood back from the shower to shampoo his hair, thin lines of blood trickled down his fingers. "What d'you expect, Camelot?"

Brad recognized this voice from the next room. Two nights ago he had gone to see him. Josh Duncan, or "Emo" as he was called, had long reddish hair and a red mustache the color of oxblood shoe polish. He had a body shaped like a brick. He was the only player allowed to break the prohibition against facial hair and tattoos.

Brad sat across from him that night reading the tattoos that lined his arms. They were advertisements for Spalding's new catcher's mitt, Red Oak Chewing Tobacco, and Wrigley's Gum.

Emo was dressed in red bathing trunks and black-rimmed sunglasses. "Yeah, mon," he said of his tattoos, "I'm more like a walking billboard every season." He had a slightly confessional tone. "But a guy's got to make a living, and as much as I hate capitalism, hey, it works, mon."

Emo didn't live in the Blue Top Motel with the rest of the team. His quarters were a huge Arabian tent erected behind the scoreboard in left–center field. "Seven seasons in the minors," he explained. "The hellish bus rides turn you into a nomad. I got so I can sleep standing up. I just decided a couple years ago not to fight it anymore, you know what I mean, mon. I gave in, went with the flow, became a goddamn bedouin."

It was early evening. A plane thundered overhead, and Emo raised a finger to the sky and stopped talking. After the plane had passed, he resumed.

"I don't compete with those bitches anymore," he said. "The devil's machines sent to earth to seduce the fine young men. Bitch goddesses."

He lit a joint, assumed some kind of yoga position on the canvas floor of the tent, and said, "So, was it Princeton, mon?"

"Yeah," Brad answered.

"I hit the Ivies myself for a couple semesters. I was in a town they called New Haven, a complete misnomer. My style was severely cramped, if you get my message. I mean, mon, I wanted to learn about *life*. They were teaching something else entirely. The hallways, mon, they were lined with moribund professors in khaki trousers. Not a one of them had ever set foot in the real world with all—" he stopped to lift both hands to the canopied ceiling of his tent, then he chanted—"with all its reeking ambitions and brutally simplistic truths." When he finished he took a hit from the joint, bowed his head slowly, and exhaled two smooth jets of smoke through his nostrils. "Oh, mon," he said. He held the joint up in the air. "Thank Allah for the United States Peace Corps. Before baseball, mon, I spent two years in the corps, long enough to set up my pipeline." He laughed complacently. "I still got me a mon over there to send me the vile stuff."

"Where were you stationed?" Brad asked.

"Stationed? Now that's a good word for it. I had a choice, mon, and I went to Thailand. I'd done my research. In 1960 they had the best dope in the world in the Golden Triangle. I'm still sending regular checks to the Thai economy. Hey, it's a fair deal, is it not? They send us the blessed drug so we can dull our brains against the ravages of Western civilization. *Ç'est bien?*"

"And what do they get?"

"The Peace Corps, mon. And good old-fashioned lucre."

When Brad declined a hit off the joint Emo asked, "So where do you and I stand, mon?"

"I just thought I'd stop in and—"

"Check it out?"

"Well."

"Hey, it's cool, mon. Everybody's got to check everybody out. I saw you pitch today. Nobody ever told you about swinging your left hip on the follow-through?"

"What do you mean?"

Emo stood up. "Like this, mon. You keep that left leg stiff and you're going to burn your shoulder bad. For every action there's a reaction. I ought to write that one down someplace, leave it behind for the next generation. But I've seen it happen. A mon's pitching great one week, the next he's on the skids. That's when they come to me for assistance. I've had them lined up outside my tabernacle. Lined up, waiting for me to fix their careers. I got the Ouija board, the tarot cards, the voodoo stuff, whatever they want to try. Got a crystal ball here somewhere, mon. I know pitchers better than any other mon alive. There isn't a creature on earth more superstitious than a pitcher." Emo stopped to root through an old black trunk. He found the crystal ball and held it up for Brad to inspect. "Spike Pearson. Ever hear that name, mon?

"White Sox." Brad said. "Cy Young winner."

"Two years ago," Emo said, laughing to himself. "Mon, he was a creature to behold. When he came to see me he'd lost the pop on his fastball. Tell you this, he couldn't break a pane of glass with his fastball. He'd lost it someplace, and the top brass in Cleveland were going to wash him out of baseball entirely. Gone, a memory. He'd tried everything, you know? Wore the same pair of socks every game for two months; they stood up by themselves, ran around his room at night keeping him awake. Ah, it was awful, a disgrace.

"I had him throw to me for fifteen minutes one day. I had him stick a few pins in one of my little dolls because he had faith in that sort of action, and I don't go around disabusing anybody, I mean a mon believes what he wants to believe, right, mon? I read his right palm, I prescribed raspberry tea before bed, that's all. He got his act together."

Emo walked to the entrance of the tent, swung open the flap and tied it back, exposing a rectangle of pale blue sky. "It's all up here," he said, pointing to his temple. "Pitching is all up here in the gray matter, mon. You get your brains scrambled up by this game. It's a question, mon, of getting the right karma, getting it to work the right way for you. They say you're going to the stars. Hey, you might not need my assistance." He walked over to his metal file cabinet and pulled out a manila folder. "I got the book on you. Top brass gives me a file on all the pitchers."

Emo was a kind of resident medicine man, Brad had been told. He still caught a game or two every week, but at age twenty-nine he was too old to move up. The Indians organization kept him on the payroll because they knew young pitchers to be as jittery as Thoroughbreds, and Emo knew how to settle their nerves.

"Hey, mon," Emo said. "Don't worry about this information in your file getting beyond the walls of my humble abode. I have strict rules of confidentiality just like the headshrinks and the quacks the other teams hire. They're carpetbaggers, mon, if you don't mind me saying that. Complete frauds. They're planted in concrete, they don't have the imagination to deal with modern pitchers. I take on a whole mon's destiny. My approach is metaphysical. I'm a mystic."

He winked once at Brad. "I'll be watching you. You ever need my services, mon, you know where I hang my jock."

In the shower room Grady was saying, "Waterboro, Maine, shit. Back home I'd be lying in the sand with my head buried in a nice, friendly crotch."

Grady barked once like a dog, then turned his attention to Spenser Morgan, the slender black boy who stood alone in one corner of the shower facing the wall. "Hey, Spense," shouted Grady. "D'you get much nookie in Alabama or what?"

Brad entered the shower and stood next to Spenser.

"I'm from Georgia," Spenser said.

To Grady the differences between southern states were subtle and meaningless. "What I was referring to," he went on, "was the general nature of poontang south of the Mason-Dixon line. Black or white poontang."

Brad wanted to get Spenser off the hook. He called to Grady, "Who taught you so much about sex, the Pope or the Virgin Mary?"

This was enough to set off an avalanche of jokes and assaults on Grady's Catholicism.

Brad smiled to himself. It had been a good day. He pitched six innings of scoreless ball on his second outing as a professional pitcher. It was all unreal to him, in a way. He was walking around with the inscrutable feeling that he had someone to thank for his good fortune.

"Hey, I got the perfect name," said Ed Beem, the right fielder from Tuscon. Beem had taken it upon himself to come up with an appropriate nickname for everyone on the team. "First I was stuck on Ivy, coming from the Ivy League and all that. But after watching you mow down those suckers today, what about this: Poison."

The name was an instant hit. But it wouldn't stick. There was something aloof about Brad. He had always eluded nicknames.

Grady finally said grudgingly, "Yeah, it's better than Ivy. Ivy sucks. Plus, there's never been anybody from the Ivy League who could pitch worth shit."

Brad's eyes were fixed on Grady's Saint Christopher medallion, the silver oval outlined against his muscular chest. Brad's brother, Michael, had always worn the same saint around his neck. The Schaffer family was not Catholic but Mike wore the Saint Christopher anyway, and Brad always kidded him about it. Now, for the first time, he wondered if his brother had worn the medal as a first step toward some religious faith.

Brad never had any inclination toward religion. He never tested the efficacy of prayer. Among the things he had done without prayer were sail a twenty-four-foot wooden Herreshoff in Buzzards Bay, win the regatta twice before he turned eighteen, ski Tuckerman's Ravine in the White Mountains top to bottom without falling, pitch two no-hitters in his college baseball career, and make the all-American team in his junior and senior years.

All this he had done with modesty and with remarkable ease, as if it had been ordained that life should be this way for him. A somewhat raffish-looking boy with piercing green eyes, luminous and wide, he had dated many wonderful, bright girls, girls stunning in their looks. But none of these girls ever really captured his imagination, and when he thought back over them, their beauty seemed interchangeable and overvalued.

Standing in the shower, he recalled some of these girls, and how they had asked him about his mother, and how he had never told them about the nights of his childhood when he awoke in the darkness and knew his mother was not home, when he knew that she had been taken back to the hospital. He would go to his parents' bedroom and tell his father that he felt sick.

"What is it, your stomach?" his father would ask.

"Yes."

"Well, you'd better get to the bathroom, then."

Brad would go down the hallway and sit on the john wishing his mother were home so that she would sit with him like she did once before, balancing herself on the rim of the bathtub. That night he sat on the john long after his stomachache had passed because he liked being close to her.

Brad and his brother were always told that she had headaches. They knew these headaches were a nuisance to their father. He was a man who loved to entertain, to host parties, and to play cards. Brad had the memory of his voice waking him in the night. It was always very late, and his voice was as startling as a siren. His father would be standing at the foot of his bed, snapping on the overhead light. "Your mother's sick again. We need a fourth for bridge."

Brad's brother was never summoned to fill in.

Brad was forever protecting Mike, and this afternoon in the shower he could hear his brother's voice. It was a voice behind a smile, an innocent and trusting voice.

A scene came into Brad's head. Mike had found a travel brochure for Switzerland, and he was sitting on the dock of their summer house on Cape Cod. He was fifteen years old and the only kid who wasn't swimming. He had some condition that caused his body to cramp in cold water. Brad hung around the dock to keep him company.

"God," Mike said. "Look at these mountains for cripe's sake."

He was forever talking about traveling somewhere, and even at this age Brad could tell that this faith in the vagueness of travel would lead to something else. "When Ma gets better we have to take her to see these mountains," Mike went on.

"You're dreaming," Brad said. There was just something about the look on his brother's face that made Brad want to tell him the truth about their mother. Or perhaps it wasn't the look on his face at all but the fact that there was a whole summer ahead of them in which to heal the discomfort of the truth.

"Ma's not going to get any better," Brad said.

"Oh, yeah, her headaches will go away."

"It's booze, Mike. Ma drinks a quart of vodka a day."

Standing naked in the shower room, Brad thought back to the last time he was at home with Mike. It was in early February, and Mike had just returned from boot camp. He was a Marine. He called Brad upstairs to his room to see something.

"Take a look at this," he said. He stood at attention in his dress uniform, a marvelous blue uniform with gold buttons and slashes of white down both arms. The uniform was as dazzling as the colored photographs in the travel brochures of his youth. "So, what do you think?" he asked. "Ma says it's smashing."

"That's it," Brad said. "That's what it is."

Suddenly, as if on impulse, Mike unbuttoned the jacket and fished around under his T-shirt until he found the silver chain upon which hung his dog tags, small strips of sheet metal with his name, service number, and blood type embossed in letters that felt like Braille to Brad when he inspected them.

Below the blood type was the word RELIGION. In the space next to this word, NONE.

Soon Brad was the only one left in the locker room. He sat on a wooden bench putting on his socks and remembered that he hadn't seen Mike's Saint Christopher medal that afternoon. There was one shower still dripping on the wet cement floor, and the dripping kept the cadence of his father's admonition to him for the last year of his life. "Don't be an actor, Brad. Don't ever be an actor."

What in God's name had he meant by that, anyway?

Brad lay back on the wooden bench wondering why it was that he had only once confronted his father. As he recalled the confrontation he wondered if he had enlarged it in his memory to favor himself.

"Make me proud," his father had said.

"I want to." Brad replied.

"Don't be an actor."

"What do you want me to do?"

"You've got the chance to do anything, why not take it. Mike doesn't have that kind of chance, think of him."

"I want to play ball."

"We all do, every kid in America wants to play baseball. I don't think you understand what's going on here. I need your help."

"I can't help you, Dad."

"What about the firm?"

"Your law firm? You've got enough actors there already."

The rest Brad couldn't remember. But he thought he'd gotten in the last word. A small victory.

He finished dressing, then passed the equipment room where he tossed his wet towel into a canvas cart on wheels.

"You shut them down out there today, kid," yelled Tubby Francis, the team trainer. A shadeless light bulb hung over his bald head. "Any stiffness in that shoulder?"

"Feels fine," Brad said.

"Put some ice on it anyway."

Behind Tubby another man entered from a side door. He carried a bundle of laundry. "Hey," Tubby called out to him. "I want you to say hello to Brad Schaffer here."

The man set down his laundry and walked toward Brad with a smile on his face. He took Brad's hand and shook it.

"This is Page Mullens," Tubby said. "He's going to help me out with all the maid work I gotta do taking care of you prima donnas."

A moment later, heading down the silent corridor, Brad heard Page Mullens say, "That boy's going to be a great one."

That night at the Blue Top, Brad fell asleep with a bag of ice on his shoulder and President Richard Nixon on the black-and-white television set across the room. It was after midnight when Charlie Stevens woke him. "Hey, you gotta come see this."

They walked down the concrete sidewalk that connected the motel rooms until they reached the room shared by Grady and a kid named Hempshaw from South Dakota. The room was illuminated only by the silver-gray light of the TV screen.

On the floor in the space between the twin beds, the black boy, Spenser Morgan, sat with his bare shoulders shining like marble. A girl sat next to him, and the beds were lined with other boys. Brad made out Grady, Whitcomb, Beem, and Delany.

"Come on, Darcy," someone said. "Just show him, will you?"

"We don't have all night," Grady said.

Darcy took the black boy's hand and drew it to the hem of her dress. Spenser tried to pull his hand away, but she held him. She pressed his hand up between her legs, and she smiled and took a swig of beer from a bottle. She began rocking against his hand. Spenser lowered his head. His shoulders shuddered. "Spense's gone fishing, you smell that fish," yelled Grady. "You got a fist full of catfish, boy!"

Brad's first steps felt like he was walking in his sleep. He pushed Grady out of his path and reached down and grabbed the girl by one arm. He yanked her onto her feet.

"You're spoilin all our fun," she cried.

"Where do you live?" Brad asked.

"What's it to you?"

"I'll call a cab."

"Cab? Who are you shittin', what cab are you going to call?"

"Cab! Oh, cab!" Grady hollered, "Prince Valiant needs a cab."

"We'll walk, then," Brad said.

He walked her several miles to a tar paper shack, and by this time the anger or frustration was out of her. "You can follow the railroad tracks back," she told him.

He thanked her.

"Hey," she said. "You're a pitcher, ain't you?"

She stared at him, and when he turned to walk away she asked, "Would you mind just hugging me for a sec before you leave?"

He held her. His arms were full of her, and before he stepped away she pressed herself against him and he seemed to hear the joints cracking in her pelvis and hips.

Brad ran back to town at a relaxing pace. He felt as if he could run forever. Out ahead of him light from the sky skimmed along the rails and turned them to silver. He thought once more of the shiny silver metal of his brother's dog tags.

The next morning he went to a small shop on Bristol Street where a nun watched over a meager inventory of crucifixes, rosaries, and small ceramic statues of Mary. He paid three dollars for a Saint Christopher medal and chain. She put this inside an envelope and said, "Father Hopkins has blessed everything we sell here."

Brad smiled at her and went to the post office and mailed the metal saint to Michael in Vietnam.

3

Page Mullens stood at the kitchen window holding his granddaughter in the sunlight and turning a gold wristwatch around and around on her arm. He found the watch in center field when he was mowing the grass before Sunday's doubleheader with the Pittsfield Braves. When no one claimed it in the clubhouse he brought it home for Zoey. How small her arm looked to him, how vulnerable the tiny bones in her wrist. He looked at the face of the watch, the handsome Roman numerals, the sweeping second hand. "Did somebody make this?" Zoey asked.

"Yes, somebody made it," he said. And he thought about a man, maybe a man like himself, sitting at a neat workbench, putting all the pieces together in the watch, then holding it up to one ear and smiling faintly when it started ticking.

From the window Page saw the old John Deere tractor parked at the west side of the barn where it had stalled ten months ago, breathing its last breath through a corroded set of pistons and leaking valves. Over the winter one of the tires had split apart at its seam. Page had spent most of yesterday afternoon washing the huge machine, and he hoped that by the end of the week a few potential customers would drift by and have a look. He wondered if Bobbi Ann had remembered to hang one of his For Sale signs at the Blue Top. He would ask her as soon as she came down. She slept in most mornings. Some nights she didn't get home before one in the morning, and Page liked letting her sleep late. He liked being the first one up in the morning and the one to greet Zoey as she crossed the floor in her pajamas, rubbing her eyes with one hand and dragging her blanket with the other. He liked fixing them breakfast. And he invented an assortment of games they played in the early mornings, games having to do with seeing who could be the quieter. "We don't want to wake Mommy," he would say to her. "Mommy needs her sleep."

He kissed Zoey on the end of her nose. "So, my little flower pot, did you sleep good last night?" She shook her head earnestly and said no. "You didn't sleep good? Oh, why not?" She shook her head again and told him that the airplanes had kept her awake. He had heard them himself, all through the night, waves of B-52s. He looked down at the watch again and thought of the precise movement of the parts inside it and the watchmaker's tidy workbench. He thought of the pilots in those planes, the amazing instrument panels, the blinking lights and switches. He thought of the order and grace in some men's work, and then he looked back out the window at his tractor. It appeared to be welded in place, a machine that would never move again. Scattered across his property were rusted tools and parts of old motors and half-empty cans of paint, a dismaying inventory that could make a man wonder if he'd ever had any order in his life.

He would probably have to let the tractor go for scrap iron. He thought, If I'd been able to put my hands on a thousand dollars last winter I'd have got that machine running and I'd have a crop in the ground by now. The Credit Bureau said it was throwing good money after bad.

It was a strange feeling for Page to stare out across his land and know that when this season's crop of potatoes came up it would belong to another man. He had leased 300 acres to Pete McQuinn, and even as he stood at the window with Zoey he could hear Pete's tractor clearing its lungs in the south field. Pete was a nice enough fellow. He understood how Page felt relinquishing his land.

Page knew he should have spent more time over the winter trying to repair his tractor, or trying to make arrangements with someone to borrow a machine. He wondered if he was losing ground in more ways than one. He just hadn't done much of anything on the farm since Gwen left. Three years, he thought. "Time flies away, doesn't it, Pepsi?" he whispered.

She had spotted the paper boy, Mitch Franklin, coming down the dirt road on his blue Schwinn bicycle, and she scrambled down from Page's arms and flew out the screen door to greet him. Getting the newspaper and reading the sports page was another of their morning rituals. There was a radio station in Presque Isle that carried some of the Red Sox games and at eleven o'clock gave the final scores of every game that was played. But in the morning, sitting with the box scores in the newspaper, Page could construct an entire ball game in his imagination with just a handful of figures in those printed columns.

For a few minutes this morning Page watched Zoey at

the end of the driveway. Mitch was teasing her. A week ago Page had spent an afternoon fixing the boy's front axle. He had been thrown over the handlebars when he rammed into a tree stump, and when Mitch told him about it, Page thought to himself that such a fall would have killed *him*. And yet he could almost recall a time when he would have survived, a time that seemed to belong to just another season. Maybe we always have the memory of being young and fit, he thought. But he had become timid. And he had always been more timid than Gwen. He wondered if it was because he was fifteen years older than she was or if there was something wrong with him. He was always telling her to be careful, to take it easy. She would tell him to stop worrying about her and he would say, "All right, all right." But inside he would be thinking how he just wouldn't be able to bear it if anything bad were ever to happen to her.

Page sat down in a cane rocker on the front porch, and Zoey crawled up on his lap with the *Waterboro Gazette*. He found the sports page, and then it was up to Zoey to find the story about the Indians' game. This morning there was a photograph of a baseball player swinging a bat and Zoey pointed to it and said, "Here it is, Poppy!"

Page smiled at her and said, "Nope, that's Carl Yastrzemski."

"Carl Yas—"

"Yastrzemski, the Red Sox player. You remember how I told you about the Red Sox."

"How they always lose?"

"Well. But over here, now here's our team."

It took a minute for Zoey to point out the words in the headline, which read, "Schaffer Shuts Down Pirates."

"Lord," Page muttered, "we're going to lose that boy."

"What boy?" Bobbi asked as she came through the screen

door in her flannel nightgown. Page turned to her, and she leaned down and kissed him.

"Did you remember to put up my sign about the tractor?" he asked her.

She took Zoey in her arms. "You should have a sweater on, sweetie," she said. "Yeah, I remembered. What boy, Pop?"

Page pointed to the headline. "Right there," he said. "That Schaffer boy won his fourth game last night. He has a wicked curve ball."

"The last time I saw him pitch he got it up high and was banged around pretty hard," she recalled.

"Well, he won, at least. He'll find his range."

"He has trouble getting it over for strikes against lefties," she said.

"Well he probably never saw too many lefties in college ball."

"The Ivy League?" she questioned playfully. "I thought the Ivy League was full of lefties." She said this and knew the humor would be lost on her father. He was not a man who could follow abstractions. "I'm joking about their politics," she said gently.

"What's politics got to do with baseball?" he asked. "You got in awful late."

"Two."

"Was it the Air Force men? I hope it wasn't ball players keeping you up that late."

Bobbi Ann glided across the porch through a gash of sunlight, then sat on the railing and let Zoey escape into the front lawn. She watched her. "She looks small to me sometimes, still," she said. "Whenever she runs I think she's going to fall right over."

Page began coughing, and Bobbi waited until he had

caught his breath before going on. "Last night one of them showed me a picture of Vietnam, Pop. The ocean there was beautiful. He had a picture of his friends in the waves. You'd never know there was a war."

"Oh," Page exclaimed. "I want to take you and Zoey to Bar Harbor some day this summer."

"You've been saying that every summer, Pop," she told him.

"But this summer for sure we'll go. Soon as we sell the tractor I'm going to get us a reliable car, maybe a station wagon, and off we'll go."

Bobbi watched her father savoring this idea. She was still thinking about the war. "It was on the news last night, two hundred and nineteen more killed there last week."

Page looked into her eyes and asked, "Who are they, Pepsi? Who are those boys they keep killing over there? I keep wondering who those boys are and thinking we have to do something for them."

There was a silence then and Zoey could be heard singing to herself. The sound of her voice brought a smile to Page's eyes, and Bobbi thought how lucky she was to have a father who loved her daughter the way he did. He had such a simple view of the world, and she wondered if perhaps love like his could exist in a man only if his vision had not been enlarged to include politics and philosophy and religion.

"But the ocean in that picture was so blue, Pop."

"Well, it's mighty blue down to Bar Harbor, too," he said. "Least it sure was when I took your Mama there." He looked past her, and the details of a memory seemed to come over him.

"You know they had a Ferris wheel there on the pier,

and when you were up high enough you could look out into the ocean. It was so clear and blue you felt like you could see straight to the bottom. We got stuck at the top of that Ferris wheel." He stopped suddenly. A lost look crossed his face. "I told you all this a million times already," he said.

"That's all right," she said.

"Gwen was carrying you then," he said. "I remember we went into a little store right there on the pier, and she bought some red yarn to make you a sweater. It was bright red, and I don't even know whatever happened to it unless we gave it to the Taylors after their fire, but anyway I remember looking at those two balls of red yarn, one in each of Gwen's hands, and thinking, My good Lord, we start out so small. I mean, seeing those two balls of yarn made me think how small this new life was going to be."

"I don't remember the sweater, Pop."

He looked confused. "Oh, sure you do, it came out just perfect. I know it was for you. It was the only sweater she ever made."

Bobbi waited, then walked over to him and said, "So, is there some good news in that paper today?"

He pointed at the headline. "There's a boy right there who's got nothing but good news to look forward to."

"You know which one he is?"

"Sure I do, I've spoken to him. He's tall with black hair. He's alone a lot." Page gave her the newspaper, then got up. "You know," he said, "you maybe ought to tell him what you think about his curve ball."

Bobbi shook her head slowly, raised one finger at him, and said, "That's enough, Pop."

"Well," he replied. "You know, Pepsi, you could think

about going for a ride on that Ferris wheel yourself. You don't have to wait for me or listen to me tell you what it was like."

"Pop."

"No, let me finish. I don't think you should be afraid—"

"I'm not afraid of anything, and we've been through this before."

"Well, then," he said. "I'm going to do some work in the garden."

He looked up at the sky, and she called out to him, "We need rain, Pop." He didn't say anything. He went down the steps and walked away. There were times when she hated to have him walk away. Just looking at him now she could see herself in him, in his eyes and his large hands. (She could hold three potatoes in each hand.) In the effortless way he loved Zoey. From this man she had learned to give. And from her mother she had inherited knowledge of things he would never understand. She had learned to hold herself back, in a way. These inheritances pulled her in opposite directions and filled her with ambivalence.

For a while, three years ago, Roy Swift had overcome this ambivalence.

She recalled now how her mother had spoken to her at the start of that summer when she had begun showing an interest in Roy. "I'm twenty years old," Bobbi had argued.

"Not old enough." Gwen said.

"Well, how old do you have to be?"

"Age has nothing to do with it."

"Pop says he's a nice boy."

"Well," she exclaimed with no indignation or scorn, "if you put a baseball cap on the head of a mass murderer, your father would think he was a nice boy, wouldn't he?"

Bobbi Ann remembers it all. It is just as if it happened last night. The pleasure and the guilt and fear are equally undiminished. She is on her back in the sand, and it is very late at night. I'm going to get in trouble, Roy. Trust me, Bobbi. I have to get home. In five minutes you won't care about home anymore. Trust me. He is standing over her, unfastening his trousers. The sand is damp against her skin. Then he touches her. Everything is different. It's okay, isn't it, Roy? Tell me it's okay. Don't worry, Bobbi. Just don't worry. Okay, Roy, but please take your hat off. He doesn't hear her or he hears but refuses. And all the rest is ruined for Bobbi because she can't stop thinking about what her mother said to her about the murderer in the baseball cap.

When Bobbi finally got home that night the first light of morning was threading the sky. The sky had never looked so vast and empty to her before. All her mother said to her when she saw her was, "You'd better go upstairs and take a good, hot bath."

Looking at Zoey in her father's arms, the guilt and fear and all the ambivalence seemed to have been replaced by love.

"It'll rain soon, Pop," Bobbi called out again.

But he was lost. He was looking into Zoey's eyes and he was lost in his own thoughts.

Then, from wherever he was, he began speaking. "Did I ever tell you that when we went to Bar Harbor we were pretty near the top of that Cadillac Mountain that your Mama wrote us about, that mountain where she watches the headlights."

He told Bobbi that Gwen had wanted to drive to the top but he was afraid their old station wagon wouldn't make it. "I told her we'd go back someday, all the way up."

He stopped and pulled gently on the cuffs of his shirt after he put Zoey back down. "You know, I've been trying ever since your mother sent that newspaper story to remember those lights on the mountain that she wrote about, but I can't."

"Maybe you forgot," Bobbi said.

"No, I wouldn't have forgot something like that."

Then it struck Bobbi why he had never seen the lights. As she explained to him that he was right on the mountainside and you probably had to stand off quite a ways in order to see them, he seemed to sense the irony in this, that in order for her to see what she wanted to see she had to have her distance, she had to stand away from him.

"But why," he said, "why did she pick a place to go where she could see that mountain? That mountain we went to together?"

When Bobbi didn't answer, he walked off toward the tractor and said he was going to see if he could find his hammer. He called back to them, "I raised two girls on this farm, and that's why I don't have any hammers left."

Bobbi smiled. It was true, together they had lost practically all his tools. She remembered how she had once planned to go into business building birdhouses.

She walked out in the grass and whispered for Zoey to keep still. Then she pointed out a flock of baby sparrows under a birch tree. Zoey watched for a minute, and then she told Bobbi that she knew where there was a hammer.

"Where?" Bobbi said.

"In the well."

"What's it doing in the well?"

"It fell down."

"You dropped Poppy's hammer down the well?"

"No."

"It just fell down by itself?"

"No. First Poppy hit the tractor with it, then he dropped it down the well."

"Oh." Bobbi said. She turned back to the birds.

"On the moon," Zoey said, "what kind of cereal do you get?"

"Oh, I don't know." Bobbi looked across the sky. "Where do you see the moon?"

Zoey pointed to the roof of the barn where a sliver of moon was barely visible.

"I see it now," Bobbi said. She wondered how much of her physical desire for the world she had passed on to her child, how much trouble it would cause her, whether this trouble would be outweighed by the joy of feeling connected to the natural flow of life.

Zoey talked in her ear. "Poppy said that's where he sees her, in the moon."

"When did he say that?"

"I don't know."

"What do you two talk about in the morning anyway?" She looked into her daughter's eyes.

The telephone ringing behind her shook the tiny birds out of the grass. Zoey ran out ahead to follow them. When Bobbi answered the phone, a man's voice said, "If you can come by about seven we can get this show on the road." The colonel's voice sagged under a Southern drawl as thick as syrup.

"Mr. Libby was supposed to contact me," she said.

"Contact? Hey, I like that word. This is me *contacting* you, and I'm sorry if I've interrupted anything important. Will you make it at seven?"

She gave him her answer. She hung up the telephone and stood paralyzed at a window. She watched her daughter sitting in the dirt and her father sneaking toward her from behind the tractor. He had a smile on his face. He knows nothing, Bobbi thought. She stood watching him as if she were in a trance. For a few minutes she had the feeling she would just stand there at the window without moving a muscle for the rest of her life. Just stand there watching. Her body had found its perfect balance in the dead center of this spring morning. Her father, her daughter. A past, a future. She was the link between them, her role was essential. Without her the center would not hold and they would go spinning off in hectic, hopeless orbits. At the window she said to herself, I will keep this from happening. I will keep this farm for you. The land beneath their feet was in her hands.

Much later she took a hot bath, as hot as she could stand. She lay back thinking about what was ahead, thinking about the way this colonel seemed different from the other officers who came into the coffee shop at the Blue Top Motel. Ten days ago, on the night of Opening Day at Veterans Park, she saw him for the first time. He sat alone. He stared at her, then introduced himself with a smile. He wore black-rimmed glasses as thick as ice. He had a crew cut and a handsome face. "I have a daughter just about your age," he said. He didn't look old enough to her. He told her he was only in town for forty days. "Forty days and forty nights in the wilderness," he said, "then back to hell. We'll go into production as soon as I come up with a motif."

She asked what kind of production. "We're going to shoot some movies," he said. "All the pretty girls want to be in movies, am I right or am I right?"

She walked naked through the late sunlight, her wet feet leaving prints on the pine floor. She had her mother's feet.

She looked down at the wet prints and thought how her mother could stand in them. They were similar in their nakedness. The morning her mother packed her things in the station wagon, she had worn no shoes. It was a summer day. She stayed in her bare feet from Memorial Day until fall. Bobbi had watched her that morning. She watched her carry armloads of books from the house to the car. She would need her books at the symposium at the university, Bobbi had thought, though she seemed to be taking more books than anyone could read in five days. On her last trip inside she took the German beer stein from the mantle above the fireplace in the livingroom. Bobbi watched her wrap it in a woolen sock, this blue enamel stein with its alpine chalets and snow-capped mountains. Her mother used to stare at it. You could be talking to her and suddenly she would turn her eyes to the stein and she would be silent. That day she had packed her things in the old station wagon and driven off while her footprints were still damp on the floor of her bedroom.

Bobbi dressed quickly in a pale blue sun dress. She pulled back her hair and braided it. She dressed in a timeless way, the way her mother dressed, immune to the wild fluctuations of fashion. The rest of North America was wearing bell-bottom jeans and denim shirts this summer. Her legs were bare. She could count on one hand the times she had worn stockings.

 Before the mirror she thought how it was said that farm girls were as horny as the day was long. She thought about Darcy and her passion. Then she remembered what Roy Swift had said to her: "Holy cow, Bobbi, you're like a damn time bomb."

 In the mirror she looked vulnerable and strong. Willful

and pliant, soft and defiant. The ambivalence at her interior had seeped to the surface expressing itself in physical contradictions. Her desires had gotten her in trouble with Roy Swift. It went back beyond Roy. When she was thirteen a boy had touched her for a long time beyond the water tower and she had liked it immediately, had not been able to contain her feelings. When she was touched she responded. It angered her to admit this to herself. It made her life complicated. In the mirror she made a little gesture of resignation. Then she turned away.

That evening at the Blue Top Motel the two-story concrete building was hung in mist. She passed the ball players' rooms. Muddy cleated shoes were lined up outside their doors. It was a raw evening. Summer was not yet fully established in Maine. Bobbi felt the chill on her thighs. Her nipples were hard. She thought about the boys from Texas and Georgia. How could they play ball in the cold weather? Each spring the Southern boys complained about the weather.

Colonel Ellis greeted her with a broad smile and a handshake. His hair was slicked straight back. He looked like a movie star. He wore his blue Air Force uniform. From the doorway she saw his cap folded like a dinner napkin on the nightstand next to the metal coin box for the Magic Fingers machinery buried deep within the bedsprings. The room was lit by a plastic lamp on the bureau. The shades were drawn. "Can I get you a beer?" he asked. His accent, his Southern drawl had vanished. She declined the beer. "Well, you don't mind, do you, if I help myself? And why don't you sit down right here." He gestured to a chair and she sat down. There was a long silence, and Bobbi began to suspect that she had been wrong, that her pound of flesh would surely not be taken by a man who smiled so pleasantly at her.

Suddenly he handed her an envelope. "Five hundred dollars," he said. "Go ahead, check it out." He flicked a wrist.

"It was four hundred—"

"Oh, I paid that. This is something extra. A bonus. Just stuff it inside your bra. There's more where that came from."

He walked to the bathroom, and she saw him straighten his necktie in the mirror before he leaned over and took a can of Pabst Blue Ribbon from the bathtub. When he came back into the room he sat on one corner of the bed and looked into her eyes. "I never thought I'd get used to drinking this stuff warm," he said. He raised the can and gestured to the far corner of the room where there was a pile of clothing and a stack of cardboard boxes. When she turned back to face him he said he'd been all over the county looking for things. He tipped his beer can and said, "Welcome to Mayberry."

"What are you talking about?" she asked.

"You don't watch the Andy Griffith show on TV?"

"Oh," she said.

"Well, do you watch?"

"I have."

"Well I'm looking for something that we've lost, something that will have resonance as time marches on. I thought of a bunch of acts, why don't I show you?" He put down his beer, leaped to his feet, and worked himself into a pose that was meant to approximate a man on horseback. He pulled on the brim of an imaginary cowboy hat and called out in a loud voice, "Major Reno, you stay here in the draw. I'll ride on ahead and check out that Indian encampment." He paused for a second, then by way of explanation said, "That was Custer at Little Big Horn."

He walked over to her, and she flinched when he reached past her for his can of beer. "It's all right," he said. "Nobody appreciates my sense of humor. But listen to this one. Shultz, the mad inventor." He straightened his tie again and swallowed more beer. "Zo! You call me a knucklebrain and you make fun of my leetle machine! Vell I tell you zometings. Edison vos a dreamer, Heinrich Ford vos a beeker dreamer. But zey made zeir dreams gome true! You chust vate undill I iron out a gubble small bugs!"

He laughed and then shrugged his shoulders. "I can do an Ed Sullivan routine that'll knock you off your feet, but since you're already sitting down—" He stopped and looked back into her eyes. She tried to show him no expression.

"Well," he went on. "Why don't we talk over the first scenes? And you're going to have to lighten up a little bit or this won't work. One girl, she was my best ever, she had a hard time getting started too. Don't worry. Each first time is like pulling teeth. I had to lay her down and put a pillow over one girl's face and sing to her before she could get into it; then we'd knock out five or six scenes at a clip. Like I told you, Bobbi, I only got forty days to shoot, then I'm back to Nam. Time is of the essence here." He put his hand on her knee. It was a thick, big hand and when he opened his fingers he took hold of both her knees at once. "First," he said, "I want you to know why I'm here and I want to know why you're here. It's important, I think. I mean people have the right to be understood."

She said nothing. He waited, then said, "Well, you want me to go first?"

"You know why I'm here."

"Well."

"You want me to say it? You want to make me spell it out?"

"Hey," he said. "No one's making you do anything. I'm just here trying to make a few dollars."

"Why?"

"Why? I need the money. We all need the money. *You* need the money."

"I don't care about money. I've never had any money."

"I have, but I still need more." He swallowed some of the beer, and when he set the can down on the table he nodded a few times then clapped his hands together once. "You look like a nice girl, you'll understand this. I'm forty-eight years old, and I'm going to have a son by fall, which is what I've always wanted. I mean I'm sure as toast it's going to be a boy this time even though I don't have any proof, but a man like me has a certain intuition about some things. I'm pretty old to be having a kid but that's the thing. I've got a new young wife not much older than you, and I want to put my plan into action after wasting a lot of years. I call it Plan II. I totally fucked up Plan I, with Emma and my daughter. They're lost, lost to me. But this time I'm going to do things different. I'm going to buy us a piece of land in Florida, and we're going to lie out in that sunshine while places like this rot and the people turn gray from too much cold. I'm going to build a big stucco house. I'm not talking about anything chintzy, I mean something with real wood, who cares what it costs to air-condition? A pool out back, and a courtyard with grapefruit trees and grass smooth enough to putt on. And I'll be home all the time. I'm finished in the service in eleven months, and after that I'll be making real estate investments and keeping tabs on things from my office at home. You put down some cash for a hunk of land in Florida, divide it a million times, throw up concrete houses, sell them to the Jews, and in a year, Jesus Christ, life is sweet. Can you imagine the room you'd have inside a house if you could throw away all your winter clothing? Everything light and airy. Pastel colors. And baseball, God! My kid will play year-round if he wants. We'll go to spring training games with our pockets stuffed with oranges."

He stopped and picked up his beer, brought the can to his lips, and spoke into the opening. "So, that's *my* plan. What's yours? I'm interested."

She told him she wanted to help her father keep his farm.

"Right," he said. *"That* I already know. What else?"

"Nothing else."

"No plan? That's a shame. My first wife didn't have any plans either. She got bored with the scenery and started sliding her ass around the enlisted men's barracks. If you don't have a plan in this world, you're out of control completely. And you don't have a future." While he elaborated on this he began unpacking boxes and throwing clothing onto the bed. He unwrapped an enormous painting of a pond surrounded by trees while he explained that a person with no future was something he couldn't understand.

"Excuse me," he said as he squeezed past her. He carried the desk chair above his head and set it down in front of the nightstand. He sat down, opened a briefcase, and handed Bobbi some typed pages. "Why don't you read these over," he said. Then he was back on his feet.

While he set up the camera and tape recorder she read from the top of the first page. "You must think I'm a pig," she said.

He turned and looked at her. "Not true," he said. "Not true at all." He walked over to her and opened his hands.

"Hey, this is a job for you, it's a job for me. Compared to some of the shit that goes on over there, this is Sunday school. Believe me."

He walked away to the camera saying, "You can think of this as my version of the Bob Hope show. Only I give them what Bob only alludes to. I'm more honest than Bob, and I'd also like to think I'm a hell of a lot more classy than he is. I give them a class operation. I put a lot of time and energy into my act. I could sell them sleazy stuff, they wouldn't care. I draw the line against sleaze and chintzy stuff. There's too much of both around."

She waited while he hung up the painting of the pond then took the mattress off the bed and laid it on the floor in front of the painting.

"You don't have any moral virtue," Bobbi Ann said.

"It's a matter of degrees," he replied. "Delicate degrees. But, hey, you can leave any time, Bobbi baby. I wouldn't think of it in terms of any morality, I'd think of it as a story. An American story, I guess. The story of Mayberry, USA, where everyone is honest and clean cut and nobody offends anybody on purpose and there's no greed to be found until you look close enough and you find out that Barney's queer and Andy's on the take and Barney's girlfriend, Thelma Lou, has been humping truck drivers at Goober's garage. The place is just like any other place in America. And that's the trouble with America, people in America think they can export all the shit to some other part of the world and keep it there, but they're wrong, the shit is everywhere. Even in Mayberry you can't walk outside without getting it on your shoes."

He handed her a red checkered dress and asked her to put it on. "You can dress in the bathroom if you want. But don't wear your bra up top. And keep the panties on."

Bobbi hesitated. He said, "You should think of me as an artist, like someone out in Hollywood. I just have a job to do. The things you're going to do in front of the camera, hey, I've seen them all a hundred times, believe me. And I wrote the damn scripts. It's like cooking a big meal. You spend all day over a hot oven and you lose your appetite. The thrill is gone, so to speak."

"What about my face?" Bobbi asked him.

"You've got a beautiful face."

"I don't want people to see it."

He straightened his glasses on the bridge of his nose.

"Without your face," he said, "I don't get to Florida." He explained that his films were for officers in Saigon, and officers expected a pretty American face. "As a matter of fact, you could say the face is the most important part. I mean there are thousands of girls over there who could use a few extra bucks and would do anything you asked them to do. But they're the enemy, you understand? They've got slanted eyes, and so no matter whose side they're on, down deep they're the enemy because they *look* like the enemy. Anybody who doesn't look like an American is the enemy. These officers pay good money to see your sweet American eyes looking right at them."

He positioned her on the mattress in front of the pond. He read the script out loud line by line, then taped her voice as she repeated them. She could hear his camera purring. When the speaking was over the rest was just a matter of gasping and panting like a dog while she touched herself and took off her clothes. When she hesitated, he called out, "Come on, Bobbi baby. We're making a movie here!"

When it was over and Bobbi was dressed and ready to go, he said she was going to have to work on the ending.

"I mean, you know, the orgasm was really shaky, and that's the part we can't afford to fuck up."

At the door he put his arms around her suddenly and started kissing her neck. When she pulled away he said, "I thought maybe you might want me to teach you some things." He had rediscovered his southern drawl.

"I only want your money," she told him.

When she was out the door he called after her, "No offense." And then in his W.C. Fields voice, "Hey, how do you like children? Medium rare, thank you, medium rare."

On the way home that night after cleaning tables at the coffee shop Bobbi stopped at Tilton's Pond. She let her bicycle fall in the grass and then walked into the water up to her armpits. It was cold enough to stop her heart. It soaked the five one-hundred dollar bills in her pocket.

She lay in bed that night unable to sleep, unable to stop thinking about herself, and her plan and how she had turned in one direction but would only go in this direction for so long before she would turn back, and she wondered when she finally did turn back what would be the same and what would be different, and if she would ever see her mother and father together again on this land she was trying to save for him. And then she remembered the sight of her mother packing her things in the station wagon the day she left, and she wondered if maybe her father had seen her, had stood somewhere off in the distance, maybe crouching down in the hayloft watching her wrap her German beer stein in the woolen sock that afternoon, knowing she was not coming back to him, and knowing he was partly to blame for this.

Finally Bobbi Ann fell asleep with the idea that she

would spend the five hundred dollars, which lay under her bed in a row drying out, on a car of some sort, a car he could drive through the night looking for Gwen, the windows rolled down, a summer breeze sweeping by his face, a baseball game playing on the radio, the moon far out ahead.

4

From the mound Brad stared in at his catcher, who called for a slider down and away from the big left-handed batter for the Brattleboro Mets who had already hit one home run today on a high fastball and then reached first base in the third inning when Spenser booted away an easy ground ball. That was Spenser's second error of the game, and it allowed two runs to cross the plate for Brattleboro. Now, in the top of the sixth inning, the Indians were down by a run.

Brad could hear the infield chatter behind him: Grady, Meechum, Stringer, Spenser, talking it up, exhorting him. They'd grown accustomed to winning on the days when Brad pitched. He was pitching on three days' rest now. For the last five weeks he had held the opposition in check. Until today.

For two innings he'd lost his concentration. He began asking questions: Who does he win these games for? For himself, for the guys behind him? He was on the verge of setting a record for successive victories by a rookie pitcher in the Northern League. He began thinking about this, about victory. About how life really was just two things, victory and loss. He tried to block out the questions during his warm-up pitches. He tried to imagine himself moving into a new time zone, actually stepping physically from his past. Like everyone else, he had a picture in his mind of himself. It was an invention, and there were moments when he suddenly felt lost to himself, unrecognizable and beyond his own understanding. But until today he had always been immune to these feelings of dislocation once he stood on the mound.

Today he'd felt like he was being drawn back, even as he tried to step forward. He was soon thinking back over his life to the unfilled days of boyhood. He remembered sitting at the kitchen window looking out at the rain. It was a summer morning and if the rain kept up, his Little League game would be called off.

He rode his bicycle through the rain, all the way to the field on Taylor Road, out past the American Tile Company, and he sat in the leaking plywood dugout wondering how on earth he would get through this day without a ball game. He was nine years old, and already the game had become a drug. Without baseball there was too much time to fill, too much to think about. There was his brother to think about. Turning over his brother's mattress in the morning before his father came into the room to check if he had wet his bed again. Swapping sheets with Michael, spraying them with Right Guard. Then, after his father had left for the office, Mike would wash the sheets in the shower, hanging them like sails, then draping them over chairs in the basement next to the furnace to dry. Mike did pushups in those days, did them the way they told you to do them in the Charles Atlas book, as if somehow to countervail with big muscles the humiliation of bed-wetting. The veins in his arms stood out like night crawlers. Brad never had to do any exercise. He never lifted weights or ran or even stretched before he threw. He had been given a body totally immune to injury. Throughout his Little League career and then in high school he pitched with only one day's rest. He had what coaches called a rubber arm.

Without baseball there was too much to think about. He had to think about how his brother's bones were forever breaking and how his mother used to say, as if bragging or trying to explain some injustice, "Brad got the best of me." Did he leave her with nothing? he wondered. Did he take more than he was entitled to?

These were the thoughts that filled his head as a boy. These were the thoughts baseball distracted him from. And if there was no game, then he invented one of his own. A game played inside his head or on the cement floor of the garage with baseball cards and a tinfoil ball. It was another world, completely self-sustaining. Into this world came Mickey Mantle, Willie Mays, Ted Williams, even Jackie Robinson. Brad kept all their averages in his head. He knew their weaknesses in the field, how to pitch them with men on base. He knew which knee Mickey was favoring. There were no secrets. This world took on such detail that it began to seem more real than the world outside Brad's imagination. That was the other world where he took the trash out for his father, out to the backyard beyond the willow tree, where a fire was already burning in the barrel, and instead of dumping the bag onto the hot coals, he threw the trash one handful at a time, and beneath the old newspapers there were strange cotton pads folded into neat squares like sandwiches, a dozen of them, and when Brad opened one of them he found dried blood, and he knew instinctively that they belonged to his mother and that he wasn't supposed to find them. He knew that he somehow had to be to blame.

He disappeared into his baseball world to get away from this. And his father would come along and find him staring out a window, just staring, and he would say, "You'd better change your attitude."

I'm to blame, Brad thought. Of course. I was the one who ruined my mother's one chance to be healed.

He had gone along with her that hot spring night, riding a bus all the way to Philadelphia to Connie Mack Stadium for the Billy Graham Crusade. He didn't care at all about Billy Graham, but oh how excited he was to finally get to see old Connie Mack Stadium where the Philadelphia Phillies played. And the place was packed. People had come from as far away as Chicago. They came in big buses with banners taped to both sides, the windows down, and the passengers singing hymns at the top of their lungs. He and his mother crammed into the bleacher seats. Everyone around them held Bibles. And down on the field the choir stretched along the base paths, many hundreds of singers dressed in bright blue robes. And Billy's pulpit stood ten feet off the ground, a wooden scaffold rising up in the air like a gallows, rising up above the pitcher's mound. He spoke for a long time. His voice ricocheted through the old wooden stands. People were sweating terribly by the time he had finished. They fanned themselves with the printed programs. And finally Billy called out for them to come down out of their seats, down to the pitcher's mound to be saved and redeemed and healed. It was an unbelievable thing to see, hundreds and hundreds of people, many thousands of people streaming down onto the field, piling on top of each other trying to reach the pitcher's mound. Brad's mother stood up and motioned for him to follow her. But he was too frightened to move. He sat watching a colored lady at the end of the aisle beating her fists against her breasts and shouting, "I love you, Jesus. I love you, sweet Jesus!"

Brad refused to leave his seat. "Well, I can't go without you," his mother told him. "I might never find you again."

In the bus on the way home he tried to sleep with his head on his mother's lap. She stared out the window at the headlights of the oncoming traffic. He went to use the toilet at the back of the bus. He stood rocking from side to side, peeing on the seat. He could feel the wheels beneath him. Going back down the dark aisle, he saw his mother raising a bottle to her mouth, her hand shaking so badly that the bottle clicked against her teeth. Beyond the rhythm of the rattling bottle and the thrumming tires, he heard his father's admonition, "You'd better change your attitude. . . . Don't be an actor."

Brad could escape all this in his fictional world, where he and Joe Dimaggio shagged fly balls side by side and chewed the fat after the game, sitting with their feet propped up on the edge of the dugout. The more time Brad spent in this invented world the less he wanted to return to the real one. And then one day the illusion didn't hold up, the fiction was exposed, all the heroes were dispersed. He was left with too much time to fill and a descending darkness that fell around him like a cold metal container whose sides were too slippery to ascend. He sat in the container while it filled with liquid, a liquid that rose slowly and then hardened around him like a cast so that he couldn't move. He could look up through the top of the container and see the other world: the view showed him too much of that world, too much of its deceit. It was all there before his eyes, the layer of life beneath the painted surface, the deception, the fraudulence and corrupted motives. And then, when he emerged from the container, when the freezing fever of confinement broke at last, he got himself into trouble by saying terrible things, contentious things to his father. "Your life really stinks, if you ask me. It's rotten and it stinks."

There was a storm raging inside him and only baseball could quiet it. If he made it to the pitcher's mound and threw hard enough and long enough he could leave the real world behind.

Pretty soon things became more complicated than that. Pretty soon there were girls in his life. They told him he was sensitive and honest. They kissed him and undressed for him. And he went to bed with them because it was easier than answering their questions. The more he talked with them, the more difficult it was for him to conceal that part of his life he had to keep secret, that part about the metal container, and the cold black liquid, and the paralysis. He was terrified of being discovered.

During his final year at Princeton he dated a girl named Sara from the prep school in the next town, where he had spent a good deal of time. She mentioned the name of a girlfriend he'd once gone out with; then she asked him how many girls he had slept with. He said he didn't know. But then he counted to himself and discovered there had been twenty-one, an astonishing number.

"Well," she said, "I know of seventeen." She whistled through her teeth. "That's pretty unreal."

He couldn't bring himself to admit that *unreal* was exactly what it was. He could barely remember them, except the way each of them had frightened him when they tried to get to know who he really was. He was tender with them, but then he vanished. He wondered after a while if he had hoped with each of them to put more distance between himself and his boyhood or to get closer to some understanding of his mother. It took him a long time finally to learn that the metal container was constructed of guilt. His own extreme guilt. The black fever, the emptiness of his days, all of this came from his guilt. Guilt over not being a good enough son, a good enough brother. The only two things he knew he was good enough at were sleeping with girls and pitching baseballs. They were the only things that could keep the black container from falling down over him.

Today he tried to clear his mind of all of this. He told himself he had come a long way. He had found his way to the pitcher's mound for a professional baseball team. The full dream was at hand. It was beyond fantasy. He had enlarged the dream with talent and given it shape with determination. He stood face-to-face with the dream and he was in awe of it. Finally it seemed near enough for him to see it whole. And it seemed to have the power to overcome the guilt that had driven him to it.

Today he thought how odd it was that these dreams, the ones we are willing to give ourselves away to have, are born in a longing for a way out, a longing to feel strong and fulfilled and good enough.

Brad threw the next pitch high and tight to the batter to try and move him away from the plate, but somehow he got the handle of the bat on the ball and drove it straight down the first-base line where Spenser misjudged it badly. The ball bounced off his kneecap and rolled into right field.

Brad watched all this from the edge of the pitcher's mound. He watched Spenser run in a confused circle before finally retrieving the ball. He watched instead of covering first base; all his reflexes were propelling him in that direction, but he just stayed on the mound. It was a mistake, a mental error, and almost no one but Brad would be aware of it. Everyone would be concentrating on Spenser, on his third error of the game.

Spenser walked to the mound and handed the ball to Brad. "Jesus, Ivy, I'm falling apart," he said.

"Don't worry about it," Brad told him. "We'll get it back."

The runner stood on second base spitting through his front teeth. Brad looked down at him from under the beak of his cap and thought to himself that maybe he was beginning to lose it. That small error, that failure to cover first base, was symbolic of some change. Maybe he couldn't lock out the world anymore, maybe he had to make room for it.

He turned and walked back to the mound thinking about his brother's last letter. It was only the second letter Mike had written him. In it he wrote: "I have to tell you, Brad, I've been so scared here that I messed my pants."

The real world seeping in. Try shutting that out, Brad said under his breath. The catcher called for a straight fastball on the outside corner, but Brad threw a curve that broke so suddenly it hit the dirt in front of the plate and skipped all the way to the backstop. The runner moved to third base. The catcher called for time-out and ran to the mound. He said to Brad, "Christ, where are you today? Didn't you see my signal? You trying to ruin my married life?"

Brad shrugged him off. He took the ball and turned away and walked to the back of the mound. He gazed up at the flag in center field, the formation of clouds shouldering across the sky. He bent down and rubbed his fingers in the dirt, then stood up and turned the ball around and around in his hand. It was all in his hand. Nothing could get to him if he bore down hard, if he let himself be completely absorbed by the game.

He heard the voice of Spenser at first base calling to him, encouraging him. He decided that he would get this game back for Spenser. Three errors in one game. He had the power to erase these errors, to make them meaningless. If the game was won, they would be forgotten. Spenser was walking a thin line; he was being watched.

For the last four innings of the game Brad threw harder than ever before. He heard nothing in the outside world. His concentration was so intense he could see the ball's rotation as it traveled from his fingertips to the catcher's mitt. He didn't allow another run, not even another hit. In the dugout after the game Doc Hill handed him the game ball, a ritual of victory. He had a ball to commemorate each victory this season.

"They're all talking about you upstairs," Doc told him. "Somebody gets knocked out of the rotation and you'll be the first called up."

It wasn't long before Brad was alone in the dugout. Then he heard Spenser's voice behind him. "I had my eye on that last one," he was saying. "I had my eye square on it."

"It happens," said Brad.

"Yeah, but I never missed balls like that before."

"Everyone misses."

Spenser sat down next to him. "You know, Ivy, I been lying to my folks back home. I was sending home the box scores for a while, but for the last two weeks I couldn't do it. I ain't had a hit in eleven days, man."

"It'll come back," Brad said.

Spenser shook his head disconsolately. He dropped his cap on the ground at his feet and began sifting dirt through his black fingers, watching it fall like grains of sugar into his hat. "I wrote my mama that I sprained my ankle and wasn't playin' for a bit. I says to myself, If you have one good game today you won't have to mail that letter home."

He stopped talking. Brad saw his eyes drift over to the game ball on the bench between them. Then he went on.

"You know, if they send me down I'll never get back up. I'll just go down and down until there's nowhere else to go 'cept home. And I'm going to have to think about it all my life then."

Brad said he wouldn't go down. "You just have to relax out there."

"But that's the damn thing, Ivy. I can't relax no more. Once I start going down I just keep going down. Down and down. Do you ever think of going down?"

Brad heard the question and thought, Victory doesn't let you think about things like that, that it will all end someday, that everyone goes down in the end. "I'll help you, don't worry," Brad said. "Stick with me, you aren't going down."

Spenser looked uneasy. "Yeah, well," he began, then turned away and was silent a minute before starting over. "Look, for a little while I need some help. I was hopin' you could throw the ball outside to them lefties so they can't pull it down the line on me. Just for a few games 'till I get myself back."

Brad could do it. By pitching a certain way he could make life easier for Spenser. "Hold on," he said. "I told you not to worry. We're in this together."

Brad sat in the dugout after Spenser went to get a shower. He was thinking how people were suddenly drifting into his victorious path, people he could make life easier for. Spenser was the second person today; before batting practice Brad had gone out beyond the right-field fence to take a leak, and he'd found a man sitting in the tall grass, slumped over with his chin down on his chest. He was leaning against the back of the fence. At first Brad thought it was a hobo, but then he recognized the man's face, the face of the fellow who drove the tractor and took care of the field. Brad asked him if he was okay. He said he was just catching his breath. "My left arm went to sleep on me," he said. "Too much sun, I was just getting out of the sun."

When he started coughing Brad went to get him some water. When he returned, the man was gone.

Sitting in the dugout, the winningest pitcher in the league, Brad had no way of knowing that Page Mullens had been thinking of him and that in a few minutes they would meet again. All through the late innings while Brad worked to nail down another victory, there was a voice inside Page's head speaking a mile a minute, trying to figure things out: Come on kid, dig down, pitch your way out of this, pitch from your damn heart! Pitch your way right into my daughter's life. You with your big heart. It takes a big heart to survive in this game, in this *life*. Mine's always been too quick to act foolish, but now I've got to think straight. I've got to think ahead to what's going to happen. Funny, you think about going somewhere after you die and the thing is, there isn't anywhere you want to be but right here. I want to stay right here, watch my grandchild grow up, watch my daughter be happy, get married. . . . The heart inside a boy like that is enough to warm up your life, Bobbi. I'm going to leave you a lot of nothing. Debt and land that's not worth much more than nothing. But that pitcher would be something. Jeeze, the way he's pitching himself out of this jam, he's going to win another one. I can feel it. He's got it his way now.

After the game Page walked just ahead of Bobbi Ann and Zoey toward the work shed. "Let's head home, Pop," Bobbi said.
"We will, we will."
"You're going the wrong way."
He waved his hand and told her he just had to get some wrenches from the work shed and then they'd go home, straight home. But a second later they walked right into the path of the pitcher with the big heart. And as they approached him, Page felt his own heart pick up speed and suddenly he was aware of the moment in front of him. He recalled another time in his life when there was a moment like this, a moment signaling great change. He had been standing then at the window of a train. It was the afternoon Gwen drove him to the train station in Brownville Junction so he could attend a big 4-H conference in Auburn. Page hadn't wanted to go but she'd insisted. And he could tell she was eager to have some time alone. She kissed him good-bye on the platform, and he hurried into the car to get a window seat, not that he cared about the scenery from Brownville to Auburn, but he wanted to get a last look at Gwen. He stood at the window, and when he spotted her in the crowd on the platform she was just walking away without looking back. This was when he must have begun to lose her, he thought. It all happened a year before she finally left home, but he believed that afternoon at the train station was when she took her first steps out of his life.

Page tightened his grip on Zoey's hand and told himself that there was always a reason for everything that happens. "This is my daughter," he said suddenly as they neared the pitcher. His voice was almost calling out across the parking lot. "And my granddaughter."

The pitcher, who was walking in his stocking feet, carrying his spiked shoes in one hand, turned to them. He lifted one hand in the air to wave, and as he did this his baseball glove fell to the ground and Zoey scrambled up to him to pick it up. "Here," she said.

The pitcher thanked her and handed her the game ball he'd been given for his victory this afternoon. "Here," he said. "Take it."

But Zoey turned and ran to her mother and grabbed her legs and hid behind them. Bobbi looked down at her and then up into the pitcher's eyes, asking, "Is it all right?"

He nodded and held the ball out to Zoey, and when she buried her head between Bobbi's knees he knelt down and tapped her on the shoulder. Slowly she turned and took the ball from him. He stood up and turned to Bobbi and sort of dipped his head and tipped his cap like he'd done on Opening Day when she first spotted him from the bleachers.

"What's your name?" he asked Zoey. She didn't answer, and when Bobbi told him, he said, "That's a great name."

Then Zoey turned to him and stared at him before she said, "Do you like your cereal mushy?"

He laughed. "You really get right to the heart of things, don't you?"

Bobbi felt him looking at her. She averted her head, but when she turned back, his eyes were still on her.

"Well," said Page. "This is Bobbi Ann." He was smiling. He looked very short standing beside the pitcher. "Now how old are you, son?"

"Twenty-one," he said.

"Well, Bobbi's twenty-three."

"Oh."

"Isn't that something," Bobbi said archly. She laughed and the pitcher laughed too.

"Well, I sure would like to be twenty-one again," Page went on. "And be able to throw like you do."

Brad gestured to the ball field. "I had some trouble out there today."

"Nothing you couldn't handle, though."

"My curve was getting away from me," he said. He seemed slightly self-conscious. He tapped his baseball shoes together and the spikes clinked.

"Your arm," Bobbi said, raising her right arm. "In the fifth inning your arm was straying out here. You weren't coming over the top."

"I don't know about that," Page said. He seemed to want to rescue her.

"No," the pitcher exclaimed eagerly. "That's always been a problem for me when I don't concentrate. She's right."

Silence. Then Bobbi said, "We'd better get going, Pop."

She picked up Zoey. The little girl held the baseball out in one hand, waving good-bye. Suddenly the ball dropped from her hand and just as it was about to hit the ground, the pitcher caught it on the top of his foot and, with a flick, kicked it up in the air and caught it. He bowed at the waist and said, "At your service, Mademoiselle."

It all happened very quickly. And Bobbi had just turned away when she heard a voice call out in a Southern accent, "Hey, this here must be your little girl. Well, what do you know!"

Bobbi's mind was so far from that voice, it took her a while to figure out it was the colonel speaking. "Great game wasn't it?" he said to Page.

"Great, *great* game," Page replied.

"We've got to get home," Bobbi said.

"Sure, sure," the colonel said. "We'll be seeing you all then." He tipped his blue, government-issue Air Force cap in Page's direction and, as he backed away, patted Bobbi Ann's bottom. "I'll catch your act tonight," he told her.

When she walked away she saw the pitcher standing at the door to the locker room watching all this.

June became one long trip back and forth to the Blue Top Motel, to the colonel's room. Often Bobbi Ann rode her bicycle through soft evening air when it smelled as sweet as it did after a summer shower, though it hadn't rained at all in June. The farmers spoke all the time of rain. It was one more thing they could do nothing about.

"I'll get Zoey ready for bed; you better get going and beat the storm," Page said. "The clouds in the north are wicked."

"I'll try not to be so late tonight," Bobbi told him.

"I wish I had a car for you to take back and forth. I hate you riding that bicycle at night."

She kissed him. He was already dragging game boards from the closet. "I love you, Pop," she said.

He held up the Chutes and Ladders game and said, "I don't think I ever beat either of you at this."

It is a four-mile ride to the Blue Top. Bobbi peddles her bicycle and thinks about what her father would look like at the wheel of a brand-new car. Maybe she should have spent the colonel's five hundred dollars and got whatever kind of car it would buy. But a *new* car would be great. For once something new. Maine's landscape was cluttered with the rusted remains of used cars that had seemed at one time like a good idea to someone. She thinks of the rationalizations you make when you are poor, and how it is one thing to be poor when you are young and a completely different thing when you are old.

Slipping by Cook's farm she begins to construct a daydream around this image of her father seated behind the wheel of a fancy red car. Passing Footman's Dairy she considers how many thousands of dollars it would take to buy this red car and what she would have to do for the colonel to raise that kind of money. She cuts by Jenkins' farm, up the hill to Union Road. She pedals past the Travis place, where there are no signs of life. Not even the windmill is moving. From the road she can just make out the letters on the billboard planted in the front yard. The red and green letters of the Pine Tree Credit Bureau. John Travis has sold out and fled with his family to Phoenix, Arizona. Bobbi tries to imagine Arizona. Roy Swift had been there before he came to Maine. He had played some ball outside Phoenix. He told her it was a place where the sun was always shining. She thinks of Mr. Travis in such a place and wonders if he has bought himself a nice car by now, now that he is out from under his farm.

She rides past Tilton Pond and looks out across the water to the Assembly of God Retreat, a collection of aluminum campers, unhitched and strung together with strings of Christmas tree lights like booths at a fair. The trailers had appeared a week ago, as they did each summer. Someone from the retreat had come to Bobbi's house three years ago after Zoey was born and her mother had left. He spoke through the screen door about Jesus as if Jesus was his personal friend. "No, I'm not interested," Bobbi had told him.

If she were to go there tonight, she thinks, if she were to turn off Union Road and walk up to the door of one of those trailers, someone would tell her that Jesus was waiting for her and all she had to do was hand him all her troubles, all her sins. Praise the Lord, they would say. Eventually Pastor Bowditch would take her by the hand and lead her into Tilton's Pond to wash away her transgressions.

At the Colonel's door he said, "How you'all been?" He had already pulled down the shades. His uniform was thrown over the back of the desk chair. "These last few weeks we've got some real beauties. Academy Award stuff. I wish you'd let me run some of these by you."

She had told him several times that she wouldn't watch his movies. She walked to the costume pile and said, "You must have no imagination."

"Are we going to argue again?" he asked. "It's too pretty a night for arguing. Why don't you just sit down and have a drink with me and relax a while."

"You sit here in broad daylight watching these movies," she said contemptuously.

"It's business. I'm perfecting the art."

She turned away. "Who am I tonight?"

"Aunt Bee," he said. "Tonight good old Aunt Bee amuses herself with every utensil in the kitchen."

Bobbi took off her blouse and dropped it on the floor. She no longer bothered to change in the bathroom. He had seen every inch of her. She felt as if she had spent the whole month in this room. When she wasn't here he was watching her anyway on film. There was almost no difference.

She tied Aunt Bee's pink apron around her waist and walked to the mattress.

"Will you miss me when I'm gone?" he asked.

"Why don't you start your machine?"

"I've got an extension, not that you care, but I'll be here an extra few weeks while my office in Saigon is being painted. My wife called from California, I'll be going out there on my way."

"She can make the popcorn," Bobbi said.

"You think I'm a pig, that's fine, but let me tell you something, Bobbi baby, we all have our good side. The first night you were here I said every person had a right to be understood."

"I understand you perfectly."

"No, I don't think you do. I'm a complex man. It's a complex world. I took a ride out by your place yesterday. I walked around for a while, and I saw your father out in the field throwing baseballs. I said to myself, *That's* a man eating his heart out over a woman. I know a lot about human nature, I really do. I lost a woman once." He sat down in the chair and took off his glasses. He propped his feet up on the bed, then cleaned the lenses of his glasses with his T-shirt. "After I leave, what's going to happen to you and your old man? That's what I asked myself."

"You've been losing sleep over that?"

"Don't be so cynical. You remind me of my daughter, the way you talk to me. When I first came back from Nam I used to hear that kind of cynical talk all the time from her and her mother. That's the thing that really bugged the hell out of me, the way they had it all figured out. They'd put their heads together and come up with all the fucking answers. *I* was a loser because I was breaking my ass, risking my *neck*, for Uncle Sam. This is before anyone even cared about goddamn Vietnam. I volunteered for that duty. I had a sense of honor."

"Don't make me laugh," Bobbi said. "When you're

gone and we've lost the farm I'm going to curse you. As long as you have your movies I won't be free from your cesspool."

He shook his head. "I'm disappointed. I really am. I was sitting here thinking how I could help your old man and now you come down on me. I was thinking I was going to figure something out. This war's going to go on and on for a long time, and I thought as long as I'm there showing the flicks I would send Libby a check each month." He stood up and walked to the mirror. With his open hands he pushed his hair back behind his ears. "Or I could take the films to Florida with me. I could maybe make some kind of deal with Libby here, and you might be on easy street the rest of your life."

When Bobbi said nothing he shrugged his shoulders and started the camera.

On the way home that night she stopped at Roby Robinson's Ford Sales. The boy working the used car lot had finished high school with her. He had been captain of the baseball team. Bobbi led him to an ancient Plymouth. "I'll give you five hundred dollars," she said. "But you have to put four new tires on it."

"Why do you want this old jalopy?" he asked.

"Because it's got some substance to it. The rest of these cars don't look like they'd last through another winter."

The boy shrugged and she saw that he had a ketchup stain on the pocket of his shirt. "Plus a radio," she said. "I want a good radio."

"Tunes too?" he said. "I'll have to speak to Mr. Robinson."

"And did you get that ketchup on your shirt eating the dogs at Veterans Park?"

He looked down, licked his finger, and tried to wipe it

off. "Saw some kid throw a two-hitter this afternoon. A kid younger than me. Shit," he said, looking back at the stain.

"You still play any?"

"No time," he said. "Some softball for Milt's Hardware is about it."

He walked off to the office with his head down. Bobbi watched him kick a stone out ahead of him, then catch up to it and kick it again.

Mr. Robinson agreed on the tires and the radio. It would take him a few days, he said, to get the car ready for delivery. "I'll be by for it," Bobbi said. "Not until Pop's birthday. Two weeks from Sunday."

When she left the car lot she saw the boy standing under the bright lights, throwing bits of gravel into a ditch, throwing them sidearm as if he were making the play on a runner going to first base. She wheeled her bicycle around and rode over to him. "Watching you," she said, "I remember how you turned the double-play ball. You were good."

"Yeah," he said thoughtfully.

"Well, so long."

He called out to her. "I'll make sure they're whitewalls, them tires you want."

The next morning Page said to her, "At least we can talk. You and I don't have any trouble talking to each other. That's something some folks can't do at all."

"What do you want to talk about, Pop?" Bobbi asked him.

They sat down in the kitchen. Zoey was upstairs. They could hear her running up and down the hallway above their heads. It was after nine o'clock, and sunlight washed the porch and spilled in through the screen door. Page stood up. He walked over to the wall where the map of Maine was hung. The map was published by the U.S. Geological Survey and sold through the mail order catalogue of L.L. Bean. In the Mullens family the most important discussions seemed always to take place in the kitchen, and Bobbi recalled how her father had made his most ardent pleas and his most impassioned speeches while framed by the margins of the map of Maine, as if he might summon to his side of things the considerable force of geography and history and the state's natural resources, as if the sheer size of Maine would enlarge his stature.

"I want to talk to you, Pepsi." He lit his pipe, coughed over it, and set it alongside the porcelain sink, where it smoked. "The three of us," he said. "I was thinking how there's still only three of us, and I always planned on a big family. We couldn't ever get past three."

"We've made a pretty good trio, don't you think?" she said.

"Pepsi, I want to know what your plans are."

She thought of the colonel asking the same question. "I can tell you that tomorrow I work from five till midnight," she replied. "But that's about as far ahead as I'm thinking."

He looked at her understandingly. She saw that she had won him over and that he would have to struggle to hold onto the point he'd originally wanted to discuss. He rapped his knuckles against the map, then said, "When I think about what's going to happen it gives me the willies."

"Happen when?"

"Down the road."

"I don't know, Pop. You're the one who talks about how things are going to be."

"Sometimes I wake up talking to myself," he said. "I try to figure things out, and then I walk down to the south field and it comes to me that everything's out of my hands now. And what on earth is going to happen to you?"

Bobbi waited. "Do you need the answer to that, Pop, because I don't."

He traced his finger along the southern boarder of Aroostook County. "Potato capital of the world," he muttered. "Things happen to change things, Bobbi. Pretty soon the chance you had is gone forever."

"You're talking about Mom."

"No, I mean *you*, your chance. What harm is there in just letting me invite that pitcher out for supper before it's too late."

"You think he's going to lose his appetite any day now?"

"I know he's going to be leaving here, that's as certain as anything I *do* know, and you know it too."

She glanced at the calendar tacked to a cupboard door and she thought, July already. "You talk about that boy as if he was some kind of train," she said. "Like he was arriving at a certain time and leaving at a certain time, and he's going to be the last train to ever stop here. What makes you think I want to leave here, anyway? I got on another train once before. I thought I was headed someplace different, better maybe. I was damn near run over."

She stopped and softened her voice. "Come on, Pop," she said. "That's not like you, talking like this. You never had any burning desire to see me go somewhere else. That was *her* battle cry."

He said, "But I've been wondering if your mother knew something I didn't know."

"She knew how to leave without saying good-bye."

"She wasn't leaving for good."

"Pop."

"She would have taken her things along," he said. "I

always thought that if she knew she was leaving for good she would have taken her things. She had the whole empty station wagon."

"She did take some things."

"Not much."

"The things that mattered to her. Why is it, Pop?"

"Why is what?"

"Why is it you and I were both left behind?"

He looked up. "It's a different thing, you and me. That boy, Roy, wasn't any good at real life even though he could play shortstop to beat the band. You saw right through him, you saw right off, and you had the common sense to let him go. You were smart to stay behind."

"My bags were packed," she said. "I was waiting for him to come get me."

He shook his head. "No, I remember. You had a choice."

She watched him cast his eyes down at the cracked and buckled linoleum floor. "He left me, Pop. I didn't have a choice except in how I remember it. I was standing there with my bags. I watched him coming down the tracks for me, expecting to be a privileged passenger on his train. All my expectations. An expecting mother." She laughed once and looked off into space and thought about how stupid she must have looked to Roy. "The thing about being the one that waits around is you get all these ideas in your head about how things are going to be. You have all this time to imagine everything. I could see that train coming for me. The dining car with its square little tables and linen tablecloths and the flower vases." She walked through an oblong of sunlight to the screen door. "I stood there, Pop, just waiting for that train to pick me up and set me down in some place where things would be easier. And the thing is, when you're waiting you don't have any choice about what happens in your life. You just keep waiting for something to happen, and when it doesn't happen like you pictured it, you lie to yourself. You lie, to make the waiting bearable."

A moment later Page said weakly, "You'll catch your train."

"What train?"

"Whatever train you want. You've got some time."

"Time," she told him, "doesn't matter. And besides, *you* never took a train out of here."

He looked at her in a curious way, as if he was seeing something in her face for the first time, something close to a reflection of his own doubt. "When something bad happens to you," he said, "you can spend a lot of time waiting for things to get better. It's bad, Bobbi. It's the surest way to waste your life."

She waited, then asked him what he was waiting for. He took a step toward her, then a half-step back and reached his right hand behind him to steady himself. His hand came down along the coast of Maine and he paused as if leaning his weight against the rocks. "I'm waiting to see everything taken care of for you," he said.

She went to his side.

That afternoon from her bedroom window she saw him walk to the orchard. She put on her bathrobe and followed him at a distance. She watched him throwing his baseballs at the tree trunk. She wondered for the first time where the bread box had come from. And this question led to the reality that he had had a life before she came into the picture. It was strange to imagine this, that he had once been young, terribly young and full of himself, the way young people are. What had he hoped for then? she wondered. She watched him going through his pitching motion.

First the elegant pause, like a man posing for a photograph. The steady gaze in at the tree trunk where he imagined a batter standing ready. Then the gentle rocking of his hips back and forth, back and forth, as if there was music playing that only he could detect in the air. And just at the right instant his arms began to lift. They rose steadily until they held for just a second above his head. Then they began a downward sweep that caught all the momentum of his legs and back and shoulders and hips and delivered it in a compressed, graceful motion with an outstretched left arm and a hand that let the ball fly free.

Page shook his head in disappointment and leaned over for another baseball. Maybe in these countless efforts he *had* once thrown a perfect curve ball, Bobbi thought. It may have happened only once, only by accident, with no one there to record it. But she knew he was the sort of man who would be expecting it to happen once more at any moment.

She thought about this ritual of his and how she had seen him do it a thousand times since her mother left the farm. But never once before she had left. She wondered what rituals she would eventually rely upon to make the passage of time less frightening. And she thought about how scared her father must be that she would be left alone in the world someday, as alone as he was now. She had a dream to free him from debt, but it was fear more than debt which oppressed him.

She watched him walking toward the tree trunk with the bread box under his arm to retrieve the baseballs. She thought about what she could do to mitigate his fear. Ever since Roy Swift, she had promised herself that she would deal with fear on her own terms and by herself. Not only fear, but loneliness and disappointment and uncertainty. In the end, she had told herself, we are all alone. But this was not a thought her father could accept, and she knew it. When you are young you can live with the possibility of being alone. Eventually the possibility becomes a dread.

She left home early for work that day. She rode her bicycle under a broiling afternoon sun and arrived at the Blue Top with her gaudy blue waitress uniform in a grocery bag wedged between the double iron bars of her boy's bicycle. She had an hour before her shift began. She checked at the desk for the pitcher's room. Then she stood knocking at his door, knocking four times, knocking louder than she had intended.

No one answered. She walked around the side of the building and saw him sitting off in the grass with the black boy who played first base. The black boy had a pad of paper in his lap and was writing down words Brad dictated to him. Bobbi stood at the corner of the cement-block building, listening to their voices.

"I just don't want to lie to Mama any more, Ivy," the black boy said.

"Okay, so you tell me what you want to say to her, then." Brad's voice was level, patient. "We'll figure out the right words to use."

"You know what I'd really like? I'd like to talk with her. I'd like to just sit down and have a nice talk with her. She's so easy to talk to."

"What would you say to her if she was sitting right here?"

"Well, I'd tell her, I guess, that if things don't work out for me and baseball, not to worry herself 'cause I'm going to make something out of myself one way or the other."

Bobbi watched him pick a blade of grass and put it between his teeth. He leaned back on his elbows. "You know, Ivy, I've been running away from a bad picture, a picture of me without any money and nothing to do with each day. The only way I can get away from that picture is to put on a uniform. I know I look real good, real fine to Mama in my uniform. I always did, right from my first one. And I remember the day that first scout from Cleveland came to see me play in high school. I got three hits, and he ended up inviting me to go to his house a couple weeks later. He flew me on a plane all the way to his house in Ohio. When the plane landed I went to the bathroom to take a leak, and I stood at the mirror and saw I looked like hell. My pants was riding up to my knees. I had that old rotten picture of myself again; it started coming back. So I put my uniform on. I had it with me in my bag. Goddamn, though, I only had my black dress-up shoes. Mama had polished them with bacon fat, polished them like mirrors.

"The scout was real nice to me, him and his wife both. And I spent the night there in his house, and the next morning he asked me what was the biggest dream I had, or what was the biggest thing I wanted baseball to do for me. I was sittin' there over these big, fresh eggs with pepper on them and he asked me that, Ivy. I said I wanted to buy Mama a house like his. A real house with an upstairs and a downstairs. We always lived on one floor, and to tell you the truth I never knew nobody with two floors to his house. But I'll tell you something, it gives a person a real good feeling about hisself to be able to wake up in the morning on one floor and go down to another floor to eat his breakfast. It gives you a whole 'nother way of looking at the world. Just that there's so much extra room in your house, rooms that stand there empty at night, a whole floor of rooms still and empty with windows that look out at different things and all. Rooms that are empty while you're upstairs sleepin'. You know what I'm talking about?"

Brad nodded his head. "I never really thought of it that way before," he said. "But I know what you're talking about."

"Yeah, it's the idea that there's extra rooms. There's just something extra. You could say there's hardly a bum in the world who's got anything extra to spare, let alone a whole 'nother extra floor. But you're rich, though, so you must know."

"Not really rich."

"But I heard pretty rich."

"I guess so."

"What do you have?"

"I don't have anything. It belongs to my family, my father actually. He's got two houses."

"Jeezum, big ones, too, I bet."

"Yeah."

"Two floors to each one?"

"Well, one of them has three actually."

The black boy whistled through his teeth. "What do you do with all them rooms?"

"They spend the summer in one house and the rest of the year in the other. Plus my father's got an apartment in New York City where he entertains people."

"Friends?"

"No, he doesn't really have any friends."

"No friends? Three places to go live and no friends? Ain't that strange to think of a man with three places all by himself."

Bobbi Ann waited to hear what Brad would say next.

So much time had passed since she'd walked in on this conversation that she no longer felt awkward hiding around the corner. She felt almost as if she'd been invited.

"I figured out that it's kind of like being in the theater," Brad said carefully. "Being rich, living like my father lives, it's like being in the theater. He pays somebody to get the summer house ready by Memorial weekend, then he shows up, and it's like the curtain goes up and the show begins. Then, while he's at that house, he's got other people getting the winter house ready for him to come back after Labor Day. It's funny, for a long time he's been telling me not to be an actor—'Don't be an actor,' he says. But he's the one who goes from one stage to the next. People with lots of money live in this sort of theater, where everything depends on a good performance."

"It don't sound so bad to me, Ivy. Having all that space to move around in."

"You can get lost in all that space," Brad said. Then he stopped and asked, "Well, what are we going to do about this letter?"

The black boy closed the cover on the pad of paper. "I think I'm gonna just wait and see if my luck changes. I'm gonna wait till there's something good to tell Mama. I don't want to lie to her no more. That's one thing about living in a small place, there ain't no place to hide from the lies you have to tell. A person can't get away too easy from his lies."

When they stopped talking, Bobbi stepped from around the corner and walked up to them in the grass. When she said who she was there was a flash of recognition on Brad's face, and he got quickly to his feet. "I know," he said. "You're Mr. Mullens' daughter, Bobbi Jean."

"Close," she said. She turned away slightly and nodded to the black boy. "I want to ask you guys a favor," she said.

"You want autographs?" the black boy asked. "Jeezum, Ivy, somebody wants my autograph."

Bobbi smiled and shook her head. When her eyes fell on Brad she discovered that his eyes were on her, and like hers exactly. Several seconds passed in silence. Then she spoke. She was conscious of her voice and she tried to reassert herself and to turn away from him. "No autographs," she said. "My Pop's been trying to throw a curve ball."

"Is that right?" asked Brad, as if this was big news to him.

"He's been trying a long time now."

"It's just like everything else," he said. "There's no magic to it once you learn." He hadn't taken his eyes off her.

"Well, he thinks you're the best thing to come up the pike in a long time," she said. They both laughed. "No, seriously, it's true. And his birthday is coming up in a week, a week from Sunday. I was wondering if you might come out to the farm, maybe show him a few tips. You too," she said to the black boy.

Brad used the word "delighted." He would be delighted, he said. Such a grown-up, rich word, she thought. And when she said good-bye and backed away she realized that he had never taken his eyes off her. She heard the black boy say, "Jeezum, Ivy, I think you can handle a little bitty curve ball without me taggin' along."

Another game was over. For Brad, these days were becoming seamless and indistinguishable. Even the days when he pitched took no shape in his memory. His field of vision, his focus on the world, had been narrowed and compacted to a rectangle of light as wide as home plate and as high as the space from a batter's kneecaps to his armpits. He saw this strike zone in his sleep. Sometimes on the pitcher's mound he didn't even notice the batter's face, the color of his uniform. He was throwing baseballs into the rectangle of light, cutting the corners of the rectangle. Nothing existed within this zone, nothing entered it or escaped it, not even time or memory.

Tonight at the Blue Top, Brad wandered into Grady's room, where most of the team was watching television. Astronauts were about to step onto the moon for the first time. Men on the moon, the face of the last batter Brad pitched to, the voice of the girl speaking to him—none of these things existed within the rectangle of light. They were equally unreal to him.

The boys were passing around a clock that had come in the mail for Colin Harris, the reserve right fielder. His father, a Baptist minister in Texas, had sent it. Christ was at the center where the two hands intersected. Each of the twelve apostles occupied a number. Peter was standing in his robe at the number twelve.

"Nice clock," said Grady. "So, does your old man sell these suckers?"

"I dunno," Colin answered. "I think he gives them away to people in nursing homes."

"We might as well be in a nursing home," said Woody. "This place is so dead. I'm going to figure out some way to get Linda up here, I'll tell you that."

"Jesus," complained Grady. "You're always talking about Linda. I told you the way to get her out of your mind is to jerk off more often. You take my advice, jerk off twice a day, and pretty soon you'll be walking around asking, 'Linda, who's Linda?' "

Brad had heard all this before. He turned to the television screen where the space module was standing on its legs on the cratered surface of the moon. Another patch of light, another reality. He was listening to Thompson telling Grady about the funeral business his father ran in New Jersey: "I get yanked out of baseball and he's got a spot for me, waiting. I know most of the business already. Last Christmas I helped him do a job on a stiff. Fucking-A, you should see the shears you use to bust open the chest. Big, fucking-A shears, and when you yank on them there's this loud crack! Splits your chest wide open. The heart's just lying there."

Grady looked up at the ceiling and said, "Hold it, shut up." He killed the volume on the TV but left the picture of an astronaut climbing down the ladder from the lunar module. From upstairs came the sound of bedsprings creaking and a voice hollering. "Jesus H. Christ," whispered Grady. "Men on the moon about to make history, and they're going at it. Nothin's sacred any more." He smiled.

For the moment the boys were more interested in the TV. But Grady was one step ahead of them. Earlier in the season he had figured out a way to cross-wire the Magic Fingers in the room above Meechum's. For a while that was the nightly entertainment. But then they'd grown tired of the prank. Now Grady had something better to show them. "Check this out," he said. Standing on the bed he reached up to the ceiling and pulled out a cylindrical piece of plaster and plywood about the circumference of a half dollar. Suddenly, light from the room above fell through the hole, and Grady raised a finger to indicate he wanted silence. Soon voices from upstairs could be heard.

"I could have been on this mission if I'd played my cards right," a man said.

"It's not real," a girl replied. "You can tell that's not the moon."

"What the hell is it, then?"

"Looks like one of your movie sets."

"Oh baby, you're underestimating the power and glory of the United States Air Force. When JFK said we were going to put a man on the moon he turned to the Air Force and they took him seriously. And I could be there. Those boys are old fly jocks, no better than me. But my eyes went bad."

"You died."

"I'm still alive."

"You screwed everyone around you, you screwed your Air Force until it killed you."

"What are you talking about?"

"You're an extortionist. They'll send you fat retirement checks for the rest of your life for screwing them."

The bed shook violently. Bits of plaster fell from the hole and drifted down on Grady's head. The man shouted, "You push too hard, too fuckin' hard, Miss America."

Gradually the television meant nothing and all the boys were standing on the bed looking up at the circle of light from above. They heard a girl scream, then glass breaking. The bed shook the ceiling. At last the door upstairs flew open with a crash, and they all ran to the window to see who was coming down the concrete stairs.

Brad watched as Bobbi Ann emerged from the darkness and ran to her bicycle. It took him a long time to open the screen door and start out after her. Then the door above him slammed open again. He leaned against the building and watched a man in his underwear come bounding down the steps. The man called out to Bobbi. "Why don't you be a little grateful? Come back and we'll start over again." When she rode away he said, "You don't cut off a man's balls like that, baby."

She had vanished completely, the night closing behind her as if she had never been there at all. The man scratched his crotch, mumbled something unintelligible, then went back up to his room and closed the door behind him. Brad was left alone, contemplating the whole crazy world. He spent a long time that night thinking about things. He thought about the man in the funeral home who drains us and ties our shoes for the last time. We are strangers to him and he is not gentle with us. He does not know about our days in the sun, our moments of extreme pride and joy, our victories. He has his giant shears and can split us apart with a snap and turn us into ashes without blinking an eye because he doesn't know us and never did, and there is no one to recall for him how one afternoon under a high sun we almost did something to perfection. All our lives we savor the memory of some good act, and we let ourselves believe it will matter in the end, and it doesn't.

That night Brad went to sleep thinking the thought of all the restless people scattered across the planet, the thought that there must be more to life than this.

6

"So, how old do you think I look?" Page asked when Bobbi came into the kitchen. She was a little surprised to find him up so early. She'd hoped to beat him to the kitchen and get started on a cake.

"Not a day older than Sandy Koufax," she replied. She went over to him and kissed him and wished him happy birthday. When she hugged him she could feel his bones. "I'm going to have to start feeding you better," she said. She pulled back from his embrace to look at his face. "You're turning into a pin, look at you."

"Maybe I look older than I should," he said.

"I can't remember you ever caring how you looked. Are you serious, Pop?"

He didn't answer right away. "I feel out of step with the times," he said. "But maybe the times aren't so good anyhow."

He let go of Bobbi and walked to the sink. He ran the water and washed his hands. "I was a lot older than your mother," he said. He dried his hands, then walked to the table where he'd spread out the morning paper. "I was kind of hoping when I took the job at the park that we'd get sort of close, you know, the boys and me. I wanted to be somebody they could talk to."

He stood with his back to her, and she caught herself wondering when he'd lost his shape and why she hadn't noticed before that he was being swallowed up by his clothing. In the seat of his pants his trousers hung straight down, pinned up only by the points of his hips.

"I'm sure they know you're someone they can talk to," Bobbi said.

"Oh," he remarked, "they talk to me, but sometimes I get the feeling they're trying to humor me. I remember doing the same thing with old people when I was a kid."

"They like you, Pop," she said. When he turned to her his thinness alarmed her. He seemed almost to turn within the boundaries of his shirt and pants.

"Why?" he asked.

"Why," she repeated. "Well, I'm not going to answer that because you already know why." He looked at her with a puzzled expression, then turned his eyes to the newspaper.

"What I'd like to know," he said in a distracted way, "is how it's going to do any good for anyone by us going over to that country and bombing everything in sight. I think about those farmers, their land."

Bobbi barely heard him turning the newspaper pages. She was thinking instead of the colonel, what he would do when she didn't show up tonight.

"You're coming straight home after the game today?" she asked her father.

"You got something planned?" He smiled mischievously.

"You won't get any hints from me," she replied.

"A little pin the tail on the donkey," he said. "The old jackass."

A moment later Bobbi watched him walk out onto the porch, and she sat down at the kitchen table aware suddenly that he would regard her surprise as an effort to humor him. Until he'd said that about the boys on the team, she somehow had felt him incapable of such a cynical observation. He is changing, she thought. And she thought about calling the pitcher and canceling her invitation. She had been looking forward for a week to seeing her father's expression when he showed his face at their door. She had been looking forward to seeing his face at their door. She had already imagined what he was like. She had imagined it in great detail. She had fantasized what it was going to be like talking with him. This fantasy had helped her survive the last three sessions with the colonel. She wondered if the pitcher would be able to tell the next time he saw her that she had been thinking of him, fleshing him out in her imagination like a character one reads about and gradually seems to know. And on top of this, she felt guilty and stupid for having relied on his image. But honest to God, she'd had to rely on something to keep the colonel from overpowering her imagination. She had made a pact with him, that he could have her body but not her soul. And then, after he had tried to force himself on her and she had fought him off, he became contrite. His contrition had enabled him to find a way into her. She had opened up for his ideas.

She had found herself sitting on the bed telling him about her mother. She recalled for him how her mother had taken her for ballet lessons every Saturday when she was eight years old. And then ice-skating lessons one winter.

"Well, she cared," he said.

"You don't understand," she told him. "I used to watch her standing there off to the side. She was trying to make me better, to improve me. I wasn't good enough the way I was. I'd skate my heart out for her, and afterward she would criticize me because my underwear was showing. Can't you do something about it? she would say. There would be a bunch of cigarette butts crushed in the snow. I was auditioning for her, and she was trying to decide if I was going to amount to something she could be proud of."

Parents, he told her, have the natural instinct to contain their children. "We all have it," he said. "The instinct to take everything for ourselves."

"Maybe you do."

"And maybe you don't, maybe you're the exception. Maybe you think about other people before yourself, but most of us are only human, we fuck things up. A father always fucks up everything, I can tell you that. I remember so many times with my own daughter. We used to go to these air shows when she was small. Model airplanes you fly by remote control. I'd take her with me and we'd have a ball. Then, when she got to be a teenager, she began accusing me of trying to make her into an engineer. I mean, my God, if I ever lectured her about becoming an engineer it was only because I wanted her to become *something* in this world. But I never meant to screw up her life or anything. A kid has to forgive her parents for those things. You might never forget your mother criticizing you, but you reach a certain age and you have to begin to try and understand *why* she did it."

"You never knew her."

"I'm just giving her the benefit of—"

"You don't have any right to give her anything," she told him. But what he said had made some sense. It bothered her that he had made sense.

"Anyway," he said, "I'm not going to mess things up with my son, I can tell you that. And if my daughter ever needs me for anything, anything in the world, I'll stand by her. I mean if she screws things up royally I'll stand by her anyway."

"You think you can redeem a life by making a few nice gestures? I could accuse you of trying to atone for a life of sin."

He looked at her from over the black rims of his glasses and said it didn't matter what she accused him of. "I know why I do the things I do. It's never too late to redeem your life."

In the afternoon Bobbi Ann played with Zoey while her father was at the ballpark, and she thought about her mother and what Colonel Ellis had said to her about the instinct we all share, the instinct to take everything for ourselves. Perhaps this was the instinct her mother had followed. She had given for many years, but unlike her husband she had held something back, just enough to allow herself a way out when the time came. Bobbi Ann had held nothing back from Roy Swift, and so he had taken everything. Page had held back nothing from Gwen, and she had taken everything but his illusion of her, his hope of her returning. Perhaps, thought Bobbi, you must always hold something back from the world. Perhaps you must preserve a way out or at least enough room in which to turn around. This was what power was all about. Power was the ability to change the direction of your life, the ability to influence the direction of other peoples' lives. She thought how, for the last three years of her own life, she had been holding back something, she had been trying to regain some power over the course of her life. Even in sex she had held back. She had obtained a diaphragm and learned how to use it. This had given her a certain measure of power, and then the pill had made power less messy.

She looked down and Zoey was playing in the sandbox and singing parts of a song she had learned a year ago. Bobbi Ann was surprised that she had remembered the song at all. How beautiful her daughter was, how fine a thing had resulted from the loss of power, from the complete giving away of herself. She recalled how very much alive she had felt carrying Zoey, how she had felt connected to the center of some great mystery, where the answer to the mystery was perfectly clear. Beyond power, beyond even freedom, there had been a remarkable serenity, a feeling of being enclosed within the margins of motion and light. True, the direction of her life had changed and she had felt powerless to stop it, but she had felt something indescribable, an assenting to a greater power perhaps, and she gave herself away in order to feel it completely.

But Bobbi Ann still didn't know what you sometimes have to give away in this world to feel anything at all. She was talking to her daughter, laughing and talking, and thinking to herself that the pitcher wouldn't show up after all. He would let her down. Her father's surprise would go up in smoke. Suddenly it seemed like years ago that she spotted him on Opening Day, his eyes turned toward her.

There's no sense being foolish about this, she told herself. She had told herself this before. Still, she can't forget certain things, that first glance in his direction. It was like light coming in.

She thought of this and smiled because she recalled how her father was always the one who entered a room and walked straight to the windows and yanked the curtains back farther to let more light in. He always wanted more light. Her mother was forever drawing the curtains. She lived in her books, and the outside world only depressed her. That was the big difference: a woman pulling the curtains closed, a man yanking them open. Each only vaguely aware of the opposite force, each asking under a whisper, Now, who keeps pulling these? Now, who keeps closing these?

Bobbi thought, If you had to lose one of these people, better to lose the one who closed the curtains. Her father had always been receptive to life. She remembered how he posed for photographs, standing there with his eyes wide open, standing there as proud as a potentate.

Zoey had drawn something in the sand at Bobbi's feet. "A face," she said.

"Oh yes, a face. Whose face, sweetheart?"

"Daddy's face."

Bobbi's heart dropped in her chest, seemed to catch on her lowest rib. "You mean Poppy's face," she said tentatively. Zoey didn't look up from the outline she had traced in the grains of sand. "Here," Bobbi said, and she leaned down and drew a pipe coming from the man's mouth, a little curl of smoke rising innocently from its bowl. "Let's give Poppy his pipe," she said cheerfully.

Zoey looked up at her. "Daddy's pipe?"

"Yes, you know Poppy smokes a pipe. You know that."

Zoey stared at the picture with a puzzled look, then quickly bent down and rubbed it away with the flat palms of both her hands. She clapped her hands together and said, "There."

There are moments like this when Bobbi doesn't know what her daughter is thinking, when she seems to be changing right before her eyes. It is one of those times when the illusions you surround a child with no longer seem adequate, when the child appears to see straight through them and to know better. It is almost as if children belong only to themselves, as if they cannot be contained by illusions and there are forces within their hearts drawing them to the truth. They play along with an adult's lies, but inside their hearts and heads there is an outline of truth that cannot be corrupted.

"Well," Bobbi said, standing up and reaching for Zoey's hand, "what are we going to do with this beautiful day?"

It was a beautiful day, but then the day stretched into an interminable afternoon. Page had come home from the ballpark and was deeply troubled by something he couldn't understand. Brad Schaffer wasn't at the park. "He was scheduled to pitch the game but he never showed up. I didn't see him in the bull pen or the dugout. No sign of him at all."

He has gone, Bobbi thought. He was called up. He packed his things and left Waterboro in the middle of the night.

"Nope," Page told her, as if reading her mind. "Not that quick. I'd have heard something." He started his pipe smoking and sort of looked around the room as if he had something else on his mind. Then he remarked that the field at Veterans Park looked real nice today. "Even without rain, I've got it pretty green. I've been getting up at midnight and watering when it's nice and cool."

Bobbi thought, he is a farmer from end to end. He has a connection to the earth beneath him. He can even figure out a way to get around the deprivations of a drought. She listened to him give an animated review of the day's game. Waterboro lost. Apparently they had the game in their reach and should have won it. There were men in scoring position, but they were stranded on the bases. "That boy Spenser," recounted Page, "that poor boy is having a rough time of it. He gets up to bat with a man on first base, and you can practically tell he's going to hit into a double play. Twice today it happened. And then in the eighth inning he was called out looking at a pitch right down the middle, with a man standing on third base, the tying run. Killed a rally every time he stepped up to bat. He might as well have telephoned in his performance today. His mind's not on the game."

It was dusk when they finally stopped talking about baseball and Bobbi Ann stopped hoping that the pitcher would show up, the car would have to be enough. She lit the candles on the chocolate cake and set it down on the oak table in the kitchen in front of her father. Zoey was in his lap, angling to blow out the candles. Her breath bent the tiny flames but didn't extinguish a single one. "Try again, Pepsi," Page told her. And this time he blew over the top of her head, timing his breath with hers, and all the candles went out in a sudden flash. "I did it!" Zoey exclaimed.

"You did it," Page said.

After she put Zoey to bed Bobbi returned to the kitchen and found her father sitting where she had left him. He had lit all the candles again and was staring at them as they melted into the frosting. Their diminishing light was caught in the lines on his face, the creases on his forehead. Finally he looked up at her and told her how pretty she looked. She was concealing her disappointment from him. It was his birthday. "Sometimes," he said to her, "I look at you and you look so much like Gwen."

She remembered how he was always telling her mother how pretty she looked. Bobbi Ann grew up half-believing that all husbands spent a good deal of time following their wives around the house from one room to the next. "My first birthday with Gwen we'd only known each other a few days," he said. "I remember it like it was yesterday. I was at her place, in her kitchen. She made a pot of tea. It was very proper, she was one to have everything just right. I remember she had sugar cubes in a blue china bowl." He cleared his throat and said he was feeling nostalgic.

"I know I'm supposed to look forward and not always think about the past. They say thinking about the past makes you old. But it's funny, though, these things we remember. That Ferris wheel in Bar Harbor, the view from the top. Your mother's perfume in the salt air. The white cubes of sugar in her blue bowl. Those little things practically seem to make up a lifetime when you look back."

In life, Bobbi thought to herself, you have to have things that tug at you, that draw you back to better times or worse times, times that explain where you have been, where you have come from, and maybe where you are going.

"Life," she said, almost to herself, "changes so fast."

They talked for a while longer and the more he revealed about himself, the more angry she became with the pitcher who had not remembered to come for her father's birthday dinner, who had not stopped to think what this would have meant to him. When Zoey began crying in her room, Page got up from the table. "Let me go," he said.

He was gone a long time. The house was terribly dark. Bobbi made her way through the living room to the open staircase. She went up three steps, then stopped at the sound of his voice. "Do me a favor, Pepsi," he was saying. "Don't forget me. Remember your Poppy, okay?"

It was after midnight when she rode her bicycle on the Union Road toward the Blue Top. By now Colonel Ellis would have made up his mind what to do to her for not showing up. The money will be cut off, she thought. Her father's land would go down the drain.

She was going to the Blue Top to find out about the pitcher. She wouldn't be able to sleep until she knew why he hadn't come. She was angry with herself for expecting something.

Up ahead of her the lights of a plane lifted off the ground and pointed straight up in the dark sky. For a second or more there was something pretty about these blinking lights, but then the sound of the jets caught up with the lights and the sky crashed over her head and the world around her seemed to be swallowed up in the noise. It was an ugly, deafening noise and it had become so familiar in Waterboro that you hardly noticed it anymore. But still, she could recall a time before there were jet planes taking off and landing here, a time when evening seemed to float in silently over the potato fields, and if the breeze was right you could hear people out on their porches four hundred acres away, the sound of their voices traveling like words over water.

She pedaled her bicycle and looked up at the lights, and she was enclosed in the noise above her head, so enclosed that it took her a while to figure out that a person had appeared across the road and was calling out a name: "Bobbi Jean," the voice called.

Bobbi Jean, she thought.

He waved his hand for her to stop. He was standing right alongside her when her wheels stopped turning. "I was on my way out to your place," he said. His hand rested on the handlebars of her bicycle.

"It's a little late," she said.

He apologized for the lateness. But Bobbi hardly heard him. She had worked up a good head of steam, and she wanted to put it to some good use. "Look," she started out. "I don't know who you are or what people have been telling you all your life about how great you are, but in my book you're another one of those golden boys who doesn't care about anyone but himself. And that's fine, that's perfectly fine with me, but you disappointed my father and he's got you up on a damn pedestal and that sucks. It really sucks because there's enough crap in a person's life to begin with, let alone having to take more of it from a golden boy who blows into town one day and out the next."

When she paused the sky had grown quiet, and her breathing echoed in the darkness above their heads.

"I didn't mean—" he stopped without finishing, then asked if he could walk her home.

"I came this far by myself," she said. She turned the front wheel of her bicycle around.

"I asked at the restaurant if you were coming in tonight," he said. "They told me you had the night off."

"I guess you took the day off, too." There was still a hard edge to her words. "My pop was looking all over for you."

He took an envelope from his hip pocket. "I got something in the mail yesterday," he explained.

She looked at the envelope. She stopped breathing. A train ticket, she thought. A ticket out of here.

He said, "I walked around most of the night last night. I was going to come see you. Anyway, I wouldn't have been worth much on the mound today."

A minute passed. "Where are you going?" she asked.

"I was going to talk to the minister. Someone said there's a minister along this road."

"Well, there is, but you must be hard up for someone to talk to."

"I am."

"Do you drink coffee?" she asked.

"You got coffee?"

"Just like the Ritz-Carlton."

He followed her. "I'll run alongside," he said.

And he ran effortlessly. Even up the hills he seemed to be scarcely breathing. He ran like an Indian brave.

At the farm she put on a light, and they sat out on the porch. Her bicycle lay on its side in the grass. The wind was rising. Above their heads a screen window rattled in its frame. A jet took off, and Bobbi thought of the colonel lying in his bed. The world was so complicated, and she wished that for once things would be simple, utterly simple and clear.

She served him chocolate cake and coffee, and he shared the contents of his letter with her. It contained a photograph of his brother in uniform. On the back were these words: "Lin, remember me. I'll come back. Mike."

"A girl," Brad said. "Mike must have given the picture to a girl and left word for her to get in touch with me if anything was wrong. She probably doesn't know much English. I mean, she probably sent this because something's gone wrong. I called home. They haven't heard from him either. There isn't any word from the Army."

"He's probably all right," Bobbi said.

"But she must have expected him to come back and he hasn't. He probably promised her."

"People promise things."

"Not my brother, not Mike." He hadn't touched his cake. She watched his hand move again to the fork and then skip over it and return to his knee. He had those prominent veins in his hand that pulsed with the cadence of his breathing. "I feel like I should be there with him," he went on. "What am I doing here?"

"He doesn't look like you," she said.

He asked if she had a map. "A world atlas or something."

"No, I don't think so," she said. "Wait, in my mother's things there could be one. She had a lot of books."

He followed her into the kitchen, where she took a few wooden matches from the stove and led him up into the attic. "I packed up her things," she told him. "Pop just kept staring at everything. He'd get up in the morning and start out walking somewhere, and somehow he'd end up in their room, going through her things again. I took all of it up here one day."

She walked just a step ahead of him in the light of each match. When one burned itself out they stopped, and she struck another on the rough floor boards and they went on.

When they were kneeling over the crates and boxes Brad held the matches. He lit them one after another while Bobbi turned the pages of her mother's books. They were looking for an answer. For a way. He let each match burn down to his fingertips, seeming to forget. They grew more and more determined to find something that had passed, something useful. She was talking to him in the slow darkness, in the sudden light, in the still room.

"When I found out I was carrying Zoey," she said, "I went and jumped into Tilton's Pond on the way from the doctor's. I walked four miles in my bare feet and jumped in with my clothes on. When I was underwater the thought came to me that I could give up, I could stay there and never see my life again. I didn't want to wonder anymore what would happen and what was the right thing to do. I opened my lips and my mouth filled with water. It wasn't even cold. It felt warm and good. I came that close. I never told anyone before.

"So you're not the only one who wonders what's the right thing to do. But if you go and do something dumb so you won't have to wonder anymore, then you might miss the chance. You might miss the minute in your life where the whole point of everything comes clear. I had that when Zoey was born. I saw the top of her head come out of me, the fluff of blond hair."

He was staring at her as the match burned out. She took the next match from his hand and lit it and found that he was still staring at her. "So," she said. "So I don't have anything else to say to you."

They carried several books and found their way downstairs to the kitchen table. They sat there under lamplight. A warm breeze played at the screen door. He looked around and said, "Boy, I could stay at a place like this a long time."

She leaned back from the table and smiled in such a curious way that he smiled back and asked, "What? What is it?"

She looked toward the screen door. "I bet I've seen a thousand games at Veterans Park," she began. "I saw Catfish Hunter and Koufax and McLain pitch there. Those guys were here one day, gone the next. They were just too good."

"What about me, then?" he asked.

She tilted her head back in that way of hers, as if she had heard a sound from far off and could not quite make it out. "You're only passing through," she told him.

He shrugged his shoulders and said, "Who knows?" He opened another book, and they turned the pages until he put his finger down on a country bordered on its right by blue water. He traced his finger from one name in small print to another. Then he stopped. "There," he said. "Mike was right there."

7

The first sunlight of morning strayed into the kitchen and slashed through the porch windows in bars that bent over the arm of a winged chair and fell on the couch where Brad had slept through the night. His feet were hanging off the end of the couch. He had slept without a shirt on and under a quilt that Bobbi found for him after they finally stopped talking. They had talked about his brother and his mother and her father and baseball and the war. To her, he seemed supremely interested in everything she said. He was the first boy she'd ever met who didn't speak only of himself. She felt free to disagree with him.

"If I don't go to the war," he had said, "I might spend the rest of my life feeling guilty."

"Guilty for what?"

"Because of Mike. He's fighting."

"For what, what's he fighting for?"

"For freedom, I suppose. The thing we always fight for."

"You believe that?"

He looked unsure. He said, "In a way."

"I believe we want to make them just like us so we can sell them our things."

"How do you figure that?"

"We don't like people who aren't like us. They frighten us."

As Brad woke he thought back over their conversation and he hoped he hadn't said anything stupid or pretentious. He had found her a remarkable girl. He had felt himself inching toward her and toward her ideas about things, crossing the space between them.

Now Zoey stood in the divided sunlight, sucking her thumb, holding her blanket. She had a puzzled expression on her face as she stared at the pitcher on her couch. She stood still for quite a long time, the sunlight making her blink and squint. Then she moved closer to him, very close. She leaned down, and her breath on his face startled him. When he opened his eyes she was staring into them.

"Do you like gum?" she asked.

He smiled and said he did. "What about you?"

"Yes."

They just kept looking at each other. He couldn't turn away. It was as if he had awakened in a new world.

"I remember you from long ago," she told him. She wrinkled her nose, and when he raised one eyebrow at her she giggled and sucked in her cheeks, trying to make the fish face that the paper boy had been teaching her. "Hey, your feet don't fit the couch," she said.

"Right," he said. He was whispering to try and quiet her voice. "It wasn't long ago when you met me. Remember, I gave you the baseball? Just the other week."

She thought hard, her thumb in her mouth, her forehead creased in concentration.

"Don't you remember that, Zoey?"

"Hey, how do you know my name?"

"Your mother told me."

"Mommy told you?" she said. Then she looked at him again and said, "But I remember you from long ago."

He thought that she had confused him with one of her mother's boyfriends. He wondered how many had slept on this couch with their bare feet hanging over the end. "Well, maybe we used to be friends long ago."

"I can get the newspaper for us," she said.

While she was gone he began to think about what he would tell Doc Hill, the team manager, about why he missed yesterday's game. He thought about how much longer he would know Doc or anyone else in this town. His life is here, but there is a strange, transitory quality to it. His brother is going to spend thirteen months in Vietnam, longer than he will spend here. He wondered where Mike spent last night while he slept on the couch in this room.

Soon Page came downstairs and made them breakfast. He acted as though Brad ate with them every morning. He cooked bacon and eggs and sat Zoey down with a bowl of Sugar Smacks that she ate without taking her eyes off Brad.

"I like to let Bobbi sleep," Page said. "All that night work runs her down."

Page said something else about how the Blue Top would be out of business if it wasn't for the Air Force. All at once it came to Brad. That Air Force man in his uniform who patted Bobbi on her rear end that day after the game was the same man Brad had seen in his boxer shorts that night outside the motel. She's mixed up in something, he thought. And her father knows nothing about it.

Page turned from the stove, and Brad asked if there were chores he could help with. "There must be all sorts of work on a place like this," he said.

"There is, only I've sort of gone out of business for a while. Temporarily, for a summer anyway. I've leased my land, but I'll be back next season."

They sat for a long time over their plates. Baseball was the common language between them. "You know," Page said, "Bobbi's mother studied music for a while. She was learning to play the piano and she could play by ear. She had perfect pitch. She told me about Mozart, how he wrote his first symphony when he was eight years old. And before that, when he was four, he wrote a piano thing. He was a genius, no one argues with that. A true genius. Now, you wonder if there was ever that kind of genius in baseball, and there was, yes. The season Babe Ruth hit sixty home runs, that was more home runs than most *teams* hit! Boston had a total of twenty-seven on the entire team that season. And there's Ruth with sixty all by himself. That's a kind of genius, don't you think?"

"You're right, but in 1961 weren't you pulling for Mantle to break Babe's record?"

"Oh, 1961, you bet I was."

"Mickey was my hero. From the first time I ever played he was my hero. And he came close in 1961. Too bad he had to lose out to Maris. I still can't believe he hit fifty-four and Maris got sixty-one in the same season. The same team."

"Well," Page picked up, "Mick would have made it if he hadn't gotten sick. Do you know that story? He had a bad cold in the September stretch and a good friend of his, old Mel Allen, the famous Yankee broadcaster, sent him to a doctor he knew about who was famous for quick cures. The guy gave Mickey a shot of something, and it backfired and almost killed him. He ended up starting in only two of the last eighteen games, and if he'd stayed healthy he might have done it. But that was the story of Mickey's career, a lot of near misses. The last season he played injured and it cost him a three hundred lifetime average. He missed by a few percentage points. And you know he would have been the only man alive to hit a fair ball out of Yankee Stadium? Still, to this day it's never been done. Mick's shot hit part of the roof above the third deck, and people at the game swore the ball was still rising! Still going up. It would have gone out. I mean it just missed. It's the near misses in a life that fill your heart full of holes. I guess that's why I always felt something special for Mickey."

Page paused a moment, then went right on. "But Mick had a kind of gracefulness about him, didn't he? I'm not sure that kind of thing exists any longer. Right till the end, when his legs were so bad he could hardly run the bases, he was still a graceful man. You'll find out someday that this is true. When you reach a certain age you hope for just one thing, to be able to age gracefully. But why am I telling you this? You've got the whole world out there waiting for you. You're going to pitch your way right to the top." He brought his hand down on the table to emphasize this prediction. And then Zoey mimicked him. "That's right, Pepsi," he said.

He turned back to Brad. "But you've got to take good

care of yourself, son. You've got to have somebody you can talk to when things aren't right. When something is getting to a pitcher he tends to shut himself off, I know this. It's like a built-in reflex or something. It's what he learns to do to survive out on the hill. Close himself off, you know what I mean? If you shut yourself off tight, out on the mound, you might get out of a bad inning. But in the other half of life you can suffocate. You've got to have people you can trust, someone you can open up to. I've seen a lot of pitchers come through this part of the world, some going up, some going down. I've seen plenty of them grow old when they were still young. A part of you goes when they go, and I always thought, If it only wasn't such lonely work."

"I know what you're saying," Brad replied.

"Good, that's good," Page said. "Well, what about us going out and throwing some, then?"

They were in the orchard when Bobbi Ann found them. Zoey was running after baseballs, having the time of her life. Bobbi caught one glimpse of her father standing on his make-believe pitcher's mound with his back arched, stretching and smiling up at the sky. He was the shape and outline of a man blowing jazz on a trumpet, back on his heels, his face turned upward toward heaven, drawing out every last bit of sound. A sight to behold. She had never seen him look so happily absorbed. She thought, He is a man who deserves to have what will make him happy.

And what of the boy, the pitcher out there with him? He interrupted Page's windup, giving him some last-second instructions, then he stepped away. Page began his motion again, leaning farther forward this time, rocking back, then swinging his arms up high above his head. It was a perfect curve ball, and it struck the tree trunk with amazing authority. "That's it!" Page yelled. "That was it!"

Bobbi called out to them. The pitcher turned his head slightly. His face was perspiring. He was smiling at her all over again the way he did on Opening Day before anything had been said or asked. It was the smile that made her feel different. It was the smile that meant a chance.

Page stood next to the pitcher with an arm draped around his shoulder, smiling again like a potentate, the way he used to smile in the old photographs before the ground moved below his feet.

Bobbi brought them lemonade from the kitchen, and they sat in the orchard telling baseball stories. "In Wrigley Field in Chicago," Page said. "You'll have to watch out when you're pitching there."

"That's the National League," Bobbi said.

"Well, he may be in a World Series there or an All Star game. They've got that big scoreboard out in center field with a man inside who puts up the numbers each inning. I've been following the Chicago Cubs' batting averages for years, and I know they hit about thirty points higher at home in Wrigley than on the road, and there's a good reason. It's no coincidence. That man inside the scoreboard picks up the catcher's signal behind home plate and tips off the batters. He's got one sign for a breaking ball and one for a fast ball."

"That can't be true," Bobbi said. She turned to Brad. "Have you ever heard of that?"

"No," he said. Zoey was sitting close to him, between his outstretched legs.

She is my daughter, Bobbi thought. She wants what I want. It is instinctive.

"It sounds like part of the myth," Bobbi said. "Baseball is ninety percent myth, isn't it?"

"That's what I've heard all my life," Page replied. "But to me it was all true."

A moment passed, then Brad began telling a story. "This happened long ago in the early nineteen-twenties in Philadelphia."

"Not *that* long ago," Page said.

"No, not that long ago. But a pitcher by the name of Roofus Blake had pitched fourteen seasons for Connie Mack, for his Athletics, pitched his heart out, and then in the summer of 1925 he just didn't have it anymore. Connie Mack was a good man, a fair man, and he gave old Roofus a chance, but finally at the end of June he had made up his mind to let him go. Roofus was pitching at home, and it was the top of the third inning and he was being hit hard, so Connie goes out to the mound to lift him. 'I just can't get on top of it,' Roofus says. 'Guess not,' Connie says. 'I'm going to have to take you out, Roofus.' 'A few days rest and I'll be back,' Roofus says. Connie shakes his head and says, 'I'm sorry, Roofus, but I'm taking you out and I'm going to have to let you go back home to Texas.' Roofus looks him in the eye and asks, 'You sure that's the best thing, Connie?' 'Yep, I'm sure,' Connie says. 'You could try to pitch for some other team, but my opinion is that it's just going to get worse and worse.' 'Well,' Roofus says, 'there ain't another team I'd care to pitch for 'cept yours. But I swear to God, I think this arm has one good game left in it.'

"So Roofus rides the train home to Texas. His career is over, he's finished. Then, lo and behold, by the end of the season Connie Mack's team is locked in a pennant race.

And down the stretch in the last week of the season his best left-hander breaks a bone in his pitching hand and Connie is short a pitcher. He gives the situation a lot of hard thought and then sends a wire to Roofus Blake: 'You told me once that you had one good game left, Roofus. I need one good game next Sunday.'

"Roofus arrives in Philadelphia. He takes the mound in the final game of the season, the game that will decide the pennant. And he has it all that Sunday afternoon. Everything goes right for him, and he wins the game, and the As take the pennant. After the game Connie Mack says to him, 'You weren't kidding, Roofus, were you? That's the best game you ever threw for me. And I want to know, Roofus, is it the last one you got in that big left arm or isn't it?' 'I'm afraid it is,' says Roofus. He looks down at his left arm and says again, 'I'm afraid that's it.' And so the two men shook hands, and Roofus went back home to Texas, and that was all."

They were all silent, and then Page stood up and started walking toward the tin bread box. "I want to show you something, son," he said. "Come with me a minute."

When Brad got up, Bobbi asked him, "Is that a true story?"

He said he didn't know. "It's probably just part of the myth."

Page and the pitcher were standing under an apple tree like two men trying to get out of the rain. Page had a ball in the palm of one hand, and he was tracing three fingers across it. "I never showed this to a soul in my whole life," he said solemnly. "But I want you to have the secret. You don't need it now, but the day might come when it'll give you a few more years, when you've lost some speed on your fastball or you can't get the rotation on your slider. This is the one pitch that can save your career, son."

Page rubbed the ball between his palms, then went on. "Let me say to you that that's the whole, entire key to life—being able to compensate for what you don't have any more, for what you lose along the way. I've spent more hours than I can count learning this pitch, and I thought for some time that it might be a way out for me, the way to make up for the bad luck. For a while I wasn't too old to make it, to make a comeback. I could have broke into baseball with this." He held the ball up before Brad's eyes and slowly turned it on his fingertips. "I'm talking about a knuckleball," he said.

Brad was surprised. "Bobbi told me you were working on a curve."

Page smiled and shook his head. "My secret. I've got something here that every curveball pitcher dreams of having. I've got something to pass on."

Page called to Bobbi. He gave her a bat and told her to stand at the tree trunk. He said to Brad, "Stand behind her so you can see how this ball hops around."

A moment later they were ready. Page was as still as a wall before he began his windup. It was as if he was onstage waiting for the music to begin. He held the first ball up in the air with his left hand and said, "Watch." He'd thrown this pitch a few thousand times, but never better. The ball seemed to jump away from Bobbi's bat. Brad took the bat, and the next pitch did the same thing.

"That's a good pitch," Brad said.

"Oh, I can do things with this that you wouldn't believe," Page said.

"Give me another one, Pop." Bobbi called out.

He threw a dozen more, and she didn't come close. His eyes were shining when he turned to Brad. "It's like throwing dice up there. It's totally unpredictable. And I can teach it to you. When the time comes that you need it, you'll have it. But you have to promise me one thing. You won't use this pitch for at least ten years. You're still young, you have bones in your wrist and tendons in your arm you could damage. This knuckleball is an old man's pitch. You'll be able to throw it without any harm once some of your strength is gone. Right now you're too strong, you'll overthrow it and that'll be that."

Brad was walking back to the mound with Page when he asked him, "What about you, why'd you bother to learn it?"

Page called to Bobbi, "We'll be right back." He told Brad to follow him. "I have to go to the bathroom," he said.

While they were walking away from Bobbi Ann he answered Brad's question. "My Gwen was a woman with a powerful imagination. I never could keep up with her. First, when I started working on that pitch, I had a dream that it would take me into baseball. I was already in my thirties, but not too old for the knuckler, and I thought it might give Gwen something to be excited about. We could have had an exciting life, maybe a charmed life."

He stepped beyond a cluster of small pine trees. He was peeing in the dry grass while he said, "My secret, I've kept it a long time."

Brad thought about that. He thought about his own secret, the past, the guilt, the dark container coming down around him. He turned and looked back at Bobbi and thought about her secret, the Air Force man at the motel. When he turned back he saw that Page's urine was red, that there was blood splashing in the blades of grass at his feet. Another secret. Brad looked away.

"Tell me," Page said to divert his attention. "Your brother, can he throw?"

8

Like mountains, rivers, and cottages by the sea, old ballparks hold secrets, the parks made of wood that creak in the wind. Birds build nests in the rafters. Couples carve their initials in the wooden seats. Sometimes the secrets rise to the surface like a word that slips out during a conversation, then sticks in your mind. The secrets—one brilliant catch, one crack of the bat, one boy outrunning a line drive—they are timeless and they have the power to deprive the world of some of its indifference.

This is the way it is with baseball. You play every day, you just play each game, float off the field and right into the next game, the next day, and life goes on effortlessly, a mighty charmed life. Unless you end up in an office under the bleachers, a room with peeling paint and old, yellowed photographs on the walls and a shadeless lightbulb hanging on a frayed cord. And there is the manager sitting on one corner of his desk, telling you you should try to do something else with your life because you're not going to make it in this game. There is no kinder or gentler way to put it. You just don't have it.

It is deep into the season and the summer horizon bursts with reddish light toward dusk; and at night the sky is salted with stars. It is the sort of sky and the kind of evening that turn people into philosophers.

Brad was called into Doc Hill's office tonight. They were sitting a few feet from each other, but they both felt separated by a thousand miles. "Everyone in this game is a philosopher," Doc said. He searched through his desk drawers for a match to light his cigar. Brad heard him but didn't reply. Instead he waited, and his mind drifted back over the game he had pitched and lost today.

"Forget it," Doc said, "it happens. It comes and goes. The concentration, I mean. You faced a pretty good team out there today, and God knows we didn't light up the scoreboard for you. You'll bounce back. The way you're throwing, I'm not going to have you much longer."

It will be an evening like this, Brad thinks, after a long summer day, when he is told he is going up to the big leagues. A train will be waiting. A cab driver in some strange, distant city will be waiting. The momentum of this event has already begun. It began the moment he assented to it.

"We're all philosophers in this crazy game," Doc said again. "You have to be philosophical about things." His head was wrapped in gray smoke, and when he stood up and walked around his desk he looked like a man passing through fog. He was gray haired and thick chested, the kind of man who would chew the barber's ear off while he was getting a trim. "Up in Cleveland when the dog days of August roll around, the old horses will be tired out from a long season, and I'll get the call for a replacement. And you and I will part company. All of this will be a memory for you, that's all. But I hope you learned a few things that'll carry you a long way. I hope I taught you something about this crazy game."

Brad could tell that Doc had something else on his mind. "You didn't call me in just to kick the can around, Doc," he said.

Doc yanked the cigar from his mouth and ground it out in a ceramic ashtray sculpted into a catcher's mitt. "I've been sending boys up and down for a long time,' he began. "Sometimes I feel like nothing more than a glorified elevator operator in a hotel where the only decent rooms are at the top." Without his cigar, Doc's voice had lost some of its melody. He walked over to a green metal locker, opened it, and took out a yellow shirt and a pair of gray trousers that matched the color of his hair. Then he began undressing. "Back in sixty-three I was in Washington, D.C., in the Senators organization. I was driving to the ballpark one day and I got caught in a big traffic jam. There were cars and buses everywhere and mobs of people. I mean thousands and thousands of people, more people than we could get to the park in a month. Jesus, baseball was a losing proposition in those days in that city. But these people out on the streets were mostly Negroes. They were swarming all over the city, every block was jammed. But they were quiet, very quiet and orderly. Each group carried banners telling where they'd come from to get to Washington. Some were from the really bad places—Birmingham, Alabama, and Albany, Georgia—places where Negroes had been shot and beaten. Those who came from the northern cities were older, family-aged men and their wives, but the ones from those hard places were young. They were singing their freedom songs, and some of them were dancing and holding hands, and I thought to myself then that these young people, they're the ones who get things changed in this world. They're the ones who take the risks. And they've got a great burden on their shoulders trying to change something that's been going on for so long. This is something I can understand real well, and I always tried to give my Negro boys the best chance I could because I knew in many cases it was going to be their *only* chance."

Doc paused and bent over slowly to tie his shoes.

"It's Spenser, isn't it?" Brad said.

Doc stood up and his face was flushed. "Yep," he said.

"How far down?"

"All the way. Kemp, Texas, population three hundred and thirty-two."

"He'll quit before he plays A ball."

Doc nodded his head. "Down there all the coaches wear Hawaiian shirts," he mused. "Exploding eucalyptus trees, volcanoes. They've got no class."

"You want me to tell him."

"I was going to give you the day off tomorrow. I thought you could take my car, maybe take him fishing or something."

They are out at Three Mile Stream, east of town. Doc Hill's red Plymouth Valiant is parked in the brush behind them, and Spenser and Brad are sitting on a public dock holding fishing poles. "I have to tell you, this is the second time in my life I ever fished," Brad says. "It's one of those things you grow up expecting to do."

"Who'd you go with?" asks Spenser.

"My brother."

There is a silence, and Spenser clears his throat and spits into the water. "If I was your brother over there I'd run away, that's exactly what he probably done. I hear about what they're doin' to boys over there. I hear about those tunnels filled with awful shit to kill a person. Your brother probably got smart and run off somewheres, Ivy. Maybe he's goin' to get home." He pauses to pull down the beak of his ball cap. "Shit, if I get me a catfish in this pisshole I'll be amazed. I'll eat a catfish on sight even if I ain't hungry. I love 'em. Probably cause they're so ugly. Hey, what'd the blind man say when he walks into the fish factory?"

"I don't know."

"Morning, ladies."

Spenser laughs, and Brad thinks to himself, The world is so precariously balanced that no one can be sure of anything from one minute to the next. A laugh, a cry. A life of planning and yet everything remains uncertain. One day you have a brother, the next day he's gone. So no wonder there's a place for baseball, for its irresistible order. Brad had tried for many summers to teach the game to Mike. After a while he could play pretty well, but never as well as Brad, never well enough to keep up. Instead of bringing them closer, baseball only widened the gap between them.

"They've got rivers over there in Vietnam, don't they, Ivy?"

"Yeah."

"Then there's got to be a way out for your brother. If there's a river runnin' through it then there's a sure way to get hisself out. I used to always say that. At home I'd fish in the river that runs right over the county line, the same river the slaves used to hide in when they was bein' chased down. I always figured that I had a ways to go myself if I needed to. Whenever you got a river nearbys you got somethin'."

"Where would you go?"
"What?"
"Where would you go?"
"That answer I don't know really. I guess I'd just follow the river as far as I wanted, maybe almost to the ocean. Only I was kinda scared of the ocean in ways."
"There's nothing to be scared about. The ocean's the greatest thing in the world." Brad looks up across the stream. He can see the wind stirring the surface of the water. "I bet you've never seen a sailboat, have you, Spense?"
"Pictures of some."
"Yeah?"
"Yep."
"You'd love sailing. I used to race my brother in Buzzards Bay. We had a couple of little prams, and we'd race around the edge of the bay, flying with the wind, water coming over the gunwale."
"Water comin' right into the boat?"
"Yeah, but not enough to slow you down."
"But there's times when there wasn't no wind, ain't there?"
"Sure. You can get caught without wind. Caught in irons, it's called."
Spenser looks at him pensively. It is as if this new world is visible in the air between them. "Well, then, you ain't goin to get nowheres in the ocean without your wind. But the river's a whole different kind of thing, Ivy. It's always movin' along. It's always waitin' to take you someplace else if you have to leave the spot you're in. It's the freest thing. I always used to feel free when I was standin' by the river. Don't need no sail, don't need no wind. Just holt onto a log or just lie on your back and let the river take you."

It takes Spenser a few minutes to reel in his line, put another worm on his hook, and cast out again. "Maybe your brother found himself a good strong river and he just laid down on his own back."

Time passes, and Brad keeps hoping Spenser will say something that will make it easier for him to pass on the bad news. Fishing has made the black boy voluble. "I was thinkin' the other night that you and me got to each have sons of our own. You know how they say if you push a boy to playin' ball he won't play? And he'll grow up hatin' the game? Well, if we both has sons I got an idea that we'll make out fine, 'cause you can be the one to push my boy and I'll be the one to push yours."

They both laugh at this. Their laughter skims across the stream like a flat stone thrown sidearm into the water. Then Spense asks, "Does it seem a long ways off to you?"

"What's that?"

"Kids and all that."

"Sometimes. Sometimes not."

"You like that Bobbi girl, don't you?"

Brad turns to him and he is smiling back. "What are you, writing a book or something?"

"Hey, come on, you can't kid me. I know all about romance. Plus I like her myself, and if you wasn't around I'd'a been findin' my own way to her door long before."

"I haven't figured her out," Brad says.

"Hell, ain't a girl worth her salt who a boy can figure out. Two different kinds of folk completely. But what I like about her is that look in her eyes. You can tell she ain't the kind of spoiled girl that's gonna make a boy wish he could hop in a river of his own to get free from her. No sir, you'd want to keep real near a unspoiled girl like her, 'cause you're gonna get understandin' from a girl like she is. You can tell. I don't care what people say about gettin' married. I know I used to think the reason a boy gets married was so's he could get it every night without havin' to go to so much trouble, but I know now that it's a lot more than that. You got to marry a girl who respects you, respects you a powerful lot. So that even if the time comes when you don't think so high of yourself, that girl is still gonna be there. Only don't you wish sometimes you was married with kids already, so they could sit up there in the stands and watch us play?"

"I never thought of it."

"Well, maybe you ain't had to worry. I mean you're gonna be playin' this game for a lot of years, and there's plenty of time for you. But I keep on thinkin' how good a feelin' it would be to have somebody up there in the stands who was rootin' their hearts out for me."

"I'll tell you something," Brad says with a grin. "The next game I don't pitch I'll sit up there myself and I'll organize a whole cheering section for you." Brad has forgotten there won't be another game, and only when he and Spenser have stopped laughing does he remember.

"I may just get out of baseball for a while," Spenser says.

"Why?"

"I don't know, but I'd like to find me a girl who knows somethin' about music she could teach me. Music's somethin' that seems good to me right now, and I can't say exactly why."

"You'll find her," Brad tells him.

"And we'll both have sons then?"

"We'll have sons."

"Only my son ain't gonna get to see his daddy play ball," Spenser says. Then he is silent for a minute before saying, "Ain't I right on that, Ivy?" He has turned to look straight at Brad.

"They want you to go to Texas."

"Class A?"

"You'll get back up," Brad says.

Spenser sighs. He reels in his line. "We ain't even had a nibble from this pisshole," he says. "If this was a river, I'd lie down in it like your brother probably done."

Brad can see the reflection of the water in his eyes. He is thinking, When the dream is gone nothing is ever the same again. Already Spenser has begun changing. Something is different.

When the dream is gone what will you become?

Perhaps a philosopher.

Bobbi Ann had her own philosophy, and she told it to Spenser to try and comfort him. They were at the train station, waiting. Someone was painting the walnut wainscoting in the lobby a horrible avocado green color. With each brushstroke the future of this room looked bleaker.

"We're all tied together," Bobbi said. "By a soul, a soul outside our own. We each have a piece of this soul, like a seed in our pocket, and we grow on our own and live independently through a life. When we die we lose our identity, and we drift back to the big soul, and whatever we've learned and experienced, all our wisdom and feeling, is given back to the big soul, and then eventually we find our way back to another planet with another seed in our pocket." She told him this, and when she'd finished he was silent. She felt a little self-conscious. She shrugged her shoulders and said she had nothing else to say.

"I'm goin' to remember that," Spenser said reverently. "You mean we're goin' to live forever?"

"A part of us," she answered.

"And we're all sort of held together, like the three of us no matter where we go is really still together?"

Bobbi nodded her head.

"I'm glad of that," Spenser said. He looked first into Bobbi's eyes and then he turned to Brad. "That gives a man a kind of hope, don't it, Ivy? Let's say that the three of us is always goin' to be together, then. And that this seed we carry around in our pockets ain't never goin' to die."

After a pause he turned back to Bobbi and opened his arms to embrace her. It was very quick and they barely touched. This was the first time she had ever felt a black boy's skin. She felt him tremble when her breasts brushed against him.

"I don't really know you that well, but good luck," he said. Then he gave Brad his hand to shake. "I want you to plant your seed on the mound in Cleveland. You get up there, don't waste no time."

"Here," Brad said, "take this." He handed him an envelope. It was an envelope from the Blue Top, and Bobbi shuddered at the recollection of the money passed to her in these envelopes.

"What's this?" Spenser asked.

"Just take it so if you need it—no, don't open it here."

"I can't—"

"Take it."

"It's a lot of money."

"Just a few bucks."

Spenser slipped it into his hip pocket. "I'm puttin' it in with my seed, Bobbi Ann. I don't want to take it, but you're right, Ivy, I'm goin' to need it. Goin' to have to get some new clothes now that there ain't no uniform to wear."

"You'll be back," Brad said.

"Maybe Uncle Sam will get me, and I'll be in a different kind of uniform."

Brad grabbed his arm. "Don't do that, don't ever do that."

"Well," Spenser said. "When you get on the mound in Cleveland and they're shinin' that big TV camera at you, don't forget to wink."

"I won't."

"Well, can you wink?"

"Sure I can wink."

"Let's see. First one eye, then the other."

Brad winked, first one eye, then the other.

"Good, that's good. Now you-all get goin'."

"We'll wait," Brad said.

"No, you get goin'. I like to be alone for a while before I leave a place I ain't comin' back to."

9

Summer seemed to start each day on the sunstruck porch. This morning Brad and Page sat there talking. The birthday car was parked nearby, its nose pointing at them, its roof and hood coated in light. Page said he had given it a good polish. "Spent the day walking around it," he declared. He paused, then with a hand on each arm of his chair raised himself slightly to look over the porch railing at a spot on one fender he had missed with his chamois cloth. "You don't get a shine like that without chamois no matter what kind of an idea you have," he said.

Brad nodded. Then he asked him where he was going to go first in his new car.

A moment later Page answered, "I hear you and I'll think about that, but I was just about to say something else. I was thinking about this the other day watching you fellows out on the field. About how a ball player has a special kind of existence in this world. You're going to live two lives, you know. One life in baseball, and then another when you can't play anymore. Most people don't ever live even half a life, they're so busy just trying to stay on top of things." He crossed his legs at the ankles. Brad saw his socks didn't match.

"But then, of course, you've gotta die twice too," Page said. "When you have to stop playing there's a good part of you that will die. Think of the players who stuck in the game too long, just for that one more season because they couldn't face giving up the game. You can't blame them, can you? They were facing a kind of death, death at a young age, and they wanted to postpone it as long as they could. And I've been there myself, I've been through that too. Watching you fellows out there the other day it dawned on me that we have that much in common. Two lives, two deaths. When I lost Bobbi's mother it was the end of one life."

He stopped and looked back at his car. Brad saw the car's reflection in his eyes. "And the new life can surprise you," he went on. "You take that car. I never dreamed I'd have another car in my lifetime. It's funny, though, before I laid eyes on that machine I had a hundred places in mind, places I wanted to go to. And I used to say I couldn't go because I didn't have any way of getting there. But now that I have this car I can't really think of a place I'd like to go to."

Bobbi came outside with Zoey straddling her hip, her bare legs hanging below a gingham dress. There were grass stains on her knees. Page said to her, "You didn't get me my newspaper this morning. Are you on strike?"

"The news is all bad," Bobbi said.

"I don't read anything but the sports, you know that."

Bobbi looked out at the car and suggested they take a picture. "We ought to get one good picture before it collapses, don't you think?"

"Don't give it any ideas," Page said. "I've got big plans for that machine."

"Well, anyway, let's get a picture while it's looking so grand."

Bobbi went inside and when she came back with the camera she had a photograph to show Brad. It was a picture of Zoey at seven months. She was dressed in white-footed pajamas. Dressed like a baker. Bobbi handed Brad the photograph and said, "Pop used to say a baby at seven months ought to be about the size of second base. That's why we took this picture."

They passed the photograph around. Page held it up at arm's length, and Bobbi chided him for not wearing his glasses. He said, "It's true, Pepsi, you look just like second base." Zoey went to stand between his knees. He put one arm around her and kissed the back of her neck. "Well, let's take some pictures, then," he said. "You're long past second base, and we don't have any pictures of you."

They photographed the car from every angle with Page behind the wheel, then with Zoey behind the wheel, then with Brad standing with one foot propped up on the bumper.

"Let's get one of you," Page said to Bobbi.

"We have plenty," she said.

Brad took the camera from her and said, "We need one more, one of you, go on." He motioned to the car. She walked over to it, straightening her dress at her sides. She opened the back door and got in. Page called to her to get behind the wheel.

She closed the door and said she was just going along for the ride. "Today I feel like putting my head back and letting someone else drive me around."

It was a box camera that you held down at your waist and looked into. Brad centered the image in the glass. "You have to hold still," he said to her. Suddenly she turned her face in the open window, then folded her arms under her chin and looked into the lens, past all of them, past her daughter whom she loved but to whom she was connected by a single improvident night, past her father whom she loved but whose life threw up a wall in front of her. She looked past Brad whom she barely knew, and she thought about his first visit to the farm that night when she told him he was only passing through, and she thought about how people's lives are bound together no matter what they tell each other. And when the shutter clicked, all of them seemed to start breathing again at the same time. It was as if something had passed between them, some understanding, maybe. Brad stared down into the square glass frame. When he turned and looked at Page he was still thinking of Bobbi. He was smiling. "You should have been on stage," he cried. And when he spoke, the spell of the moment was broken. The photograph would show her face centered in the car's rear window, her features sharply cast in the blue morning light, her expression showing curiosity, happiness, perhaps some slight impatience, not what you would easily call contentment. She would look like a healthy girl, eager to get on with life, to live all that was ahead of her. The sunlight would be caught on the narrow strip of chrome beneath the window and in the oval hubcaps.

The photograph would show the dark, sparkling car slouching forward, its shoulders rounded and wide. It would be seen sitting on a sea of green land.

Much later, after Zoey was asleep and Page was in his bed listening to the last innings of some baseball game on the radio, Bobbi sat on the porch with Brad. The moon floated above the pitched roof of the barn. "I was thinking," she said, "how we take pictures and leave them behind hoping someone will remember how we were."

"A part of history," he said. "A permanent record."

"But a lie, really. A myth. Things are arranged before the lens, things are omitted."

He wondered what she meant by this. Then he told her how his family had always taken photographs. "Not just my parents, but all their friends. There were always lots of pictures. Maybe they couldn't really believe how lucky they were. Their big lives, they had to *see* them in order to believe them."

"A kind of proof, then?" she asked suddenly.

"Yes. Evidence. Only it was so phony most of the time. Like you said, a myth. The happy faces, the hugs, arms around each other. I mean, two minutes later people could be trying to kill each other. So much was missing, maybe they took all those pictures to hide what was missing. I remember each year getting together for the family Christmas card. The Bickharts, the Kayes, the Millers, we all had the same kind of cards, the same photographer. He must have made a mint. He had to put makeup on Doctor Miller to hide these bad marks he used to have around his eyes. He's a brain surgeon who does this special kind of brain surgery. People fly in from all over the world to have the operation. It takes hours and hours. He does it all under a microscope that cuts into his face, deep bloody circles around both eyes. The only time I ever saw him without those circles was on the family Christmas card each year."

Bobbi told him that the lens captured both the presence and the absence of things. "It's just as much proof of what is missing as what exists, each picture, I mean. I was thinking of the pictures we took this morning. Fifty years from now, a hundred years, someone will pick them up and wonder where the mother was, the wife. They'll think she died." She asked him what else was missing from the pictures his family took. "I mean," she said, "besides the bloody circles on Doctor Miller's face."

He told her that with his family the pictures showed a soft life. "I have a theory about all those people, about why the rich people have so many problems. It's because they're soft. The good life, all that good luck, makes them soft and then when the problems come along they fall apart."

Brad walked over to the porch railing and put one foot up on it. "That's the thing I worry about too, that I'm not tough enough inside. I worry about Mike for the same reason. But I envy him too, because he's going to get the chance to find out."

"Everyone gets the chance," she said. "Sooner or later the good luck is gone, and you find out what you're like inside."

"But you ought to be able to find out first. Before the lights go out it would be nice to know if you can see in the dark."

"I think you know," Bobbi said. "I think everybody knows what's inside."

"Not Mike. I don't think Mike has any idea."

"But you do."

He didn't say anything for a minute, and then he told her that she had looked perfect sitting at the window of the car. "I bet it turns out to be the kind of picture you could put on the cover of a book or something."

It was late and they were barely talking when Zoey appeared at the door. She had dressed herself in the gingham dress. Light from the kitchen threw her shadow onto the porch, outlining the dress where it flared at her knees, making the shape of a letter A. Bobbi took her in her arms. "It's not nearly time to get up yet, sweetie," she said.

"I have a busy day," Zoey said.

A minute later she was asleep in Bobbi's arms.

"It's my fault," Brad whispered. "I was the one who told her she had a busy day tomorrow. That's what my mother used to say to me."

"Is that what you wanted to hear?"

"More than anything. Sitting around with nothing to do was like a prison sentence for me. I was probably hyperactive."

"That's what *we* do," she said. "We've been sitting around for hours."

"Well," he said.

Bobbi Ann looked down at Zoey. "She's in never-never land," she said. "I remember when she was light as a feather. She was born early, seven weeks early. I could dress her in my doll clothes."

He asked if he could hold her, and Bobbi carried her like a puppet and laid her in his arms. In his open hands Zoey looked very small again to Bobbi. She said, "You want to know where you're going and how things will turn out, for their sake."

"I can see why," Brad said.

"Well, for your own sake too. But she's going to live way into the next century. I want her to play the violin in the twenty-first century. Then I want her to teach me. We can sit together in a room playing a concert for each other. In the year 2009."

"I'll be sixty-two."

"I'll still be twenty-three. I'm not going to get any older, this is as old as I get." She reached over and brushed Zoey's hair back from her face. She said, "Once you have a child you think about time a lot more, about time passing. I can't even remember now what I used to be like. It seems like hundreds of years ago that I was pregnant with her. I can't remember what my life was like before her." She looked up at the sky beyond the porch roof and said, "You know, we're here and then we're gone. Do you ever think of that? How fast it all goes?"

"Most of my days are pretty slow," he said. "A lot of waiting around for a game to start."

"The individual days, maybe, but then you look back and four hundred of them are missing. Another year."

Brad looked at her a long time. It was the intelligence of her face that struck him, a serene quality in her eyes.

"But I think about this," she said. "How you live your whole life, in a town like this, say, and after you're gone, on any given day not a single person in town thinks for even a second about you. You're completely forgotten unless you have children. They might remember you, be able to describe you and what it was you stood for. That's the great chance you get with children. And I guess you have the same chance with baseball. You could be remembered in some way. I mean, no one ever remembers a farmer, but if you make the big leagues there'll be some record that you were there."

"But how?" he asked.

"What?"

"*How* will you be remembered? That's the important thing."

"Yes," she said. "Of course, you're right."

He told her he didn't ever want to live the kind of life everyone lived. "I wanted to be different," he said.

"I know," she told him. "Someday I'll tell you things about the next life, and the life after that."

She wouldn't go on even when he asked her to. The expression on her face was suddenly so similar to the way she had looked in the car window that morning. He asked her what she had been thinking then. She said she couldn't remember. He didn't exactly believe her, but he let it go. He kept thinking about her face framed in the glass of the camera. He had already forgotten certain things about it.

Brad thought about photographs, how they have the capacity to outlive us. If he were to discover photographs of these people after never knowing them, after only reading about them, would he recognize them? Would he recognize her in the window of the old car? Would the picture show, as she said, the presence and absence of things? The passage of time was too fast for him to observe it. You can only look back over life, over the accumulated happiness and tragedy of life, he thought. Do others see photographs the same way, with some slight apprehension over the fear of discovering what's been lost? Maybe the photograph proves that certain things were this way or that way, just as he had always sworn they were. But isn't it too bad that everyone needs this evidence to persuade the world of what they once were, and to persuade themselves as well?

If he were to ask Bobbi Ann what she would hope to find years from now when they held up the photograph to see how things had been that day, would she really know how to answer? It's not a question meant for young people to whom the present is still unfolding. But he could suggest a few things. Things like health, excitement, self-respect. Things that are often lost.

She let Brad carry Zoey upstairs and put her back to bed. He thought about what Bobbi had said about seeing into the future, and when he came back out on the porch he asked her if she believed in fortune-telling.

"You're talking about Emo Duncan," she said.

"Yes."

"Our resident catcher in the rye." She smiled. "Whose fortune are you interested in?"

"My brother's."

"That's a little out of Emo's league, isn't it? I've never known him to deal with anything outside baseball."

"But you don't believe it, do you?"

"I didn't say that. I heard a story once about a pitcher who broke his hand the night before his biggest game, his *pitching* hand. The game the next day was going to determine his future. He went to Emo and supposedly his hand was healed." She became silent.

"So he's a medicine man as well as a soothsayer," Brad said.

"I guess he's whatever you want him to be. I don't know how anybody in this world can say for sure that something can't be true."

Brad was quiet. The middle of the night grew cool. They started a fire in the living room hearth. He told her he expected his brother to last only a few minutes under fire. "I can't see him shooting back," he said.

In the next breath a bat came flying out of the chimney. They both jumped. One of its wings scraped Brad's cheek. Bobbi yelled, "Zoey! We can't let it get in her room!" Brad turned on the overhead light. They saw it stuck like a black star on the ceiling. Bobbi got a broom from the kitchen. When she took a swing at it, the bat circled their heads wildly, then drifted up the stairway. They charged up the stairs after it, turning lights on ahead of them. Page's door was shut. When they found the bat again it was above the window frame next to Zoey's bed. "We need a flashlight," Bobbi said. Before she went for one she pulled the sheet over Zoey's head.

A few minutes later Bobbi had captured the bat in the bedspread while Brad blinded it with the flashlight. They took it outside and set it free. It disappeared above their heads. Brad took a step away from Bobbi. "I'm sorry I wasn't much help," he said.

She walked up next to him. "There's nothing wrong with being afraid," she said. "Where you come from you don't run into bats every night of the week."

"I've always been scared to death of bats. Particularly bats from Louisville."

It took her a second; she saw he was smiling at her. Her hand brushed his arm. "The Louisville Slugger," she said. "I understand they can't touch your fastball this summer."

"I *was* afraid," he said.

"So what."

"Could you tell?"

"Yes."

"That's what I meant about being soft." He kicked the dirt with his right foot, then his left. "I was always the one rescuing Mike from everything, I wasn't allowed to be afraid of anything. Mike looked up to me."

"You can be afraid," she said. "He'll look up to you anyway. And you don't have to pretend anything with me. You don't have to strike me out."

He sighed and looked up at the stars. He walked in a circle around her, then told her how much he liked being on the farm. "I've never seen stars like this," he said.

She pointed out several constellations to him, the names sounding like explorers from an old world. She stood close enough to him to feel him breathing. It started something inside both of them. He thought about Mike looking up at certain stars. He wanted to cry for him. He told her this. "Go ahead then," she said. She made it sound so easy.

They spent the night talking. In the first light of morning he took her bicycle and went for a long ride. The green fields were endless. It was like dawn at sea, only none of the countryside was familiar to him. He turned the bicycle into a meadow and rode for hundreds of yards. The ground was hard, like a road, after the rainless summer. With the sun, suddenly everything was colored. He passed cows going out; back on the road, two children—a boy and his younger sister with a hand-painted sign. The scent of berries followed him a ways. He turned around and went back and bought a pint. "How much?" he asked. Neither of them knew for sure. The girl looked at her brother, surprised at his silence.

Brad asked her if she knew the girl down the road, Zoey.

"Yep," she replied. Then she asked, "How much money do you got anyways?"

He paid them and asked what they were going to do all day. The boy shrugged his shoulders dolefully. "Stuff," his sister said.

He rode back with the strawberries resting on the handlebars like a box of jewels. At the door Bobbi joked with him. "Gone all week and that's all you have to show for it?"

"But they're the best berries money can buy."

"How's a hungry family going to survive on a few berries? Have you forgotten we have babies to feed?"

"But you don't understand, each one of these contains the essence of a full-course Thanksgiving dinner." He held one up and turned it before her eyes. He touched the end of her nose with it. "I bought these from an old Indian down by the river. He told me these berries had the power to elevate the spirit so much that you forgot about being hungry."

"But there is no river," she said slyly.

"You must believe me."

"Yes, okay then, I'll believe it all," she said.

Page cooked them pancakes for breakfast. They read the sports page and talked about baseball. Brad thought to himself that if it weren't for baseball he never would have come into their world. He couldn't remember a morning of his life that had started more calmly than this. He felt something lifted from him. He felt part of a well-arranged world.

After the dishes they took turns pitching and batting baseballs into the fields. Page had almost a hundred balls, they were scattered everywhere. Then they all jumped into the old car. Brad was behind the wheel, Zoey was between his legs pretending to steer. They drove across the fields with all four doors wide open, driving very slowly so they could just lean out of the car and pick up the baseballs. They were all laughing. The strawberries had stained their fingers. Everytime Page leaned over for a ball he began coughing. He finally asked Brad to stop the car. He got out and told them he was going to take a walk. He gave them a little wave, then turned away. "Leave the dishes for me," he said. "Just leave the dishes. I'll be back soon."

10

In those days Brad's suitcase was kept in the living room behind the couch. He didn't go to the Blue Top anymore. Neither did Bobbi. Those days they were waiting to hear about Michael. His absence, his disappearance, drew them closer. Under the morning sun Brad practiced the knuckleball in the orchard while Page sat in the grass smiling, acknowledging the passage of his secret. Bobbi had taken over for him driving the miniature red tractor at Veterans Park. He was tired, and she insisted he take some time off. He went to the park only on the days Brad pitched. He sat down the third-base line with Bobbi and Zoey, like old times.

The days were flying by. The next full moon, they said, would be a frost moon. The old times were accumulating. They took long walks at night to slow time down.

Tonight they walked all the way to Veterans Park. They sat in the darkened bleachers, watching the jets take off across Route 1. Below them the white baselines and the boundaries of the batter's box were outlined against the shadowless field. They sat, as in a darkened theater. The irony was not lost on Brad. He recalled his father's call to arms and said to Bobbi, "I've never purposely put on an act."

"Not even for yourself?" she asked.

"I don't think so."

"Not even that first night, in the attic?"

"What do you mean?"

"I thought for sure you knew I wanted you, but you were pretending not to know. You didn't want to look smug."

"You're wrong, I didn't know anything."

"Then you're as guileless as I thought you were." She laughed a little. "But down there, on the field, you have something up your sleeve. What kind of magic tricks do you have anyway?"

Brad remembered the time his brother asked him the same thing. Brad had been named for the second straight year to the all-American team in college. No pitcher from Princeton had ever come close to this before. Brad told Mike it was just luck, but Mike had pressed him to reveal his secrets about pitching.

"You really want me to bore you with this?" he asked Bobbi.

"Why would I be bored?"

"Well," he said, "I have a few things. You'll be the second person I ever told. I told Mike once." He stood up and walked to the railing. He pointed down at the circle outlined in white in the grass a few yards from home plate.

"The on-deck circle," he said with satisfaction. "I study batters before they get up to bat against me. When they're taking their practice cuts in the on-deck circle, I'm watching out of the corner of my eye. And before the game while they're taking batting practice. A guy who carries his bat high, his wrists way up here like this, up around his chin, he won't be able to get down and through a tight fastball; it'll take him too long. A guy who holds the bat flat and low, who sweeps it over the plate, he'll jump too early at my breaking ball, he'll beat it into the ground without any power."

He was eagerly telling her this and each time he turned from the field back to her, she showed him an animated expression intended to urge him on.

"Hitting is all timing," he declared. "And pitching is throwing off a batter's timing. If a batter can figure you out, you're finished. Dead. It's not the fastball that strikes out a good hitter, it's the unexpected fastball. Batters have these expectations. When the count's at two-and-two, it's the end of the line and they're thinking the pitcher's going to try and finish them off, they're expecting fastball all the way. That's when I'll drop them a curve or a change-up, the off-speed stuff. When I'm in a jam I've got two pitches I rely on. Most pitchers have one and it doesn't take long for good hitters to figure out what it is. When it's two-and-O, or three-and-one, I mix up between the fastball and the slider. I don't let myself rely more on one than the other. I want them both there to choose from."

His smile showed the pleasure he was getting from this. He seemed to have forgotten everything but baseball.

"So you're an enigma out there," she said.
"In a way."
"An illusionist?"
"I suppose."
"But not an actor?"

"No," he said patiently. "Not an actor. A magician maybe, but no actor."

He moved closer and took hold of her, his hands cupping her elbows. He leaned back against the rail and pulled her to him. "And then," he went on slowly, "halfway through the game, just when they might start catching on to my strategy, I change the whole thing around. When I'm ahead in the count and could ease off, I throw the real heat, I turn up the gas. I want to catch them off balance."

He drew her elbows together slowly until the backs of his hands were pressing against her breasts. She watched him. He kissed her knuckles and said, "You've got the makings for a great knuckleball yourself."

"From a pedigree of knuckleballers," she replied.

Each kiss, each time his lips touched her fingers it was like a step taken, a stair mounted, a slow ascent.

"I'm taking Pop in for tests tomorrow," she told him. "He's so stubborn about going to the doctor."

Brad already knew him well enough. A man who denies pain and illness with a mixture of irony and scorn. "I'd be the same way," he said.

She looked straight down the length of his legs, their kneecaps were touching. His shoes looked enormous to her and suddenly very comical. She had not noticed before how long they were. The sight of them made her feel like laughing. "They should sell you the boxes," she said. But he didn't hear her. He was speaking of something else.

"What you said to Spense about the soul, do you believe it?"

"I believe we belong to the earth," she said. "We're given off by the earth and then drawn back, like something thrown up on the beach by the tide. But we only belong to the earth. The people from Mongolia wandering around Asia eventually developed tough skin and slitted eyes to be able to stand the winds. Someday my great grandchildren might be born with even tougher skin and narrower eyes to survive the winds on Mars. The earth provides us what we need, or a way at least to compensate. Think of it," she said, then paused. "My mother leaves, but then there's Zoey in her place, someone new for me and Pop."

He was thinking about Mike again. If he lost his brother, who would there be?

She walked down the row of wooden seats a few steps before she leaned out over the railing, gripping it with her hands and rocking gently on it. "I believe that up there, all of that up there, is beautiful. And our children's children are going to see it all. To those places that are so far away we'll send robots first. Great machines with incredible strength and brains, already programmed to build entire cities for us to live in. When we finally arrive, everything will be finished and waiting for us. Right down to the last detail. Right down to mailboxes on the street corners.

He pointed to the field and asked if they would build any ballparks.

"Not like this one," she said. "Pretty soon this will be a rare thing."

She looked out over the field. There were fireflies near first base where Spenser had once stood. "So," she said, "it all comes down to expectations, then. Knowing what the batter is expecting, and then giving him something different?"

"Yes, that's it, that's all it is really."

"Like life, then."

"You believe that?"

"Don't you?"

"It wasn't really that way for me. Things were pretty even in my life," he said.

"Everything you wanted came true?"

"Not everything."

"And what you couldn't have, did you pray for that?" she asked.

"I never prayed," he said.

She told him that she had prayed for her father, but only recently. "And I don't know," she said. "Do you think we should be praying for ourselves?"

"Now," he said, "since I've come here, things are different, I'm believing different things."

She looked straight at him. "Do you pray for Michael?"

"Yes."

"Every day?"

"Yes."

"And you pray to God?"

"That's all I know. And you, is there a God in your picture of things?"

"Yes," she answered. "When I was carrying Zoey I prayed constantly to God that she would be born healthy. I prayed every day for that, and the minute she was born I counted toes and fingers to make sure she was perfect. When you have that kind of perfection right there in your hands, you never doubt the existence of God again."

She was lost momentarily in her own thoughts. She drifted away. She floated above the ballpark and hovered above the place beyond the outfield fence where the shortstop had gone inside her. She wondered what God had thought about her then.

"You're very pretty," he said.

"You are too."

"I'm supposed to look mean, I'm supposed to be intimidating out there."

"Well, to me you look pretty." She leaned up to him and kissed him on his lips. "That first night," she went on, "that night in the attic when we were looking for your brother, you could have had everything. It was all there for you, you could have taken it. I wouldn't have stopped you. But now that I know you so well, it's different, it feels different to me. It's something to give."

They talked all the way back home. They talked about Michael, the war, the men who had gone to the moon this summer. "I feel attached to all of it," she told him as they reached her porch. "It's strange how so much in the big world has gotten caught in the web of this small place."

He stopped her to kiss her. He reached beneath her blouse. She felt his palms against her. "Come on," she said.

She took him through the dark house, up to her room, into her bed, and she told herself that even when he would leave her, when all this was over, it would be all right. They would remember. She thought of her mother. If she were ever to see her mother again she would tell her about this boy, and how she lost him to his dream. He had some place to get to, she would tell her. She and her father fell in love with people who were moving toward their own dreams.

"The world," he was saying to her. "It does seem small, I know what you mean. So much is happening."

There was some light in the room when she stood in front of him helping him undress her. It took him forever. She kissed him and placed his hands on the hem of her dress, and inch by inch he gathered the material into his hands. She felt the light on her thighs.

"I'm sorry," he said. "I'm better at baseball."

"Well, that's admirable." She laughed, then dropped down slowly onto her knees. She felt the breath rush out of him. When she stood again she went up onto her toes. His arms went around her, he lifted her off the wooden floor. She looked down at his feet standing in her clothes and said, "I'm on my way to Mars."

Eventually they slept. But then, sometime before sunrise, she opened her eyes and found him standing at the window. A jet plane was exploding in the whitening sky. She whispered his name and he turned. "Those other worlds you believe in," he said. "I was just thinking that Michael would believe you."

11

"Twenty-four hours and I'm out of here," he said. Bobbi sat next to him on the front seat of a government van he had borrowed to move his belongings from the Blue Top to a room in officers' row at the base. It was early morning. They were parked on a side street, a few blocks from the Pine Tree Credit Bureau. A few minutes ago Noel Libby had come by to confirm to Bobbi Ann that the payments on her father's account had been made for the next nine months.

"So," the colonel said, "counting everything, you bought your old man eleven months and a car. Not bad for forty days' work. You still have the rest of the summer for a good time. Live it up. Of course, life won't be as sweet without me around."

He smiled at himself in the rearview mirror and asked, "You think these glasses make me look like Superman, I mean Clark Kent?"

When she didn't answer, he went on. "Well, seeing you in a rearview mirror is going to make me sad, baby."

Bobbi was silent. She was thinking about Brad and about her father, and about waiting. She hadn't realized before how you can reorder your life around waiting, never knowing what to expect, as if waiting were an action. Time passes and you wait for something to happen, but all that happens is that more time passes. She was thinking how she would ask the colonel to help her and what kind of a person she was to turn to him for help.

Looking at the people passing by on their way to work, she felt lost in this town, lost to herself. It was as if the person she had always wanted to be was far away again.

You give up, she was thinking. You give up on this world when you just can't wait any longer for things to get better. So then, she was sitting here in this man's company because she didn't want her father to give up, she didn't want Brad to give up.

The Colonel fiddled with some loose change on the dashboard. "I hoped maybe you'd have something for me, some parting gift, maybe a silk scarf to put around my neck and send me off to war with. I've never seen you in the sunlight, you look very pretty."

She looked down at the floorboards, a crushed candy box, and cigarette butts. "You soldiers wear the worst shoes. Flub-a-dub shoes right out of Disneyland."

"They'll outlive all of us," he said ruefully.

She waited. "What do you do there anyway, in the war?"

He was surprised. "What do you care?"

"I'm curious."

"Curiosity killed some cat," he said.

She wondered what she could ask him, how she could win him over without giving away anything more.

"Anyway," she went on, "how long before you'll be settled in Florida?"

He looked off through the blurred windshield and held his gaze a long time as if trying to see that state from where they sat. "Florida," he told her, "is a long ways off. You can't ever be sure about something like that. I may get out to California and find she's split too. I'm not the kind of guy women actually get down at my feet and roll around on the ground for. And actually we're not married yet. We've got to work out the details."

"So, it's just an idea then, your son and all that?" He didn't say anything. "But what you told me about your daughter, that was true?"

He said it was and then asked, "Why do you all of a sudden care about my life? You need a new battery for the car or something?"

"No," she said. "The battery's fine."

"So tell me, are you in love with this cat?" He turned and faced her. "This baseball man?"

"Boy," she said.

"Boy, then. If that makes it more innocent."

"What do you care?"

Drumming his fingers on the steering wheel, he said, "Well, I have a feeling you're in love with this boy and maybe he's in love with you and you're thinking if you can pry a little more cash out of me you'll both live happily ever after."

"I don't want your money."

"Oh, really? Maybe I should go have a little talk with Libby then."

"I want your help," she said.

He looked at her and sneered. "There's two kinds of women in this world, or *girls*, if you want to call them girls. The kind that will give a guy a blow job while he's driving down the interstate and the kind who won't. If you want to keep your baseball boy, be the kind that will. And that's all the advice I have for you."

"I don't want your advice either."

"Well, you got it anyway, free of charge."

"I want to know if you can find someone. His brother's lost over there."

"Where?"

"Vietnam."

"Oh Christ, you make me laugh Bobbi, baby. Everybody's lost over there."

"Well, who goes looking, I mean when somebody's missing?"

"You're kidding. Nobody goes looking, who has the time to look?"

"There must be somebody in charge."

"They're all watching our movies, remember?"

"I want to know if you can help find somebody."

"Jesus H. Christ, I may *look* like Superman, but come on! You expect a hell of a lot from me."

He paused and began peeling one corner of the inspection sticker off the windshield. He raised a finger in the air. "Let me tell you something, Bobbi. I haven't been kidding you about how the world works. You want something in this world, and you have to pay for it. And if you don't have cash money to pay for it then you pay some other way."

A woman in a red sweater walked past the car, and when she looked in the windows, Bobbi put her head down.

"I'll tell you what," he went on. "Maybe I'll drive out

on the highway and you'll put your head down here and get in some practice for your baseball boy while I think things over, what do you say?"

"I was asking for your help," she said.

"Well, what the hell are you asking *me* for, I'm in the Air Force, for Christ's sake. You think I'm speaker of the House of fucking Representatives?" He turned away and looked out a side window.

A moment later he said, "He's a goddamn Marine, he ought to be able to take care of himself."

"How do you know he's a Marine?"

He laughed a surly laugh through his lips. "I know a lot of things," he said. "What are you two doing, running some kind of mutual admiration society? He's trying to save your ass, you come to save his brother's ass. I was going to spare you the gory details. I mean I didn't think you'd want to hear about how that handsome pitcher of yours took a left turn into hell to save your pretty ass. Jesus."

"What are you talking about?"

"But isn't it a hell of a note though, the two of you dealing with me like this? I'm the big pig, but you both get right down in the mud with me. That's one hell of a note."

He shook his head wearily and said they had worked out an arrangement. "You want to know any more, ask your pitcher. And stop being so righteous. You've racked up quite a score yourself, you know. The whole world's waiting to hear why a sweet girl like you would ever believe for a minute she could save her old man by spreading her legs for the United States Air Force. Jesus, let's be honest about things, baby. You're using me and that makes you as bad as I am. And now you want to use me some more."

When he was silent, she answered. She measured her words. "There are things you have to do when you have someone else to think about besides yourself. You don't know anything about that, you couldn't know. I never believed I was saving anybody by coming into this cesspool of yours. But I was buying time. A little time to figure out what to do next."

The rest she had never admitted to herself. She wanted to buy this time because if there was a chance her mother might return, she wanted to make sure there was some place for her to return to.

The colonel reached for her hand. "Look," he said. "I can give you more time. I don't want to be alone tonight, my last night in town. I can give your old man all the time he needs."

"There's no time left," she said.

"Sure there is, there's always time."

"No there isn't. He's dying."

"I'm dying too, for Christ's sake. I want a little companionship before I die from a broken heart."

She took hold of the door handle. "To me you're already dead," she said. "It's in your eyes, I can see it."

"I may fool you. I may come back to life."

"You'll never see me again," she told him.

She opened the car door and stepped out into the street. She heard the motor start up and the van rolling down the street behind her, rolling very slowly. It seemed to take forever for him to pick up speed and pass by her.

12

"Number twelve doesn't look too sharp today," Darcy said to Bobbi as she sat down along the third-base line. "Your boy doesn't look so good," she said again, shaking her head. She and the kids were devouring an enormous bag of orange sugar-coated popcorn. "You want some, help yourself."

Bobbi took one piece just to be friendly. Looking out at Brad on the pitcher's mound, she didn't notice anything unusual. He struck out the next batter on three pitches. When the crowd stopped clapping Bobbi asked, "What do you mean, Darcy? What do you mean he doesn't look good?"

She had a mouthful of orange popcorn but she spoke right through it, scattering orange sugar down the front of her. Flakes of it settled between her breasts. "He walked a couple of guys in the second inning, couldn't get the ball over the plate. Take a look." She gestured to the scoreboard. The Indians were trailing by two runs.

"It's only the third inning," Bobbi said. "We'll get back those runs."

"Hey," said Darcy, "you didn't do the infield today. I saw Buttsy out on the tractor."

"I was with Pop. I asked Buttsy to cover for me."

"Your Pop ain't feeling better yet?"

"No."

"Well, when's he going to be back anyways, because if you guys don't want the job no more I could sure use the extra dough, and I can drive tractor better than Buttsy."

"I didn't know you were interested."

"You ever seen Buttsy try and drive a straight line? He's got them wicked thick glasses, lenses so thick they'd stop a bullet. But why are you thinking about giving up that job, anyway? It's easier money than working tables at the Blue Top, isn't it?"

The Blue Top. Bobbi thought how she had earned more money there in the last two months than Darcy would see in any three years put together. "I want to spend time with Pop," she said.

Darcy drew her large, mobile mouth into a sympathetic frown. "Well, once your boy gets called up, you ain't going to be too happy here at the park, anyway." She shook her head thoughtfully and pulled one of her children up onto her lap. "I remember how every time I tried to make myself think it wasn't going to be that sad when my boy left, it never worked. It was always sadder even than I could have thought. It's just the idea that the big leagues is so far away from here. You think of Cleveland. Cleveland, Ohio. It's a great big place, Bobbi. They got department stores bigger than this ballpark. Department stores, I'm sure of it." She paused for a minute, thinking hard about something. "Hey,

Bobbi. You suppose they even got one of them Saks stores from Fifth Street?"

"Fifth Avenue, you mean?"

"Yeah, Saks from Fifth Avenue. Wouldn't you just about give your left tit for a little cash to spend in a place like that Saks on Fifth Avenue? I hope you don't mind me saying this, but that's the kind of store I suspect your mom does her clothes shopping in these days. She was wicked smart, wasn't she?"

Bobbi nodded her head.

"And you always done so good in school yourself. You must have been born with some of her smarts. Probably you gave some already to Zoey. That's a nice thing to give."

"I'm not sure brains have anything to do with shopping at Saks," Bobbi said.

"D'you see that? See that right there!" Darcy exclaimed, and when Bobbi looked out at the field Darcy said, "No, no, I mean there, the way you said that, 'Saks,' as if it was the most natural thing. It fell right from your mouth."

"I've never set foot inside Saks."

"Doesn't matter. The thing is if you ever did get the chance to go, you'd know how to behave once you got there. You'd know what to say to the salesladies, and they'd treat you like you were a regular." Darcy shook her head, then swatted one of her boys who was fighting over the popcorn with his sister.

"I think you'd be surprised who shops there," Bobbi told her. "As long as anybody has the money to spend, they'll fit in fine. Nobody cares who you are in this world if you have enough money."

"But it takes more than money to fit in. It takes smarts. And that's the thing I never did understand about you,

Bobbi. Why do you suppose it is we both stayed in this place? Why is it your mom could leave but we never could?"

"There's nothing stopping us," Bobbi replied.

"Well, I got too many mouths to feed. I got to stay someplace where I know who my friends are in case I need help."

"But if you really wanted to leave, Darcy—"

"Oh, I really *did* want to from time to time when I was bored or when I was in love with a boy who was leaving. But there was always somebody else I had to look out for besides myself, and you know, Bobbi, I think maybe God gave me these babies so I'd stay put and not go running all over hell's half-acre, making a damn fool of myself. He gave me no choice or else I'd have probably run off with the first boy that laid me down, and I'd have ended up a terrible misfit."

Darcy looked into Bobbi's eyes, then turned and looked around to make sure no one was listening. Then she said softly, "You know I'm as wild as the next girl, and I enjoy playing with a boy as much as anyone in town, but I'm not never going to be accused of leaving somebody who loves me. I could have stuck something up inside myself, or found somebody to do it for me to kill my babies. But I didn't. Maybe I'm never going to see inside Saks of Fifth Avenue, but I'm taking care of my babies. A lot of girls might not have left them be born in the first place."

Suddenly Darcy was silent, and when her eyes drifted down to the field she began to smile. It was a serene smile, a smile of satisfaction that reached up to the corners of her eyes. When Bobbi turned to the field she saw a boy leaning against the back of the dugout, a boy who worked for the concession stand. He had an aluminum tray of hot dogs hanging from a canvas strap around his neck. He was smiling up at Darcy, all the way up at her. His eyes passed over everyone else to find her. He was a bony boy with knobby knees and a bad complexion. When he moved on with his tray of hot dogs, Darcy sighed.

"Who's that?" Bobbi asked.

"Phillip," she said happily.

"I never saw him before."

"He just moved to the base, his Daddy's in the Air Force. They came all the way from Seattle." She stopped, then told Bobbi that they were in love. "This isn't just some dream, this is the real thing. We ain't even done anything together except talk and walk around. I decided to save it all this time so we have something else to look forward to. And plus that, he's shy. We haven't even really kissed yet. But I feel like I know him real good. I feel like he isn't never going to leave me no matter what happens."

She rose up in her seat, craning her neck to get a glimpse of him selling hot dogs way off in the bleachers. "I don't know what's going to happen to the rest of the world," she said, "but we're going to be right alongside each other, I can feel it."

As she said this, someone hit a baseball high into the cloudless sky. There was that fine, true sound of the ball cracking against the wooden bat, a sound that seemed to silence all the other sounds. And Bobbi turned her head and raised her eyes and caught the ball in its upward flight. It looked as if it would go up forever to reach a height so far up in the sky that someone far away, were she to look up at this moment, would see it too.

Everyone was waiting for the ball to descend. Everyone but Bobbi, who was lost in the idea that somewhere her mother had stopped whatever she was doing and had spotted the ball. Perhaps she had put down her pen on her desk and looked out the window up at the sky and seen the ball. Only, to Bobbi, it was no longer a ball, but an instant in time when her thoughts connected with her mother's in one still point of clarity and understanding.

In this moment Bobbi imagined seeing her mother again, imagined what she would say to her: "There are things I have to tell you. You were always beautiful to me, even to the end I couldn't have loved you more than I did. My God, it was the purest kind of love, I wanted to be like you. Pop and I, did we torture you with love? We wanted to draw a circle around you and keep you to ourselves. A circle just big enough for us all to turn within it. You wouldn't be loved, you wouldn't be contained. You had this big, wide-open dream. You never shared it with us but I knew it was there. You dreamed of turning round and round inside a bigger circle. I could see you spinning on your heels, spinning free from us.

"Well, I can honestly tell you I have never wanted this for myself. I have not inherited your—what shall I call it? Disloyalty, dishonor? I remember when Jay Gatsby died in the end, and I wanted to blame Tom and Daisy for his death, and you said they weren't to blame. You said that they were just careless people. That got them off the hook. And in *Madame Bovary,* Charles has every reason on earth to blame Rodolphe for Emma's death when she kills herself, but when he meets Rodolphe afterward he says, 'I don't blame you. Fate is to blame.'

"You read these books to me. You must have been trying to make me see something about your own carelessness. You were always so careless. I remember how determined you were to make me understand the people in those books. You were preparing me for your own departure scene. You wanted to be blameless.

"The really crazy thing is that Pop and I ended up blaming ourselves. We couldn't blame you. We still want you to be on our side. I always dreamed of having a mother who would take my part. Isn't this only natural? The time I started my period in school and I ran home crying. I stained my dress, and you told me I could have hidden it if I'd thought of taking off my sweater and tying it around my waist so that it covered my bottom. That was all you would give me, a way to hide the accident. You sent me out into the world with a sweater tied around my waist. And when it came again and I wanted you to put your arms around me and explain things, you told me that was the only good thing about being pregnant. 'Not having to go through the Civil War each month,' you said.

"Whatever made you so unsympathetic?

"Maybe you think that since you left we've made a mess of things. Well, we've had some grace without you. You have to pay us credit for that. You have to give Pop some credit for holding on.

"But there is one thing I hate you for. I've never understood it until now. All this time I thought Pop was the reason I could never leave this place. I had to look after him. I had to pick up the pieces. But I can see now that it was you. I've been waiting here just like Pop, waiting for you to come back with some explanation. There are things you have to explain to me or I'll never be free from you."

"There's only one thing I'm scared of," Darcy said. And the sound of her voice called Bobbi back to a world that seemed to have changed. The joy was gone from Darcy's voice and her eyes were sorrowful.

"What are you afraid of?" Bobbi asked.

She nodded her head in the direction of the Air Force Base and the jet that was taking off. "Phillip got his papers from the draft board. They want him to come for his examination. He's not a soldier, Bobbi. He's too shy for that. He's the only shy boy I've ever known."

After a moment, Bobbi said, "Tell him not to go."

"But if they want to find you they will, and there ain't any place you can hide."

"Maine's a big state, they can't look everywhere."

"Are they looking for your boy or how come he ain't been taken away?"

"His father knew people," Bobbi told her.

"Would his father talk to those people about Phillip?"

"We'll do something," Bobbi said. "We'll figure it out."

Darcy looked down into her daughter's brown eyes. She spoke again without looking up. "Maine *is* a big state, you're right, and I was wondering, Bobbi, what is it you're going to do when they call your boy up to the big leagues?"

"I have to stay with Pop," she answered. And she could see that this answer disappointed Darcy, that it didn't fit her romantic picture of things.

"Well, maybe all of us can hide somewhere together. There's places on the map where they don't even have roads yet. But what I meant was, what if they boy asked you to go with him?"

"He hasn't asked me."

"But if he did, would you go or would you be too scared?"

"Scared of what?"

"I don't know exactly," Darcy said. "Scared of getting lost maybe. Scared of going out to the A & P to do your food shopping and not being able to find your way back home. All those people crowding in on you, and they all know where they're going but you don't." She shook her head dramatically. "I guess that's what I'm scared of. Being lost scares me practically to death. So I can't follow my boy if the Army takes him. I heard about girls going off to basic training, getting a motel room, and then hoping their boy is sent somewhere where they can follow along and live with him. But all the boys are going to Vietnam anyway and even if they wasn't, I couldn't sit all day in a motel room not knowing one thing about where I was, not knowing any neighbors or nothing."

Darcy sighed heavily and looked out across the ball field. "The air's so clean here, isn't it, Bobbi? I'd miss this air something wicked if I went away. But before they'd take Phillip from me I'd put him inside me and keep him there for a whole, solid week so I'd get a baby from him. I wouldn't save myself no longer if he was leaving me. I'd want to give something to this place, something that would say that we was in love, that no matter what happens to us from now on, we was together and things was good for us."

"Yes," Bobbi said. "A confirmation."

"What?"

"Yes, you're right. That's the way it's supposed to be. I'm sure of it." This is how it has been with Brad, she thought. Holding him, making love with him, it is all a confirmation of everything she has ever wanted to believe. It has been enough to overcome her skepticism. It has been some kind of triumph over the disappointment of the past and the uncertainty of the future.

She thought back to the first time with Brad. The shape of his arms, the outline of his shoulders, the lines of his ribs. The words they'd spoken:

"I'd sworn off this," she said.

"What do you mean?"

"Well, I'd taken up a life of abstinence."

"I don't want you to feel bad about this, Bobbi. Tomorrow will you regret this?"

"What I regret is that we didn't do it sooner."

Bobbi let her mind race over all this, and then when she opened her eyes to the ball field she saw Brad in his windup. It was a motion she knew well, a motion that began as thoughtfully as they had begun together. Then his body gathered speed and power as it turned within itself, his legs and hips working together, creating a rhythm and form, creating this out of air and then spinning under its influence like a top, like a fine top set spinning on a table. Both his arms were straight up over his head forming something like the eye of a needle. It was the epitome of grace and power.

Only today something was different. Something was missing, she could tell. It was barely perceptible, a flaw, one tooth missing in a gear, one link in a chain. But it was enough to throw the timing off.

Bobbi couldn't tell where the flaw is, she could only see the effect of it. The baseball was straying from its target, it was floating from his hand. Brad seemed to be throwing each ball with only his arm. He walked one batter and then another. He paced around the back of the mound. The order and flow of the game were disrupted. The catcher went out to the mound, said something to Brad, then returned to the plate. Then Brad threw one more pitch, and the batter was waiting for it and he swung from his heels and drilled it deep into right center field, and two runs scored. Somehow he got out of that inning, but then in the eighth with two men on the bases the catcher went back out to the mound, the catcher, Emo Duncan. They both watched a batter with shoulder-length hair walk up to the box.

The batter took ball one. Then ball two. The crowd was nearly silent. Bobbi left her seat. She stood beyond the concession stand, watching. She was trying to get a closer look, a clue. The count was even at two balls and two strikes when Brad threw a slow, high curve and the long-haired batter clouted it with all his might. The ball rose and rose in the sky. It was still rising when it hit the scoreboard.

On Brad's face there was a look of complete resignation. And this convinced Bobbi. She was certain what had happened. She didn't wait at the clubhouse door for him this time.

13

After the game that same day, Brad dried off with a stiff white towel, combed his hair in front of the mirror, and prepared to return to Emo's tent. As he pulled on his socks he listened to Gus Blanchard, the center fielder from Memphis, teaching the new first baseman how to rip off the Coca-Cola machine. It was one of those machines where you could reach up through a little square trap door, between two iron arms, and twist a bottle free from the gear mechanism. "It's like learning how to reach up a lady's dress," Blanchard was saying. "Once you get it down, you never forget it."

Brad recalled his last visit to Emo's tent, that hot night back in late June after he'd seen Bobbi Ann running from the colonel, running across the parking lot of the Blue Top. That night Brad walked along the deserted country roads for hours before he wandered into Emo's tent. "I need to find out about somebody," he said to Emo.

"Hey, mon, you got trouble?"

"I want to find out about some guy in the Air Force. He hangs around here. He wears the same kind of sunglasses you wear."

"Tell me this, mon, a pitcher with stuff as good as yours, if you got trouble then my guess is that girl's involved, the one you've been putting the pork to."

"Listen, you can talk that way about somebody else, not her. You understand."

Emo raised two fingers in the air in the peace sign. He apologized negligently, then asked, "What is your trouble with the United States Air Force?"

"This officer's been hanging around the Blue Top."

"So what's the big surprise?"

"I want to know what he's doing there. I'll pay you. I'll sign over my next pay check, whatever you can find out."

It had taken Emo two days. In the bullpen before a twilight doubleheader in which Brad was scheduled to pitch the second game, Emo took him aside. "This mon of yours, he's buying a farm for your honey," he said. He waited, then said, "There's more, mon."

They had talked through the first game. When Emo had given Brad the whole story he shrugged his shoulders and said, "Mon, I'm sorry. My advice is you tie him up against the backstop and throw fastballs at his crotch."

Brad asked how much money it would take to buy him off.

"Not money," Emo said. "That one is into power with a big P. And control with the big C. You dig?"

By the third inning of that first game, Brad had decided what he was going to do. Emo looked into his eyes and said, "I get the bad vibes from you, mon. You're going to make a deal with the devil. I'll tell you what, you let me make the deal. I got nothing to lose."

"I can't let you risk your neck," Brad said.

"Risk what? We throw away a few games, we save your sweetheart, no big deal. I'll call for a few fat pitches, we'll let somebody on the other team look good for a change. Hey, and look mon, I'm sorry about your friend there, Spenser. I could have saved him if he'd been a pitcher, I only work with pitchers, you know, mon?"

Now it was over and Brad found Emo stretched out on his air mattress drinking tequila. It had been simple, surprisingly simple for Brad to do something he never had thought himself capable of doing. Emo was behind the plate calling for fat pitches. They gave away three runs in the second inning. When the Indian batters got all three runs back in the bottom of the fifth, they'd had to give away two more runs to lose the game.

"So we both lose a little innocence," Emo said, looking up at Brad. He took off his sunglasses. "This team can lose a few games. In the whole cosmic scheme of things what does it matter? There's half a billion people in China who couldn't care less. It's all relative."

"How much did he make off me?" Brad asked.

"Not you, mon. That's the wrong attitude. And I don't think it's the money at all with this guy. He wants to be able to sit up in the stands, you know, and for once in his life be able to say he *fixed* a ball game. He knows how the game's going to come out. He's like a god or something."

Emo passed the bottle of tequila to Brad. Brad took a swallow, Emo told him to take another. "What I think," he went on, "is that a power freak like this toy soldier gets a real rush to think he can penetrate the world of baseball. You remember that guy Rothstein who fixed the nineteen-nineteen World Series? The Black Sox?"

"Rothstein and I," Brad said, "were two of a kind."

"Bullshit. Your guilt trip is a dead end. I look at you, mon, and I'm seeing all the guilt of the world in your eyes. You better leave it behind or it'll eat your damn guts out. Now look at me—I'm a happy fellow today. We made some progress against the crap in the world. Whatever we can do to deprive this world of some of its greed, that's fine by me, even if you have to cheat to do it. This colonel made a few bucks he'll piss away on cheap beer. But in exchange we got your girl, free and clear."

Emo tossed Brad a paper bag with the colonel's films inside. "The soldier was downright contrite. He said he was wrong about everything. He told me he was going to look for your brother. He said he knew some people. She asked him to try and find your brother, mon."

Brad thought for a minute, then said he was going to shower up. "I owe you a paycheck," he said. He started to walk out.

Emo stood up. "Look, mon," he said. "You're not going to be here much longer, you'll be at the top and I'll be sitting right down here. When you get up there, remember this: You've got to have steel in your heart when you're on the hill staring in at those hitters. You go around feeling bad for everybody, mon, and it's going to weaken you. It'll kill your nerve. You'll lose it, I've seen it happen, I know how it goes."

At the dinner table Bobbi watched every move he made.

"I'm glad none of you were at the game today," he said. "I felt like I was throwing from second base."

"I saw a squirrel today," Zoey said.

"Eat your beans, honey," Bobbi told her.

"They'll make your eyes green," Brad said. He looked at Bobbi and smiled faintly.

"How many runs did they get off you?" Page asked.

"Seven," Brad answered.

"I heard they were hitting the ball pretty hard," Bobbi said.

"But how do they remember?" asked Zoey.

"My fastball was," Brad said, shaking his head, "well, I don't know where it was."

"Were you keeping that shoulder back?" Page asked.

"How do they remember?" Zoey asked again, her voice rising.

"Shush," Bobbi said. "Don't talk when someone else is talking."

"Your shoulder," Page started to say.

"I don't know," Brad replied. "Look, I got us some ice cream for dessert. I'll go get it." When he got up, Page excused himself to go use the bathroom. He walked across the room, the floor boards cracking under his steps. Small, cautious steps. As Bobbi watched him, she thought, he is waiting for this, it is inevitable. It is like an army advancing against him. The army has already reached the front field and has a view of his house.

When Page started to pee, Brad dropped his spoon into the sink and the clinking noise made the room silent. They listened. He started and stopped a half-dozen times, then flushed the toilet. When he flushed it a second time Bobbi knew he was trying to conceal something. Water rushed through the old pipes in the ceiling overhead, down the wall.

Finally Bobbi got up from her chair and went to help

him. Brad said to her, "I'm going to take him to Bar Harbor." He waited while she searched his face. "He asked me. I thought I'd get the car fixed, and we'd go as soon as I have a day off."

For some reason Zoey began crying. She laid her head down on the table and through her tears she said, "How do they know?"

"Know what, sweetheart?" Bobbi asked. She turned towards her, torn between going to her and going to her father. "Know what?"

"Where they put the nuts."

"Oh, baby, I don't know. I'm sorry."

"But how?" She was crying from the bottom of her heart.

Bobbi got down on her knees and tried to console her. At last she laid her head down on the table next to her daughter's. "God tells them," she whispered in her ear. "God reminds them."

Later, while Bobbi gave Zoey her bath, Brad helped Page upstairs and into bed. For a long time Bobbi heard him in her father's room, reading out loud from his baseball encyclopedia, quizzing him on the statistics he had memorized over a lifetime. After each question there was a short silence, then his answer. Their voices were low, rhythmic, as if in prayer. She thought how her father must have always wanted a son, and how she had wanted a brother, and how this boy had been assimilated into their lives so quickly, almost as if they had both been waiting for him, as if the timing of their coming together had been fixed years earlier and all they had to do was keep living long enough for their lives to cross.

Coming out from her father's room, Brad met Bobbi in the hallway. "Sometimes when I'm reading to him I forget where I am," he said. "It's like I'm back home reading to Mike during one of his asthma attacks, still at home, and none of this has happened. I can almost hear his breathing. I used to read very slowly. He'd be wheezing like mad, but gradually the sound of my voice seemed to relax him and he'd fall asleep."

When Brad turned away, she saw there were tears in his eyes.

"He must have wanted to be like you," Bobbi said.

Brad shook his head. "He was like your father. They're the kind of people who never ask for much. Not like me, I ask for everything. My dream ends up costing everybody else."

"So you're going to throw it away?" she asked. She drew back from him and stood against the banister. "You think that will save anyone? You give up your dream and the rest of us automatically live happily ever after? That doesn't make any sense to me."

When he said nothing, she went on, "The world ends up then with one more person with a shattered dream, one more person who could have really done something. You talk about reality."

"It's a game, a myth, remember? It's not reality."

"It's reality if you make the dream come true, if you make it real. And then the rest of us get to say to ourselves, Yeah, it can happen, it can really happen. It's something for people to believe in."

"Your mother had a dream, look what it ended up costing him," he gestured to Page's door.

Bobbi told him it wasn't her dream that broke them apart. "It was that she denied the dream for so long. It made her sick inside. I remember how sick she was over it. One night in my room she told me she and Pop were married on an ocean liner, in the ballroom of an ocean liner out in the middle of the Atlantic. She described it all to me, right down to the engraved silver and the linen tablecloths, then she kissed me good night and walked to the door of my room. She turned the light out and she said, 'It was the Titanic.'

"Just when she had won me over, she destroyed me with her bitterness. You deny the dream too long and it fills you with bitterness."

"I'm going to take a walk," he said. He started to turn away from her.

"You worry about being an actor," she said. "My mother was the greatest actor of all. You turn your back on your dream and you'll be an actor for the rest of your life."

"I'll be back in a while," he said.

"I'm going with you."

Under moonlight she rode on the crossbar of the bicycle while he pedaled for all he was worth. "The next full moon will be a frost moon," she told him.

"Your father already told me that."

This means to them both that summer is running out.

"When I leave here," he said, "I'm taking you along, all of you." His words were spread out by his breathing.

"I have to stay," she said.

"I'm taking Pop too," he said. "I'm taking you and him and Zoey and everybody else who wants to come along for the ride." He paused, then said, "I'd like to take Mike too."

They went sailing downhill a moment later, and Bobbi raised her voice above the rushing wind. "You know what life is," she said. "Life is getting used to things, hard things, terrible things. It's getting used to people leaving!"

They took the long, tarred road beyond the lighted runways, into the center of town, and out the other side to a neighborhood of identical houses placed in rows. It was Bobbi's idea to stop. They sat down on someone's front lawn under a maple tree with rustling leaves. "It sounds like applause," Bobbi said when the leaves picked up. "It's the sound of a thousand cheering fans. They're on their feet, wild with excitement." She was acting out the scene for him, playing the part of a radio announcer. "Two outs, two men on base, top of the ninth inning in a one-run ball game. The pitcher looks in, gets the signal from his catcher. Wait a minute, the catcher is coming to the mound. They're talking something over. Finally the pitcher's ready. He checks the base runners, then starts his windup. He delivers. Crack! The batter blasts a line drive to deep centerfield. It's going, going, it's *Gone!* Can you believe it? One strike away from the third out and the pitcher threw up a fat, hanging curveball. What do you think of that?"

The joke was over. Bobbi folded her legs and sat before him. She waited for him to say something.

"You were there," he said.

"You laid up some of the fattest pitches I ever saw," she said.

He turned away and looked off at the house behind them. "Well, my shoulder was a little stiff."

"Oh?"

"And if you believe that—"

"I don't," she said. "You were just pulling back. You were taking something off. How come?"

At first he didn't answer. He glanced down the street, down the row of identical houses, and said he had always wanted to live in a neighborhood like this. "I wanted to be able to just walk outside and have a bunch of kids around. We lived way off by ourselves. That's probably why I became a pitcher, you could do it by yourself. Plus I had Mike to—"

She cut him off. "You know what I think?" she said, "I think you let them beat you out there today."

She paused and lowered her head. Then she looked back at him, and he started to get to his feet. She took his hand and pulled him back down. "You made a deal with him," she said.

"It was going to be between him and me."

"He bets money on the other team and you make sure he wins?"

Brad was silent.

"You want to explain something to me, please," Bobbi said. "You tell me please why you play baseball anyway, so maybe I can understand what's happening here, because I thought it was something big for you, your dream that we talk about all the time. But if you can throw it away...."

She knew he was going to tell her he had done it for her, and she kept talking because she didn't want to hear him say it. "Everybody I've ever known went into this game because he had a lot to gain by playing it. But that's not the way it is with you. You had everything all set up for you in the real world and you turned your back on that for baseball. You went into baseball with a lot to *lose*. And maybe you're determined to lose it, if not for Mike, then for me. But I'm not going to let you do that. You can't go around paying some kind of penance because you have the chance everybody else dreams of having. You don't waste it."

"There are reasons sometimes," Brad said.

"No. There's never any good reason for wasting a gift." She lowered her voice and glanced down at his hands. "You blame yourself for Mike the same way Pop blames himself for my mother and I blame myself for *Pop*. None of it makes any sense."

She stopped while a jet passed overhead. In the lighted window of the house a man craned his neck, looking up at the sky.

"You're trying to save me," she said. "I've been trying to save Pop. Where does it stop?"

"Where did it start?" he asked.

She looked at him and knew the answer to this. It was the answer she had figured out at the ballpark this afternoon. "It started with her," she said. "One person comes barreling through your life, one person poisoned by some broken dream, and then there's hell to pay. Everyone is left blaming themselves."

She walked to the bicycle and spun the pedal with her toes. It made a clean, smooth sound in the night. "I've been waiting for her to come back, just like Pop. It's the unanswered questions that hold you back, that keep you waiting. We're both waiting for answers."

Riding back home, Brad told her they could be anything they wanted to be. "Sometimes I think about the guys I knew at school. They lived under the great weight of their parents' expectations. Obligations. Things were decided for them. That's the one great advantage coming from a broken family, you can become whatever you want to be. You can be different."

"You always can," she said, "no matter what anyone else expects. You can have your dream."

"And you, what about your dreams?"

All the way home she didn't answer him. They were back when she told him what it was she dreamed of having. She lifted her head and gestured to the stars. "I'd like to have a lot of children. Seventeen years from now when

Halley's Comet passes over I'd like to have a child Zoey's age, three years old. Old enough to see it and maybe remember. But young enough to live another seventy-six years to see it happen again. You think of it, seeing it twice in your life. That would be something."

14

One after another as the first days of August wore on, the batters fell before Brad. He had hit the peak of his abilities on the pitcher's mound. The whole game, the dimensions and fairness of the game, had been thrown out of order by the brilliance of his performances. When he pitched, the distance from the mound to home plate seemed to have shrunk to an impossibly short space of air and light through which his pitches flew with impunity. He saw the batters as Goliaths, expanded with hot air and so sluggish they couldn't move. Each had a strike zone the size of a refrigerator. And the balls Brad threw into this zone were barely visible, nothing more than a few molecules of heat wrapped in white horsehide, traveling at blinding speed.

Wednesday he rode to the park with Page. He would pitch today, and he planned to prepare for the game like any other day. He would sit behind the backstop and watch his own team take batting practice while going over the opposing batters in his head. He would draw a mental picture of each one, then work out a strategy. He would pitch the entire nine innings in his head, and then when the real game began it was simply a matter of trying to get this game to imitate the one he had already created.

When they parked, Page didn't open his door. Brad waited. "No, go on," Page said. "They gave me a few days off. I'm going to sit right here and listen to you on the radio. I'm a little pooped today."

"I can get you a seat in the dugout, out of the sun."

"No, that's fine, I'm fine right here. Remember that kid Angel who tagged you last time. He's a golfer, anything low and he'll rip it."

"High and tight," Brad said, and then he tipped his cap. "Beep the horn each time I strike him out." He saw Page tap the steering wheel with one hand, his face seamed and dark.

In the clubhouse Brad had almost finished dressing in his uniform when someone yelled that there was a phone call for him. He carried his spikes and cap and walked to the equipment room. Tubby handed him the phone then ducked out the side door so he could have some privacy. Brad thought to himself, Is this how it's going to happen, the word comes like this and I'm off to Cleveland? But he knew better. Doc Hill would be telling him face to face.

The voice in the telephone was his father's. It was level, muffled by the thick Persian rugs, the leather furniture in his office. Brad pictured him standing in sunlight, the light sweeping over his broad desk. The handsome leather-bound books in rows and stacks from floor to ceiling.

"You freezing your ass off up there?" his father asked.

Strange thing to ask, Brad thought. He told him it was hot.

"It's August," he said.

"Yeah," his father said. "But every time I've ever been in Maine it's been cold as hell."

"Well, how's Mom?"

"Oh, you know, the same, about the same. She's worried about Mike."

"I haven't got a letter in five weeks," Brad said.

"Yeah, well, Christ, he probably doesn't have time to sit around writing letters. In the Philippines they kept us hopping. So what are *you* doing with yourself?"

"What do you mean?"

"I mean how's life up there, anyway?"

"Fine, it's okay."

"Look, your mother'd be a lot better off if you could get down this way once in a while."

"Why don't you bring her up for a game, I'll show you around. What do you mean, 'better off'?"

"I don't know. You know what I mean. A woman likes to have her children close by. With Mike gone it's tough on her. They must give you a day off. You know, school doesn't even start till the end of September on the West Coast. I know people out there."

"Why?"

"Why what?"

"Why are you talking about law school again?"

"Your season's going to be over by then, isn't it?"

Brad didn't answer.

"Look," his father said. "I'm worried about your brother. I think he's going to go AWOL. Don't say anything to anyone about this."

Brad imagined his father already plotting out the steps he would have to take to bail out Mike. Forms could be filed. Letters. Evidence collected. He went on.

"He wrote a letter about marrying some girl over there. D'you get anything like that from him?"

"No."

"Jesus, you fall in love in the middle of a war and, well, you never know. But Mike's not strong. He could get himself in a lot of trouble. It could be a real mess."

"What do you want me to do?"

"It's a rough time, Brad, that's the reality of the thing."

"I hope he gets away."

"What?"

"I said I hope Mike gets away."

"He won't, there's no place to get away to. You know they shot someone for desertion once."

"You should bring Mom up once."

There was a pause. "I've got another call, can I put you on hold?"

"Sure," Brad said. A moment passed before he hung up. He walked out of the room, down the cool, dark concrete corridor that led like a tunnel to a square of light at the far end, where the green of the grass and the blue sky were as bright as a promise, a chance. What were the chances that Mike could ever find his way out of a war? Brad could imagine him trying to run away if he'd met a girl and fallen in love, or if he'd just gotten too scared.

The first time Brad faced the kid named Angel he hit a home run to left center on a curveball that hung over the outside corner of the plate. Then Brad bore down and struck him out three times in a row on ten fastballs up around the navy blue letters on his uniform.

In the empty locker room he sat staring at Spenser's old locker. There was still a faint white gash across the metal door where there had once been a strip of adhesive tape with Spenser's name printed on it. He thought about how nervous Spense used to get before a game, sitting here getting into his uniform. Brad had seen his hands shake near the end when his destiny hung on each game, each time at bat, each ground ball hit toward first base.

Brad pushed the locker door shut with his foot. The door swung back open. He kicked it shut this time, thinking he should have been able to do more for Mike, for Spenser, for his mother. His dream was drawing closer, but the people he cared about were drifting beyond his influence. How many people could he lift up as he ascended? He had always seen a longing in his brother's eyes, a longing to hang on. It had been there even the night before Mike left for boot camp on Parris Island. Mike was talking optimistically about what was ahead, but you could tell he was only trying to bolster himself. Brad could see how scared he was. The next day, just after sunrise, they stood together at the end of their driveway waiting for a Marine lieutenant who was to pick Mike up and drive him to the train station.

"He's a decent guy," Mike said. "He's the one I talked to first, the day I signed up at the recruiting office."

"Has he been there?" Brad asked.

"Oh yeah, twice. He said it wasn't so bad. He kept telling me about the girls in Saigon." Mike laughed, but Brad could tell his heart wasn't in it. He could tell that the idea of girls in Saigon was as foreign to Mike as the man in the moon. As hard as Mike might try, he wouldn't be capable of fleshing out his vague idea of girls in Saigon with any consoling detail. And behind his smile there was a wariness that gave itself away in brief grimaces, that swept over his face and cast him off from the moment at hand. These were the gestures that conveyed the longing to Brad.

The old longing that said, "You're going someplace, Brad. Please take me along. Can't you take me? I'm your brother for Christ's sake."

That morning Brad could see in Mike's eyes something like a prayer that the Marine lieutenant might never find their driveway, that he might get lost and then just give up and go back to his office and throw the signed papers away.

"It's too late now," Mike said cheerfully.

"Too late for what?"

"They could probably send you to prison. It's like breaking a contract or something, isn't it?"

Brad put an arm around his shoulder. "Everybody gets nervous about now, waiting, I mean."

"Cold feet," Mike said.

Brad looked down at Mike's polished, black shoes. "Yeah, cold feet," he said.

Off in the distance a car with its headlights on high moved toward them. They were silent. He looked up the driveway, he thought about how they used to race their bicycles back and forth. The time Mike flipped over the handlebars, the blood all over his face. Brad washed the blood off. It was only a gash in his lip.

He heard the car's tires on the road, like a dull whistle, like an ache in the center of his chest. Part of him wanted to grab Mike by the arm and pull him into the ditch by the road. Run off through the woods with him, never turn around. He was still free. The whistle grew louder, more distinct. Brad turned and watched the car speed past them. He felt his breath returning.

"I'll probably learn a lot of new jokes," Mike said.

The passing car had restored him. It was like the angel of death passing over him. Then a loud screech tore through the stillness. Just as it happened, Brad was looking up the driveway, and he could see only one piece of their house and one lamp going on in a window. The screech was the car, its brakes as it came to a dead stop. Then the white reverse lights went on.

"Looks like I'm going to be a Marine," Mike said.

The lieutenant backed up all the way to the driveway. He glanced out the window at Mike's suitcase, reached behind and unlocked the back door, then looked straight ahead down the road.

Mike put his hand out. Brad shook it. "He was pretty friendly when I met him," Mike said hopefully.

"Take care," Brad said. "I'll write you."

"Me too," Mike said. As he turned away Brad saw that the lining was hanging out of one of his pants pockets. Mike opened the car door, threw his suitcase on the seat, then got in.

Brad saw the driver's lips move. The car shot ahead, and Mike jerked back against the seat. His hand flew up at the window either to steady himself or to wave. Brad waved back. The rest of the day he wondered where Mike would be standing at attention when someone else noticed his pants pocket hanging inside out.

Brad kicked the door to Spenser's locker. As it was swinging back open he kicked it again. Then he stood up and kicked it for all he was worth. He leaned against the metal door, both his hands flat against it, and kicked it again with his right foot, then his left. In the empty locker room it sounded like a gun being fired. He was thinking about the look on Spenser's face as he dressed for his last game, he was thinking about his mother's face, the sweat beading on it, while Billy

Graham spoke of salvation, he was thinking about the promises that Marine lieutenant had made to Mike, and the ditch beside the road where they could have hidden together. He kicked the locker door again and again until he became aware of both legs going numb. He was trying to put his feet right through the metal door, to blast a hole in it. All he could see was Mike's pocket hanging out and someone yelling at him for it, making him feel like a fool. Laughing derisively. Mike fighting back tears. Mike wondering why Brad hadn't told him, hadn't stopped him from getting in that car that morning.

He felt a hand on his shoulder. When he turned, Page was standing there looking up at him. After a minute Brad told him what Mike had said that morning, how he was probably going to learn new jokes. Page said "All the locker-room jokes, all the jokes men tell about girls, I know why they do it. They do it so they don't have to talk about love, that's why. Let's go on home now."

They found the front porch set for tea. In the kitchen Bobbi was washing Zoey in the sink. "The latest fashion, cookie batter from head to toe," she called to them.

"I baked for you today, Poppi," Zoey yelled.

"Poppi's getting fat from all your baking," Page said. He went to her and kissed the top of her head like he always did. She was dressed only in her underpants and a striped white T-shirt that Page called a ditchdigger's T-shirt. When she saw Brad standing in the doorway she hid behind Bobbi. She looked back at him from under Bobbi's armpit. She asked, "Mommy, did you remember to invite everyone?"

"Yes," Bobbi said.

"Did you invite the governor?" She asked this, then turned to Brad and said, "We always invite him."

"The governor of Maine?"
"Of course," she said.

She seated Brad next to the empty chair meant for the governor. "Do you go to school?" she asked Brad.
"Not anymore, but I did once."
"Where?" Bobbi asked. "Before Princeton, I mean."
"I went to boarding school, a place called Exeter."
She and Page both said they knew of it. "A great school," Page said.
Brad looked at Zoey and said, "But no girls there." She looked puzzled. Brad said, "They used to bus them in for dances on the weekends though. They matched us up by height. A list of names and heights came the week before each dance. No weight, just height."
"No girls," Zoey said ruefully.
"Well, before that I went to a school with girls, a day school."
"I've always liked that term," Bobbi said. " 'Day school.' It sounds nice, doesn't it? Like short pants. It sounds old."
"It was," Brad said.
Page looked across the table at Bobbi. His face was in hers. You could have picked them out of a crowd as father and daughter.
"Why do we invite the governor when he's always too busy?" Zoey asked.
"You wanted to invite him," Bobbi said.
She shook her head and said, "Not any more."
"But if he had come," Page said, "What would you have asked him?"
Zoey was silent.
"You can imagine he's here," Page went on. "You could talk to him about—"

"About the snow," she finished. "We don't get enough snow."

"It's my machine," Brad said. "My snow machine broke."

Brad moved into the governor's seat, drank his tea and ate the cookie.

"You're not the governor," Zoey said.

"You can pretend he is," Page told her.

She looked up at Brad and told him she had been waiting for him.

"How long?" Brad asked. "How long have you waited for me?"

She turned to Bobbi. "How long, Mommy?"

"Oh, he's missed the last six or seven tea parties."

"Six or seven," Zoey said proudly.

"Well, I've been very busy." Brad pulled his cap down.

"Why?"

"Why? Well, I've been busy waiting," he said. "I've been waiting for you."

"Why?"

"I've been waiting for you to grow taller so that when I came to your tea party we could dance together a little."

She thought for a minute then said, "But we don't have a song." She was shy then. She said she was going to pour more tea. She picked up the tin watering can and pretended to pour them each a cup.

"The teapot went the way of all teapots," Bobbi said.

"It just broked," Zoey said.

"This is a fine pot," Page said. He raised his cup to his lips, swallowed, then sighed with satisfaction. He looked at Zoey and said, "I'll sing, you dance."

He hummed his baseball tune for them. They danced on. It was a nice picture—a table set for the tea party, Bobbi sitting there, leaning slightly to one side so she could see her father, and her daughter dancing with the governor of Maine, her bare feet on his shoes as he waltzed her around the porch. Everything was peaceful. But there is a question such a picture provokes: When are we pretending and when are we lying to ourselves? Bobbi thought to herself that we stop pretending and start lying once we fall under the influence of love. The giving or taking of love, the making of love, the waiting for love and running from love, and even the memory of love. All these require a capacity to lie to oneself and to believe the lie.

They danced on, and Bobbi said, "You look wonderful to me."

That night she and Brad lay in a hay field just beyond the barbed wire fence at the end of a runway at the base. "When Mike was in eighth grade," Brad told her, "he tried out for football. He'd never seen a jockstrap before and some of the older guys got together and told him it was a nose guard. He came running out onto the field with the jock over his face, the straps behind his ears. It was awful."

They lay on their backs when the jets took off. They plugged their ears and could still hear the noise and feel it ripping through their bones. They had to hold their breath against the incredible, monstrous weight of the planes only a few dozen feet above their faces. The ground beneath them shuddered like a great animal falling off its feet. It was like lying below a building that starts falling and only at the last instant veers off and spares you. The planes were so close that Brad and Bobbi could see the red and green light bulbs revolving inside their glass globes.

When the sky was silent again Bobbi asked, "So what did he say, your brother, after that happened?"

"I can't remember, really. I think he made a joke of it, or tried to make believe it never happened."

"Make believe," Bobbi said. "My father making believe my mother will return. You making believe your brother will be all right. Zoey making believe the governor will stop by for tea."

"There's a big difference," Brad said.

"What is it?"

"I don't know, some intellectual basis, some reason to believe."

She told him it went beyond reason. "When the reasons don't hold up we still have the lie to count on. All over the world, millions of liars in love, telling themselves what they need to hear, believing whatever it is they need to believe."

"Not always," Brad said. "Sometimes the truth is enough." He stopped and put a blade of grass between his teeth. "Maybe it's not enough when someone puts a jockstrap over your nose, but the truth is good enough sometimes."

Another jet was taking off. Brad clamped his hands over his ears. She rolled on top of him and waited until the jet had disappeared. Then she locked her legs around his and said she wouldn't ever lie to him.

"Good," he said.

"Unless it's absolutely necessary."

"Not even then."

"You're sure?"

"I'm positive," he said. "And when I can't play this game any more, don't let me tell myself some lie to keep going."

"I may not even know you then."

"You will."

He unbuttoned her blouse very slowly. With one finger he traced a circle around each breast, then a Figure 8 around both. "And what do you need to lie about?" he asked her.

She didn't answer because at that moment there didn't seem to be any reason for a lie.

"Well," he said, "I'll have to lie to myself about my brother and my mother or I'll spend the rest of my life feeling like I abandoned them."

"They made their choices," Bobbi said. "They have their own lies and reasons. Think of all the possible pain that comes from love. There's the person who loves someone who doesn't love her back. Then the one who doesn't love the person who loves her. The girl who loves a man who loves three other girls at the same time, and after years she finally gets him out of her system only to have *him* find *her* and swear that now he loves only her. Then there's the one who needs to love in order to be strengthened by love, and she stays with a good man only until she's strong enough to walk out his door and live without him."

She paused and confessed, "I'm taking these from books I've read. I've read too many books. And there's one more, the saddest of all. The girl who has the love in her heart for a man, but she can't give in to love because he doesn't look right. That will require a good lie. It goes on and on, I'm only getting started."

Another jet was taking off and she said, "Let's give the pilot something to think about." She pulled her dress up to her waist. His jeans were warm against her. He told her the stars were out. She said, "When the time comes for you to leave here you can't lie to me."

"I wouldn't," he said.

"Just the same, promise me you won't."

"Okay," he said. "But in the end, when our parents are gone, when there isn't any lie we'll believe any more in our old age, what do we owe them? I mean, to be a good person, a good son or daughter, what do you have to do for them?"

After a while she answered. "I think you just hold good thoughts of them, one or two, or a hundred if they've left you with that many."

"No lies?" he asked.

"No. There must be something good everyone can be remembered for. If you're willing to remember that, that's probably enough. And so, how would you remember me, if I were gone and you were old?"

He thought a moment, then said, "Pretty. And smart. And unhurried."

"Unhurried?" She laughed.

"Yes," he said. "You seem to just live each day."

15

In the morning the wind turned to the north, and a chill entered the house. Brad stood at the kitchen door looking out, thinking that summer had gone so fast. It was the eleventh day of August, already it was a month being outrun by fall. Already, to the north, winter was awake and grumbling.

Brad held a postcard in his hand. He had read it over and over since it arrived yesterday.

The rest of the house was sleeping. Now that Page slept late, everyone else did the same. Zoey seemed to have no reason to get up. The morning newspaper lay in the sun, its front pages damp with dew.

Brad drank a cup of black coffee in the presence of a dog of the same color. The dog had strayed into Veterans Park, and when no one claimed it, Page had brought it to the farm. She was old with gray around her mouth and eyes.

A board creaked, and one of her ears flew up like a sail.
"It's nothing," Brad said.
This afternoon Brad was taking Page to Bar Harbor. Page was like a farmer with holes in his pockets walking across his field, his seeds scattering everywhere. His life now was only what he would leave behind, what would grow after he was gone, what would replace him. How he would be remembered.
Morning. The smell of coffee. The whiteness of the sunlight across the pine floor. Things that are repeated, taken for granted. Life. No matter how many mornings a man has had, Brad thought. No matter how much disappointment has waited for him on those mornings, he will always ask for one more, one more like this one.
Brad stared back down at the postcard. It was a photograph of Niagara Falls in an eerie violet light. On the back, the card was addressed to Brad Schaffer, Pitcher, The Waterboro Indians, Waterboro, Maine. It was a card from Spenser. The whole thing was written in pencil in what looked like a child's early attempt at cursive writing. It all looked terribly innocent at first glance, but there was something behind this innocence and that is why Brad kept going back over it:

> *Ivy,*
> *I'm sending back your money to you as soon as I get an envelope. Many whites not allowing black men to be proud to make things on his own way. You can keep your money. I am my own boss. I been here in Woodstock, been to a big music festival. I seen babies born in the rain here. I found a girl, we're going to Canada to be free.*
> *Spense*

Last night when Brad showed this to Bobbi, he said, "He means the draft. Free from the draft."

"He means more than that," she said.

"I feel like I should go after him," Brad said. "Go up to Canada and—"

"And save him?"

"Maybe."

"We already talked about that."

"But it goes on and on."

Bobbi held the postcard out in front of her and stared at the water rushing down over Niagara Falls. "That's the thing about them all, isn't it?" she said. "If my mother failed in her life, then she had only herself to blame. And Spenser, if he falls short it'll be on his shoulders. And Michael, he went his own way too. You and I are the ones who are dragging our feet."

Brad ate a bowl of cereal, then pedaled his bicycle to the Blue Top Motel with two cardboard containers of Morton's salt in a paper bag under his left arm. He was going to meet someone at the coffee shop. This was a favor to Bobbi. His whole day was planned for him. First this, and then the trip with Page to Bar Harbor. He had a strange feeling about this day. Strange, but satisfying. He felt connected to the world in a way, connected beyond baseball. Riding along, he recalled all that Bobbi said to him about his dream, how his dream held the chance for him to do something for the world. As if when he attained it, he would find himself standing on a new piece of earth. She said he had been set apart for a special reason. Some people, she said, are known by their dreams.

Brad had been following a dream for as long as he could remember. Now it struck him that one day, years from now, his children will say of him, "My father dreamed of playing baseball in the major leagues." And they might be able to say that he had reached his dream, or that he had fallen short. It was all in his hands. But regardless of whether or not he reached this dream, he would be remembered by it.

Then he thought, there are times when you reach for your dream, and times when you let go in order to turn to your children and nourish theirs. You may not let go easily, perhaps only one finger at a time, prying your fingers from their grip on this dream.

In the parking lot of the Blue Top, Brad found Grady sitting on his suitcase smoking a joint. "You're up pretty early," Brad called to him.

"Got a big day ahead of me, you want a hit?"

Brad shook off the offer. "Going somewhere?"

Grady was holding his breath. His eyes were watering. He nodded and then exhaled and told Brad that this was the big day. "I'm taking the express to New York City."

"Traded?"

"Midnight, last night. Sold. They wanted to get rid of me. Nobody wants a troublemaker, nobody but New York City."

"Up or down or what?"

"Up, man!"

"The Yankees?"

Grady shook his head with a scornful expression. "No way, man. I don't play in the Bronx. The *Mets*."

"A contender," Brad mused.

"And I got the feeling that when the rest of you guys are pulling your puds in October, I'll be playing in a fuckin' World Series. Can you even imagine that, a rookie in a World Series?"

"You're lucky."

"Hey, maybe I'll run into you some summer, you never know."

"You never know," Brad said.

Grady shook his head and said, "Man, there's nothing about this scum-bag place I'm going to miss. The minute I'm on that plane it's going to seem like I was never here at all. Hey, look for my name in the papers."

Brad smiled to himself and thought if he ever got the chance to pitch against Grady someday, he would put a fastball about half an inch below his chin.

Walking away from Grady, Brad thought about what it would be like to pitch in a World Series. It was part of the dream he had described many times to Bobbi. The dream draws you into the future, he thought. Away from the past. and once you assent to it, much of life becomes only a matter of waiting to see how things will turn out.

Inside the Blue Top coffee shop Brad found Phillip sitting alone at a booth, pressing a wad of paper napkin against his chin to stop the flow of blood from a sore that had erupted. Brad offered his hand to shake and Phillip took it wearily, his eyes cast down at the floor.

"So," Brad said, "how do you like salt?" He set the containers down on the table.

Phillip nodded tentatively. "I have to go to the men's room," he said. He made a little gesture with one hand and then got up.

"I'll be right here," Brad said. Then he looked around the room, remembering his first days in town, the awful food he had eaten here, how glad he had been to be here. Drinking a cup of coffee here that first night in town he had savored the feeling of absolute freedom. And now as he recalled it, he wondered if this is what Spenser had felt at Woodstock and had tried to convey in his postcard.

When Phillip returned to the booth he had a small piece of toilet paper stuck in the blood on his chin. Brad asked, "Are you ready for this?" Phillip just looked at the containers of salt.

"It's just one way," Brad told him. "You could go home, pack your bags and disappear in Canada."

"I can't do that. My father would kill me," he said. Then he added shyly, "Plus that, Darcy can't go to Canada."

Brad nodded. "Well, look, there's not much to this."

Phillip interrupted. "My father won't be able to tell?"

"They'll reject you for high blood pressure, you'll flunk the physical, that's all. It worked for every guy I knew who tried it." A faint smile came to Phillip's lips. "You'll have a whopping headache for a day or two and you might see double for a while."

"We going to do it right here?"

"They've got eggs here," Brad said. "You like hard-boiled eggs okay?"

Brad ordered six of them to begin with, and when the waitress delivered them he asked her for six more. Then he opened one of the salt containers and filled Phillip's coffee cup.

An hour later both containers of salt were empty and Phillip's face was purple. His eyes were as red as hot coals. Brad led him out the door and drove him to Houlton. He parked in front of the post office. Phillip was in the basement only a few minutes. When he returned to the car he was smiling even though it looked as if the top of his head was going to explode. "I could use a drink of water," he said.

They drove back to the farm. Bobbi and Zoey and Page were in the front yard. She had him all ready for the trip to Bar Harbor. He was dressed in a new flannel shirt and khaki trousers. "Isn't he the cat's meow?" she said.

Brad motioned to Phillip and said, "I'm leaving one ill, ex-soldier in your care."

She took him by his hand. "Make a day of it, you two," she said.

They drove past miles of potato fields not as green as they should have been. Page was silent, looking at them. The sun was high and had lost its early morning chill.

"Isn't this quite a car I own?" Page said.

They passed Tilton's Pond where children were splashing. One boy stood on the end of a wooden dock, his hands pressed together as if in prayer, framed at first in the car's windshield, then a side window, and then in only the rearview mirror. Come on, Brad thought. Dive!

Route 1 was busy with tourists. The traffic swept them along, and their drive began to feel like a journey. It would take four hours, Page told him.

"But that was in the old days," Brad said. "You couldn't go very fast then."

"It was the 1950s," Page said, "and we could go as fast as we pleased."

Soon he fell asleep. When the car shuddered over a bump in the road he opened his eyes and talked in midsentence, like a man waking from a dream. "The whole time I was on the ship it was like this," he mumbled.

"What ship?"

"The Navy ship, the destroyer. We floated to Japan. It felt like this."

Brad waited.

"We were scared. I had Gwen's picture, a little square picture. I begged her for it. But she wouldn't write on the back."

Page stopped, then turned suddenly to Brad. "You know,

you should know all you can about a girl before you marry her."

This seemed to be all he wanted to say. He slept again with the sun on his forehead. Bangor was still an hour south, Bar Harbor an hour east of there. Along the highway there was nothing but trees now. Brad thought, with all the talk of a population explosion, someone ought to come here and see how much space is left.

Outside the town of Carmel they stopped for Page to pee. Brad pulled over to the side of the road. He opened the door for Page and walked with him into the brush, then turned away. Page unzipped his trousers. "That day Lou Gehrig took his last bow," he said, "you should have seen that. There he was in Yankee Stadium. He was a hero there so many times, so many years, and they were clapping and cheering for him again, everybody on their feet. The applause went on and on, it came from heaven. It was never going to stop." Page looked up at the sky, his eyes were wide and bright. "There you were, the greatest ball player who ever lived, and he's dying of that horrible disease and he says: 'Today, today I feel like the luckiest man on earth.' Then he said good-bye to all those people, not just a good-bye to baseball, he was saying good-bye, tipping his cap to this world. I cried for an hour. I stood by the radio crying like a baby."

Back at the car Brad opened the door for him and he took Brad's wrist and said, "You're going to have to nail down the knuckleball, nail it right down so you have it. Your talent will be judged by ten or fifteen years in the big leagues, not ten weeks in Waterboro. You've got to last, you've got to stay around to be remembered in this game."

Later they ate lunch on the side of the road under a stand of dying elm trees. "It's all the exhaust from the cars,"

Page said. He went around examining their trunks, going from tree to tree, running his fingers over the bark. "Someone should have done something sooner."

He wouldn't eat his sandwich, it sat in silver foil on the hood of the car. Looking off into the woods, he said, "The farm is lost." His voice was steady, and he said this as if stating a fact. "It wasn't that I didn't know what I was doing, it wasn't that. I borrowed too much money. I borrowed against the farm too many times."

He stopped and walked up to Brad and took hold of his wrist again. "I have to tell you this so you can tell me what I should do. You're smart, you'll know. I don't want to leave with all these secrets. I'll tell you, and you can help me."

They were driving again when he told Brad that he wanted to talk about Gwen.

"Tell me," Brad said.

"It was nineteen forty-five, in New York City," he began. "I was a buck private on a weekend leave. She was the prettiest girl I'd ever seen. We drank some wine, I loved her right away. When I came back home after the war she had moved out of her place, there wasn't anyone who could help me find her. That was the first time I ever borrowed against the farm. I needed two hundred dollars. I took a room in the city and went searching for her. I kept telling myself I would bump into her on the street somewhere if I kept looking."

Page sat in silence. They pulled into a service station for some water. It was time for Page's medication. Two boys on bicycles were filling their tires with air. Page saw them and smiled. They seemed to distract him from his story. "You'll have children someday," he said to Brad. "You'll love them, they're such characters."

He shook his head and waved to the boys as they rode off. "You can't spend your life worrying about everything. It's a waste, a complete waste. I used to worry about things. A lot of things. The tractor, the bank, the roof on the barn. But it doesn't really matter. When you're sick you see that it didn't really matter at all. You see that you should have jumped up and down a lot more all those days you had the chance."

After a minute, Brad asked him what happened in New York.

Page leaned back against the seat. "We'll be able to see the Ferris wheel from outside Bangor," he said. The medication had made him sleepy. He closed his eyes and said, "I'm going to tell you about New York."

The afternoon was clement. The sun moved ahead of them warming the interior of the car. Page's breathing was unsteady. It suddenly struck Brad how difficult it was going to be to move him to Cleveland. He tried to picture him sitting comfortably in a chair in that city, by an opened window, noise from the ball park a few blocks away drifting in.

For several weeks Brad had imagined this scene, and another at the airport where Bobbi and he would be waiting to meet Mike and his mother and father who had flown in for the day to watch him pitch. Everyone was smiling. A great rapprochement has taken place. A healing. They have all been healed by Brad's dream.

They drove straight east, the sun behind them and the sky ahead bruised purple. "September twenty-seven," Page said when he awakened. He was looking ahead as if for something he had lost.

"What?" Brad asked.

Page straightened in the seat. He put his hands out on the dashboard and leaned forward as if in anticipation of the memory coming back to life. "I was driving down on the twenty-seventh. I had a game on the radio. How old's Bobbi now?"

"Twenty-three."

"Well, it was forty-seven, in the fall, the leaves were almost gone. I was going to Connecticut." He pronounced it incorrectly, hitting all three Cs. "I drove for hours and hours, I remember. I was trying to keep everything straight. It was confusing me."

He told Brad that a letter had come from Gwen that same morning. She had written in the letter that she had a child, his child, and that she had given the child up to the Catholic church. "She sent me the name of this orphanage in Connecticut and told me it was my child. She had changed her mind, she wanted me to have the baby. It's a girl, she wrote.

"She was almost a year old. Gwen thought they'd just turn her over to me, but I didn't have any way of proving anything to them."

His words began to trail away. A hot breeze blew through the car and Brad rolled up his window so he could hear what Page was saying. He asked if he wanted to stop for a while. "We can pull over here."

"I told them I was the father, I said one of your babies is mine, it was a mistake, an accident."

The nuns had been eager to help. The orphanage was terribly crowded. They took Page on a tour of the place.

"Every room was full. All these faces looking up at me. I had no idea who I was looking for. Someone who looked like Gwen or me, I guess. I had Gwen's picture with me.

I can still see their faces looking up, all those eyes, beautiful eyes. Take me, take me, they were saying. I wanted to take them all.

"They had on little blue and white dresses and the older girls curtsied for me. I was no Santa Clause, I had nothing but a hard life to give. But they acted like I was something special. You wonder what children see in you."

He paused and looked earnestly across the horizon. "We'll see it soon," he said. "The Ferris wheel will be right there."

"I'm watching, I won't miss it," Brad said.

"I can't remember how we get there."

"Don't worry, we'll just head toward it once we see it. I'm watching."

Page leaned forward, folded his arms across the dashboard and laid his head down. "These old cars," he said, "can't beat them can you?"

Brad asked him to go on with his story.

"You have a car of your own?" Page asked him.

"No, I've never wanted one."

"Oh boy," Page said with surprise. "I've always wanted wheels under me. You need wheels to get somewhere these days, or else you stay in one place. Women like men with wheels, always have."

He sat up suddenly and raised a finger in the air to underscore what he was about to say. "You have to live your own life, follow your own lights. You'll be fine. But as far as one thing goes, I'd tell any man to be true to the girl he loves. Don't go falling in love with somebody else either. A man just naturally looks around, you see girls all over the place, but going from one to the next doesn't bring anything good, not in the long run. You've got to live for the little things, the regular times with a girl that understands you. A Sunday morning newspaper with the box scores, the kids playing in your bed while you read it, your wife next to you. That's what makes life good."

His hands were purple, the knuckles white. How can he be cold? Brad thought.

"Those children," Page said. "Bobbi Ann was there in a room filled with cribs. There were two to each crib, lying side by side. A whole acre of babies. Each of them had a few little things that someone sent with them, little pieces of jewelry, things they would have later on. Things to wonder about. I went through their things with the nuns.

"And then I knew. I gave Gwen a gold ring before I left for the war, for Japan. She'd sent it along with Bobbi Ann and I recognized it right away. It was there in the bread box with the rest of her things. The nuns put them in the tin bread box I've saved for my baseballs. I remember there was a pair of silk stockings wrapped in silver foil. They were for a full-grown girl, long legs, too. Gwen must have thought they would help someday.

"I had no proof but I said to the nuns, I must have this baby. This is my baby. It was fine with them. I had to fill out the papers, and then I drove home with Bobbi, back to Maine.

"One afternoon, two years later, I came out from the barn with a bucket of fertilizer and Gwen was standing there. She had a red scarf tied around her neck. She smiled at me and looked toward the house. I saw her suitcase standing there by the porch. She said, 'I was hoping I could borrow a pair of silk stockings.' She was just joking with me."

Page stopped to look around for the Ferris wheel. Then he went on. "Bobbi Ann saved them for the longest time. She said she was saving them for a time she wouldn't ever forget. And that bothers me because I can't remember if she ever wore them or not. Maybe she's still saving them. But they were there in the bread box with all the other things from Gwen. There was a few shells from a beach, and a sand dollar that she'd bleached in the sun.

"On the drive home from the orphanage I held one of the shells up to Bobbi's ear. I held it there until she fell asleep. And while she slept, her eyes moved like she was having a dream. It amazed me, because what did she know to dream about?"

Brad was thinking, how could a mother part with her child and how would she select the things to send along with her to the orphanage, how would she ever choose? Maybe you wouldn't do it yourself, maybe you would call in a friend, someone who could be objective. But what would be the point anyway? Was the idea to provide useful things? This would explain the silk stockings. And the gold ring would have some value in exchange, it was something that could be sold for a few dollars as a kind of insurance against hard times. But how do you explain the shells and the sand dollar unless they were sent along to be a reference to something or to the person who gave them.

The shells and the sand dollar would suggest that there had been a trip to the beach, perhaps they'd gone to the beach together, mother and daughter. The mother dipping the baby's feet in the sea for the first time, then covering her toes with warm sand. One day at the beach evoked by a few shells.

Or maybe the mother had gone to the sea alone, and had spent the day walking along the shore, trying to decide what to do. Imagine this mother walking at the edge of the surf, her head down, her heart full of questions, her hands knotted together behind her back, or holding up her dress, hiking it up to her knees. Two shells and one sand dollar chosen from the hundreds of things washed up with the tide.

Brad wondered if maybe Gwen walked along the beach with all her questions, and then out of the blue she paused and bent down and picked up something at her feet. Three moments, three pauses in a long walk along the shore, three questions being weighed and each marked by something belonging to the sea.

"That trip to Connecticut," Page said, "that was the last time I ever left Maine."

When they reached Ellsworth the sky was clear, the air was different in some way. It was salty and it carried the scent of a world at sea. Page rose up and looked out every window.

"Maybe it's been moved," Brad said.

Page looked skeptical. "Well, once they start sending men to the moon I guess folks aren't much interested in Ferris wheels."

It was true, Brad thought. The world was changing and soon nothing would be the same.

From Ellsworth the road to Bar Harbor was bordered by gift shops, snack bars, motels. Everything had the look of transience, like it was built in only a few hours and could be dismantled and carted away at a moment's notice if the tourists were suddenly to go elsewhere.

"All these folks here," Page said, "These folks root for the Red Sox and dream of going to Fenway Park just like I do."

"You'll be there when I pitch in Fenway," Brad said. "You'll be in the front row. I'll get free tickets, won't I?"

"Sure you will," Page said. "You get one ticket for your father too. Get him a good seat behind the first-base dugout, him and your mom. Your brother too. I can see them all there, and you out on the mound burning up the Boston batters, sawing off their bats."

Brad said, "Don't count on my father."

"Oh, but once he sees you out there on the mound it'll all be different," Page said. "You went your separate ways, but it'll work out."

"I'm not sure baseball can work any miracles," Brad said.

Page didn't answer right away. He leaned back again and the sun was on his face. He was thinking about something else. "I can't tell you how many nights in my life I sat in our room by an open window, thinking about what I should have done different, what maybe we could have talked about. There were lots of times when I wanted to say something, but Gwen was in her own world and the closer I tried to get to her, the more she pulled away. And those nights after she was gone, I used to think maybe I was wrong, maybe I should have said something to make her believe in something different."

"You can't make someone believe anything," Brad said.

"But just to try. Just to try anything. You've got to try or else you always wonder. And all those nights sitting up alone, those nights when it would have been so good to have Gwen there. The wind at the window. I'd turn on the radio and sit it on the windowsill facing out, and turn the dial real slow, and listen as closely as I could for some sound of a game from somewhere. The fuzzy sound of the crowd cheering in some far-off city. A ball game coming from somewhere I'd never get to see.

"I remember nights when there would be so much static in the air that I could only get a little bit of real sound, a few words, and then nothing for the longest time. But I'd sit there anyway, waiting for the game to come back. And I'd fill in the space with my own thoughts."

"You still wait for her, don't you?" Brad said.

"I always hoped that one day I'd come out of the barn, carrying something, and there she'd be, standing there just like once before. Now I know I'm going to miss it."

"Bobbi says we keep coming back," Brad told him. "We go on and live different lives, many lives."

Page smiled. "Let me come back a pitcher, then," he said. "A real one like yourself."

They took the back way into town, staying close to the water where lobster boats were tied to the piers, traps piled on their sterns, the paint chipped from their gunwales. In the boatyard an old, gray seagull was resting in the H of the Hardware sign. It had turned the H into a four-poster bed.

Up ahead, a policeman waved them on. He gestured furiously when Brad reached him. "We're looking for the Ferris wheel," Brad said.

"You can't stop here. We're rerouting traffic for the vice president."

"We're not interested in the vice president," Brad said. "We're looking for the Ferris wheel that used to be here."

"There's no Ferris wheel," the man said. "Move along."

Brad turned onto a narrow lane and parked the car. Above them roared the sound of a helicopter landing. Vice President Agnew was heading for the dock where a crowd of people had assembled. "Maybe we ought to go down and see this," Brad said.

"You go," Page replied. "I'll catch forty winks so I can stay awake on the way home."

Brad was a hundred feet from the platform on the dock

when the applause subsided and the vice president began his speech. Then, out of nowhere, a man began shouting at the top of his lungs. The vice president whipped his head around as if he'd been shot. Another shout escaped from the crowd. The next thing Brad knew, a man was running toward him, a man in a priest's collar and army fatigues. The police were gaining on him but he was still shouting, "Criminal! You liar! You're killing us all!"

He was a young man, Brad saw. A man about his own age. There was a puzzling disparity about him. He had a handsome face and the look of a reasonable man, and yet his eyes were wild with rage.

Brad was looking into his eyes when four policemen surrounded the heckler, taking hold of his arms and legs. One man clamped his forearm against his throat. Brad watched his face turning red, then purple. Brad moved toward him, pushing through the crowd. It was like running through water. He stumbled and came down on his knees on the hot, macadam parking lot. At last he reached the man, he reached his foot, his sandal. The body was being dragged away from him, and all Brad could do was hang onto this sandal. He tightened his fingers around it, but in seconds there was nothing left. The stranger receded from him. Brad was looking up into the face of a policeman whose club was tilted down at him. "One more inch and I'll give you the stick, buddy," he said.

When Brad returned to the car, Page opened his eyes and asked at once, "Your contract, how long is it good for?"

"One year, or until I pitch my first inning in the majors, whichever comes first."

"The majors will come first," Page said. "You'll have to ask for what you're worth. Don't ever be afraid to ask for what you're worth."

"We should talk about money," Brad said a moment later. "I'm going to take care of everyone. There will be plenty of money. I'm going to take care of the farm too. We'll spend time there whenever we can."

Page looked at him. "When I think of it, the three of you going to all those cities, all those fine ballparks, oh, it'll be a real show won't it?"

"The farm," Brad said.

"The farm," Page said. "The farm will go on, won't it? I'm the fourth-generation farmer, did you know that? It just keeps going on despite everything."

A group of kids ran past the car, and Brad watched them until they rounded the corner, out of sight.

"Who *is* the vice president now," Page asked. "I can't remember." He didn't wait for an answer, but took a folded sheet of paper from his shirt pocket. When he opened it, Brad saw that it was a page from a newspaper, a page neatly mounted on white paper with a nice black border drawn in by hand. It was Gwen's "Rituals of Summer."

Page read it to him, then said, "This place where she can see the headlights going up and down Cadillac Mountain, it must be a place somewhere near here. She looks across the bay, it says."

Page handed Brad the piece of paper and said, "I thought she might be near here again this summer."

They drove on. The brightness of the day had turned to the west. Brad drove to all the points of land shown on the map. Lamoine, Sorrento, Sullivan, Hancock Point, Welton's Reach, Black Point. Each was a small community, a colony of big summer houses, a dock, a post office, a few tennis courts, children in white shorts and tops, the insignia of a yacht club embroidered on small pennants flying from the masts of boats in the harbor.

The car's muffler had come loose and they rumbled into these sanctuaries, drawing scornful looks from the summer people. It was as if they had come in their old car to lay siege to these colonies, a pirate ship wedging into the harbors with its guns blasting.

Page was watching everything with a look of wonder. They finally made a U-turn in a driveway near a sloping lawn where people had gathered for cocktails. The men wore red trousers, the women long, flowered dresses. "I remember," Page said suddenly, "when I was here with Gwen I felt like a hayseed. But you know, it's only the land that makes these people different from me. One man buys a thousand acres of land and plants potatoes on it. Another man buys one half-acre lot on the shore. A hundred years later the half-acre lot is worth a hundred times more than the whole thousand acres of potatoes. It's a strange thing, but I don't know, Brad, do you think these folks are any happier?"

Another hour passed and the sun became beet red, an enormous ball that seemed to have drawn into itself every bit of light from the water. At a stick-frame general store that also served as a Texaco station, Brad stopped for gas. A small, white-haired man emerged from a screen door that slapped shut behind him. He put on a pair of leather gloves.

"If you wanted to see the cars on Cadillac," Brad said, "where would you go?"

"Grindstone Neck," the man answered without looking up from the meter on the pump. "D'you say five dollars worth?"

Three miles beyond the store they turned right, down a wide road, and drove under beautiful overarching shade trees past old white houses spaced far apart, their windows and walkways trimmed with flowers. The road went on for five miles, then narrowed as it led into the colony of Grindstone Neck. Across from a village green, Brad turned down a dirt lane that took them to a dock that looked right across the bay to the mountain. It rose up ahead like something unreal. "This has got to be it," Brad said. He shut the car engine off. "Want to take a walk?"

"I'll just sit here," Page said.

Brad walked onto the dock where a boy and girl were fishing in bare feet. "What do you catch?" he asked them.

"Mackerel," they said.

"Hey, can you see the cars at night over there?"

"Yep," the boy said. "Watch them a lot."

Brad walked back to the car and found Page turned to the window. He had both hands on the window frame. Across the lane from him, at a cottage whose cedar shingles had turned silver with age, a woman was walking from the porch to the front door. She was bathed in red sunlight. Then the door opened and closed behind her and then, one by one, she drew the curtains at the windows.

"I'm as tired as can be," Page said. "Let's go home."

16

His fever began that week. For five days Bobbi and Brad took turns sitting with him in his room. They put cold cotton washcloths on his forehead. They brought him ice chips in a glass bowl. Zoey picked wildflowers for his room, their stems crushed in her hand.

Then on Thursday, Page seemed unaccountably better. He sat on the porch, and they all listened to a Red Sox game on the radio. When the last out was made Bobbi took him upstairs. She leaned over to kiss him goodnight and he said, "All the times I planted things in the soil here, I was always surprised how many rocks there are in Maine dirt."

"They didn't stop you," she said. "You kept on planting."

"Yes," he said. "But you should think of something else, you don't have to stay here."

"I'll get you more ice," she said.

She went downstairs, and the black dog followed her, her nails clicking on the wooden floors. The house was terribly quiet. Zoey was asleep. Brad was outside walking. Bobbi knew he was thinking about Michael. He had called home again and there was no news. He and his father spoke on the telephone in short, tense sentences that revealed far less than the silent spaces.

Bobbi stood at the kitchen sink looking out at Brad. She was thinking that there would be an end to this, to the disagreement and misunderstanding. She imagined a time when they will all talk to each other.

But even as she thought of this, there was an emptiness hanging over everything, like the emptiness in Brad's shadow spread out behind him under the sweep of the porch light. It was the emptiness of this house, the world her father would leave behind.

Later Page called her back into his room. When she was standing next to him he asked her if she remembered any stories. She asked what kind of stories and he said, "Something about us, just something you remember."

She set the glass of ice chips on the table, and while she fluffed the pillows under his head she told him about the time she first took Zoey into the potato fields and how she reacted to the first scarecrow she saw. "She just walked around it in a circle, looking up at it for the longest time. Then she touched the hem of its coat, and she got down on her knees in the dirt and looked up inside the coat and she gasped, 'Mummy, we're going to have to feed him better.'"

Page smiled. Bobbi filled the silver teaspoon with ice and pressed it against his lips. When his lips opened she could feel the heat rising up his throat.

"What's the first thing you remember?" he asked her.

"About Zoey?"

"About you."

"Oh, I don't know."

"Think hard," he said. "I want to know."

She looked off across the room. At the window the white curtains stirred in the breeze. She looked out to where a star was caught in the top of a maple tree. The screen door wheezed shut in the kitchen.

"What was that?" he asked.

"Brad coming inside."

He looked at her. "You should tell him not to worry. Everything will be all right."

She nodded and said, "I remember sitting in the bathroom watching you while you shaved. You used to make a seat for me on the window sill so I could watch. It looked pretty, the white foam on your cheeks. That was before I'd ever seen snow, but when I saw it for the first time I thought it was the same."

"You don't remember anything before that, though?"

"Not that I can think of."

"Your mother, what about her?"

It took Bobbi a while to put her finger on anything. She was half-listening to Brad's sounds below her and to Zoey turning in her bed down the hallway. But then something came to her. "We built a fort together in the living room. We took all her books down from the shelves and made walls and a tower. It was big enough to sit inside, I remember."

He remembered too. "You were four or five then."

"And the times she read to me at night in your bed."

"Yes."

"They were good times."

"When you see her again," he said, "you must tell her."

He waited a long time before he said there was something he had to ask her about. "It's hard," he said, "it's hard for me to ask, but will you tell me, when a boy makes love to you . . ."

He paused and closed his eyes. "I come from a different time and I don't know about this at all. But does he make it feel good for you, too?"

"Why are you asking me that, Pop?"

"I need to know."

She felt his hand turn within her grasp. "Well, it depends on the boy, but you don't expect too much. I mean, when you love a boy it's nice to be close and—"

He cut her short. "But more than that, I'm wondering—"

"I know," she said. "I know what you're asking, and, yes, sometimes it happens the best way without even trying. If you care for the boy and he cares for you and there's a kind of understanding between you, it's like chemistry."

He turned his head slowly, and she could hear his whiskers brushing against the cotton pillowcase. "We didn't have that," he said sadly.

"It takes two people."

"I've been thinking that I let her down that way, right from the beginning. I never knew much."

"You loved her," she said. "You cared for her."

"But when we were together, I don't know if it felt good for her." His voice trailed off.

"It's not such a big deal," she said. "It's not. Boys think the wrong way. They think that once a girl has done that, once she's made love and he's made her feel good, that she's shared her greatest secret, her greatest intimacy. But it's not true. It's talking with a boy, telling him your dreams and what you think life is about, that's the kind of intimacy that counts. You didn't have that with Mama because she wouldn't let anyone get that close to her."

She lost him to his own thoughts. She let the time pass between them and then tried to call him back. "What do you think the odds are for the Mets anyway?" she asked.

He answered her right away. He said it would depend on pitching. "I like that kid Seaver," he said. "But I'm glad Brad won't be playing in New York. Cleveland is a better place. Old Hank Greenberg's town."

She knew he was wrong about this, that Greenberg never played for Cleveland, but she let him go on. It felt good hearing him talk, even if in illness he was starting to fail.

"Hank was as big as a tree and he had a big heart," he told her. "I remember back in 1947 when Jackie Robinson first broke into the game with the Brooklyn Dodgers, there was all kinds of problems because of his color. The fans were getting on him, some teams even threatened to go out on strike rather than play against him.

"But there was a game early in the season when Hank was playing first base, and he accidentally ran into Jackie on a play at the bag. Hank walked up to him and apologized and asked if he was all right. Then Hank said, 'Don't let them get to you. You keep up the good work, you're going fine.'

"Hank was a man with honor. And he knew what it was like being in Jackie's shoes. Hank was a Jew, he knew the whole story."

Bobbi watched him when he finished. She thought how these old baseball stories ran through him, how many had poured out of him. She wondered how many she had not heard, how many he would take with him and she would never know about.

She waited for him to fall asleep. She watched the ice melt in the glass. She saw the star break loose from the maple tree. She thought about Brad who was waiting for her downstairs. She thought how she wanted their lives to be long. This morning Brad had asked her what it was like to have a child, and she told him it made the passage of time seem different.

"It makes you feel older in a way," she said. "But when I first accepted the fact that Zoey was coming into the world, I thought it was time for me to move away from the center of the stage, off to one side, that I had been the center of attention long enough and now it was someone else's turn. I wouldn't face the audience as much from now on, and my lines wouldn't be as important. I was tired of thinking about myself, though, and it felt fine being replaced."

Suddenly Page opened his eyes. "It's not right," he exclaimed, "what they say to the Negroes and the Jews."

It took him a long time that night, but eventually he told her everything about Gwen, everything he had told Brad. When he'd finished she tried to fit the pieces together.

"You told me once that you remembered her knitting the sweater for me when she was pregnant, that red sweater. You said the two balls of red yarn made you think about how small I was inside her. But you never saw her pregnant."

"It was your brother," he said. "We lost your brother. I remember now, the sweater was for him."

She pushed him then for the whole truth. "No more secrets, then, Pop. As soon as Brad told me what happened when you went to Bar Harbor, that woman in the cottage closing the curtains, I knew. You found her."

He didn't deny this. She said, "All this time you kept telling me she was going to come back here, you kept hoping. Then you find her and you don't even talk to her."

"There was such a beautiful sunset across the water," he said. "And she pulled the curtains."

She didn't have to tell him why she'd done this. They both knew by now that she was a writer, and the world she imagined in her head was always more vivid than the real world. The real world never measured up.

"Why, Pop?"

"Oh, you know your mother."

"No. Why didn't you go up to the door at least?"

He shook his head. "I didn't want her to see me like this. I know how funny I am to look at now."

"I'm going back there," she said. "Maybe not right away, maybe not tomorrow or the next day, but I'm going to find her and I'm going to pull open all her curtains and show her everything she couldn't see."

"I don't know what to say," Page said. "I was going to send Brad to tell her I love her. I still remember the minute I fell in love with her. Things happen in a person's life, and only after you live long enough can you tell that those were the things that changed everything."

Outside, the jets were taking off again. When they were gone there was a great stillness in which Bobbi could distinguish the sounds she would remember all her life. The windmill creaking, the barn door straining on its hinges, Zoey stirring in her bed, her feet searching for the cool places in the sheets.

Bobbi listened and wondered what sounds she had made in her mother's house, her mother's Manhattan rooms, before she gave her away to the orphanage. What a strange thing, to find out at age twenty-three that your life is not at all the way you always believed it was. To find that you were brought into the world and then sent away.

Sitting on her father's bed while he slept, Bobbi thought to herself that children are the one consolation in life, seeing your children at peace and growing in the world. It was what her father wanted for her and what she wanted for Zoey.

But what about her mother, who had given her up twice? Perhaps her life in New York City was elegant in some way; perhaps she hosted parties and entertained friends and couldn't be bothered with a baby to care for. Or maybe she was poor and could see no hope of providing for a child.

But why, then, hadn't she aborted the pregnancy? Why had she gone through with it? And this question brought on the most difficult possibility for Bobbi to consider. Had her mother waited until she was born and then found that she was not what she had expected?

She remembered what it was like after she became pregnant with Zoey. At first she had tried to hide it. She had dreams night after night, awful dreams from which she awoke screaming. It was her mother who finally said to her, "I used to have dreams like you. It's the baby inside you."

When it was out in the open, Bobbi was relieved in a way. But only for a little while. Then her mother began cornering her, trying at first to tell her about her options. She had used the word "options." "You only have three options. You can have this baby, you can have the baby and give it up, or you can end it now."

They had argued. It had seemed to Bobbi that they would never stop arguing. Her mother accused her of promiscuity. Bobbi first tried to deny the accusations but then began fighting back with a defiant, desperate candor, shouting details at her.

Eventually they said nothing to each other, and that was the hardest thing for Bobbi.

Now Bobbi could see that Gwen had accused her of everything she'd once accused herself of.

Bobbi got off her father's bed, and the black dog followed her down the hallway to Zoey's room. She took a stuffed bear from the bureau and placed it under the covers. Then she went into the bathroom and stood in front of the mirror combing her hair for a long time. She braided it on one side. She let the water run until it was very cold, then she washed her face. She stared at her reflection in the mirror, unable to see even the palest trace of her mother. She thought, When I go to see you, I'll wear my hair like this. I will look nothing like you.

At the foot of the stairs Brad stood with his chin on the railing. He watched her descend. Her footsteps on the wooden stairs were almost silent. She leaned down and kissed him. Her face was upside down and the braid hung down. He took it in one hand. He leaned his head against her breasts. She told him exactly what came to mind.

"I wish we had met sooner. I wish I had been a virgin. It's silly, but it would have been one thing in my life that would have pleased Pop."

He let her go outside by herself. The moon was passing across the fields, and Bobbi thought of all the rocks her father had turned over in his soil. She could stay here forever and not be afraid of anything, she thought. But there was a part of her that had already left or that had never belonged or that was ready to leave.

She wandered into the west field, and when she turned back toward the house she saw that Brad had lit a lamp in the window for her. The instant she saw it, she took her first step back to him, wishing she was already there.

It seemed to take forever to reach him. Standing up in his arms she pried off her shoes. He stroked her hair and unbuttoned her clothes. When his fingers grazed her belly she missed a breath. She took hold of his wrist and put his fingers on her. When he touched her it was as if her heart was suddenly shut off. She couldn't move.

She made love with him, then they were still. She was aware of the house around them, the fields outside the walls of the house, her father above them sleeping with a black dog, her daughter sleeping with a bear.

In the moonlight she sat naked in front of Brad, her breasts heavy and firm. She felt the stiffness leaving her nipples.

"I'll drive you there tomorrow," Brad said. "We can leave right now."

"When I go," she said, "I'll have to go alone."

Toward sunrise her father called for her. She had not really slept. She left Brad and went to him. He asked her to stay with him. She brought the black dog up with her onto the bed. "What did she say?" she finally asked him. "When she came back and saw me again, what did she say? Did she pick me up?"

"She was glad to see you," he told her.

"But what did she say, Pop?"

At last he confessed that he couldn't remember.

17

Her mother stood on the cottage porch, her head down, her shoulders pitched slightly forward. She was digging in her purse as if she were searching for keys to the front door. Then, at last, she found a cigarette and lifted it slowly, almost reverently, to her lips and, lighting it, dropped into a wicker chair. It was very early morning. The sun was up but it would be several hours before it climbed above the east flank of Cadillac Mountain and made any difference to this point of land.

From the dock Bobbi watched everything. She felt the sea beneath her, its dampness settling into the soles of her feet, its cadence already running through her. The shifting in the cedar underpinnings of the dock rose up her shins, into her hips. It was like riding on a train.

Driving to the coast in darkness Bobbi had thought of another train, the train that would soon take Brad away from Maine, through Canada and down to Cleveland. And now, standing here looking at her mother, watching the smoke from her cigarette drift off the porch, Bobbi's life seemed divided into parts, four parts. Four people. Each had a pull on her. For a long time she had denied to herself the influence of this woman. But standing here she could feel the force of her presence. It was as if Bobbi had wandered back into her magnetic field.

Well, something had to be done about this. From the moment she'd learned of her mother's presence here she felt herself turning in her direction. Bobbi came here this morning to break the influence, the spell, that a mother casts over her children when she turns her back on them. It is like the spell of royalty, their allure is the direct effect of their aloofness.

From where Bobbi stood her mother looked like hell, unkempt and disoriented. She had always looked so much younger than her father, too young and too pretty for him. It was satisfying to Bobbi to see her like this, and to consider that the distance between her parents might have narrowed a little by now.

She watched carefully. The tall masts tilted all around her in the harbor. She was standing in a world completely foreign to her, a world of bobbing sailboats, a world of summer people. Her mother's world, the world she must have dreamed about. She had once told Bobbi that some people consciously choose unhappiness over happiness in their lives. Bobbi looked over at her on her porch and wondered which choice she had made. Was this her dream, the dream of gaining access to this world?

In the last few days Bobbi had given much thought to the whole idea of dreams. And she had stood on the dock for over an hour trying to organize her ideas and compose a kind of speech to make to her mother about dreams.

Dreams with their power to transform, deceive. You have to know when the dream is worth following. To dream of getting somewhere is not enough, it is just another trip to the moon. But if the dream is noble, if it gives something back to the world, then all the sacrifices made to reach it will be pardoned. If a mother's dream is good, then, in order to reach it, she can walk away from her children and they will find a way to forgive her. She will be redeemed.

Bobbi came here to tell her mother this, to find out once and for all what kind of dream took her away and whether she was ever coming back. She came for explanations, and to explain things.

She wanted to tell her about Brad. For some reason she wanted her to know. Is there ever a time in a daughter's life when she no longer cares what her mother thinks of her?

After her mother left the porch and went inside the cottage another hour passed. Bobbi pictured her sitting next to a lamp, reading. She waited. She decided to wait until the sun reached the cottage. She thought of her father sleeping in his bed. Before she left the house this morning she pulled open the curtains so that he would wake to sunlight.

The curtains. Her mother's curtains were drawn. Bobbi couldn't wait to open them. She would cross the street, and once her mother had opened the door to her and kissed her and invited her inside, she would pull all the curtains open and take a good long look at her mother's face.

The geraniums were dead in the window boxes. They have died from neglect, Bobbi was thinking. All at once she saw smoke seeping out the windows. Smoke billowed out the screen door. Clouds of it poured onto the porch. The cottage looked as if it was on fire.

Bobbi ran the length of the dock and crossed the street at top speed. She climbed the porch steps three at a time and was reaching for the screen door when her mother burst through the smoke with a bundled-up blanket in her arms and a faintly amused expression on her face. She stopped in her tracks, raised her eyebrows and turned one cheek to Bobbi. "Kiss me," she said. "Kiss me, sweetie, before I positively expire!"

She turned away just as Bobbi's lips brushed against her. Bobbi recalled to herself how her mother, when she was feeling her oats, would slip into a theatrical vernacular. "Kiss me, sweetie, before I positively expire," Bobbi repeated under her breath.

"I was trying to get some heat in the damn place," Gwen said. "It's as cold as a grave this morning." And she went on to explain that there was some problem with the damper in the fireplace. "It's that same old problem," she said, and then she backed away wearily and sat down on the wicker chair. Shaking her head, and waving the smoke away with one hand, she set the blanket on her lap, and Bobbi looked down at this. Her mother held it like a baby she had rescued from the smoke.

"Do you know something about dampers or shall I send for a man?" she asked.

"I'll look," Bobbi said.

She went inside. It took her only a few minutes to open the damper in the fireplace and then all the curtains. When she came back onto the porch her mother was gazing off into space with a calm expression. It was as if every one of her mornings began this way, with smoke and a visit from a daughter she hadn't seen in nearly three years.

"These things happen to me," she said with resignation. "I was riding around Beverly Hills in a giant limousine when the engine or something just blew up. We were practically incinerated on the spot."

She looked up at Bobbi and a smile slowly appeared. "Now when did you start wearing your hair in a braid? Don't tell me it's a sign of something, you young people are so angry these days."

"It wasn't ever long enough to braid before," Bobbi said.

Her mother opened her arms and unfolded the blanket, revealing stacks of paper, typewritten pages. "It's so unpleasant, all this anger and rebellion," she went on. "Max was just telling me the other day that one of his sons took over the chapel with a bunch of black students at whatever college he goes to, Williams or one of those. The point is that nobody ever went to the chapel in the first place so nobody knew they'd taken it over. They had to send out word. Oh, I think that's a riot, don't you?"

She stopped and thought a minute. "I always wanted you to go to college somewhere, but now I think they only waste brain power, don't you?"

Bobbi walked over to her chair and stood across from it, leaning back against the railing. "Who's Max?" she asked.

Gwen lifted her chin and looked puzzled. A moment passed. "I was sure you'd met Max," she said to herself. "Well, my life's been so mixed up I can't really remember who's met who and who knows what."

Her voice trailed off, and she looked back down at the pages on her lap before going on. "Max is my agent," she said. "He's in Manhattan screwing somebody." She stopped abruptly and then told Bobbi that she looked pretty.

"In a different way than I'd remembered, but very pretty, very young. You're lucky."

"Who's Max?" Bobbi asked.

Gwen craned her neck and peered in through the screen door.

"Oh, look, the smoke's almost cleared."

"Does Max live here?"

"It belongs to him. Everything belongs to Max. When he gets tired of screwing people in New York City, he'll come back here and screw me. Are you shocked?"

"Is he the one you left with?"

"I hope I haven't offended you. What? Oh God, no. That was nothing. Max is an old friend, very old, very dear. He looks after me, we look after one another. He has a bit of money," she said slyly. "It helps."

She looked past Bobbi then, turning her attention to a mahogany-colored sloop that was raising its sails just off the end of the dock. "You see that boat right there?" Gwen said, suddenly animated. "Pokey Steinbach had the wood for her hull shipped all the way from Africa. Same wood the Kennedys chose for John's casket. Tunisia, I think, or Rhodesia, it doesn't really matter. But if Pokey doesn't take a few lessons, he's going to be buried in that boat somewhere out beyond the bay and we'll never lay eyes on him again."

"That would be ironic," Bobbi said.

"Ironic? Yes, exactly." Gwen looked pleased. "But no great loss to mankind. Tell me though, how did you find me here?"

"Pop came looking for you."

"I don't remember that. He didn't drive his tractor all the way. No, I suppose not." She lit another cigarette and said, "So, did you come to have it out with me, then?"

She raised her hand and stroked the braid in Bobbi's hair. "Did you come to give your errant mother holy hell?"

Bobbi stepped out beyond her reach.

"I'm sorry," Gwen said, "my cigarette smoke probably bothers you."

"I don't think of you that way," Bobbi said.

"As your mother, you mean? I've been demoted, then?"

"I'm sure it doesn't break your heart."

Gwen squared her shoulders. She looked back out at the boat and pointed. "You watch, Pokey's going to try and jibe that boat around the buoy. He's a complete fool on the water." She stopped when Bobbi turned away. "You never know what it is," she said softly, "that breaks a person's heart."

"That sounds too easy," Bobbi said.

"Easy? Well, easy or not, you can stand on my porch telling me how many hearts I broke if you want, but I'll tell you something you don't know. I was young, younger than you are now, and I had all the promise in the world."

She stood up suddenly and walked away.

Bobbi called to her, "And?"

"And nothing," she said over her shoulder.

"Don't say *nothing*."

Gwen turned slowly. She opened her hands at her sides. "And then there was this man standing in my kitchen talking about tractors and fertilizers. He painted a rosy picture."

When Gwen looked back at her Bobbi could feel her mother's eyes warming. "You know, Bobbi," she said. "The best thing I ever did was not try to separate you from your father. You think of me leaving you behind, but it really wasn't that. You belonged with him, not me."

After a long silence Bobbi said, "So, does that get you off the hook, then?"

Gwen regarded her with a skeptical expression and didn't answer. "Have you ever thought about the nursery rhymes a mother sings to her child? I missed out on that, but you sang them to Zoey. All the children are taught the most dreadful nursery rhymes. Jack falls down and cracks open his head. The old lady who lives in a shoe and has so many children she doesn't know what to do, so she gives them all broth without any bread and whips them all soundly and sends them to bed.

"And Peter, Peter, pumpkin eater has a wife and can't keep her, so he puts her in a pumpkin shell and there he keeps her very well. Ah, now that's what your father needed, a great, insurmountable pumpkin shell."

"He would have done anything to keep you."

"We had nothing in common."

"He would have changed for you."

"I wouldn't have changed him for the world. He was one of a kind. And all my life I've made it a point never to try and change anyone. But these nursery rhymes, they're all so awful, and I've been thinking that they're intended to be awful as a kind of way for mothers to prepare their kids for all the disappointment that lies ahead. I think it's really a pretty good idea, don't you?"

"We weren't prepared to lose you."

"Oh Bobbi, I make no excuses for my exit, but I'd thought that was all over and done with by now."

"What about the other baby, what about that?"

"Your brother," Gwen said slowly. "A moment of delirium."

"That's not good enough."

"No? But it's true, perfectly true. I was careless. We're all careless. Some of us are capable at any time in our lives of making a complete mess of everything in five minutes."

"Your life was already a mess."

"Let me finish. It was a moment of weakness. It was just easier for a moment to stop saying no. And I was willing to leave it all up to the gods. When I lost that baby there was nothing holding me back."

"What about us?"

"I had to go."

"What did you want?" Bobbi asked her.

She waited and thought and then smiled derisively. "Maybe just a thrill," she said. "But why don't we take a walk together? Let me put my face on and we can take a walk down by the water. You never get to the sea."

Bobbi waited on the porch while Gwen sat at a table just inside the screen door putting on lipstick, eye shadow, rouge. She called out to Bobbi, "Talk about a losing battle."

Soon they were walking in the sand, their shadows falling off to the west, onto the rocks. The sun was on its side in the water. "We could get some mussels and cook them for lunch," Gwen suggested. And then she remembered she had to go somewhere for lunch. "It's one of those things I ought to just back out of. How often do I get to see you?"

"It's all right," Bobbi said, "I'll have to get back anyway."

"I suppose. But you know, all this talk about dreams and broken hearts, it's all terribly complicated to me now. For me, it was much simpler than that. It was 1949, the world was as perfect as it's ever going to be, Bobbi. The depression was over, the war was over, the cure for polio soon to be discovered in a drop of water on a sugar cube. But I wasn't content. Definitely *not* content. I wanted big things in my life."

When they passed a couple sitting in the sand with their child, Gwen looked back and said how lovely the child was. "Perfect," she said with delight.

"Zoey would have loved you forever," Bobbi said. "And forgiven you."

"Forgiven," Gwen said. "We're shooting my theory all to hell. I have this theory, you know, that when people get together after a long silence, a long time, they're determined to discuss something but they end up talking about the weather, about anything but the thing they'd wanted to talk about."

"Not everyone," Bobbi said.

"Well, in my theory it's everyone. You know when you're young you figure that the time will come when you've gotten old and when pride and vanity are long gone and you'll be able to discuss all the old forbidden things with your old friends from childhood. But you can't. Those things never get discussed."

"Anyway," she went on. "Let me just say this, another theory. In our world there's no greater crime than a mother abandoning her children. That's what everyone says. But I—" she stopped suddenly.

Bobbi waited, then stopped walking. She watched her mother walk away. She called, "You what?"

Gwen turned back with a smile. "Oh, everyone wants to be able to explain everything about people. Why they do the crazy things they do. Some people are too complex for that."

She turned her shoulders and hips and faced the water as if addressing someone at sea. "Those people you can't explain so easily, they're adding to the mystery of life, the great, wonderful mystery."

"Your theories," Bobbi said, "they don't hold any water. It's the same old thing for you, you're like Daisy, you're too careless to be depended on."

Gwen lifted her chin again in that theatrical way. The wind caught in the collar of her blouse, then passed. She looked enchanted when she turned to face Bobbi. For a moment Bobbi was certain that she would tell her it was true, that she was like Daisy. But she didn't say anything. She just stood still as if luxuriating in the idea that she might be like a character so real and resonant in her imagination.

"You've taken it as a compliment," Bobbi said.

"Well, I always forgave Daisy," she said. "But really, I'm more like Gatsby himself. I've seen life through a kind of romantic film. I *had* one kind of life, and I imagined another entirely. I wanted to find it."

"Did you?"

She smiled and said she wasn't sure. "But to me, the thought that my life could be completely different tomorrow from what it was today, that thought was always too powerful to resist. The freedom to change. And those people in your father's world hate change more than anything."

When they reached the dock Gwen was first to spot a car parked on the lawn of her cottage. She yelled and waved to the driver. A horn blew back at her and she turned to Bobbi with the clear smile of a child. "They haven't forgotten me," she said. "They've come to take me to lunch."

"I should go," Bobbi said.

"Why don't you wait for me, I won't be long."

Why *does* she wait? For one last look, for something more?

She stands in the sunlight going through the papers her mother had rescued from the smoke. Dozens and dozens of copies of the newspaper piece she had sent them, "Rituals of Summer." Other pages with a few typed words, false starts. Bobbi is looking for her name, her father's name, among these words. There is nothing, no sign of them.

At last she walks around the rooms of the cottage. She opens a drawer. It contains only an acorn that rolls away like a marble. In the bedroom, the bureau smells like mothballs. One red dress hangs on a rusty hook in the closet. The rest of her clothes are on the floor in a heap. Bobbi stares down at this for the longest time, trying to figure out why it makes her sad to see her mother's things in a pile like this.

One by one she hangs up the dresses, folds the blouses. Picking up a blue sweater, she runs her fingers over three letters embroidered in pink thread. GLP. Tiny letters that would stand over her mother's heart to identify her in some way. The same letters are sewn on each blouse, on a pair of gloves, a scarf, a handbag.

In time there was a sound on the porch. Bobbi found her mother sitting crosslegged on the bottom step, her feet in the grass. Her legs were bare, very tanned. Her toenails were painted red. "I threw my shoe into the Atlantic," Gwen said. "The heel broke off again. That's three times. What are you going to do?"

Gwen called out "Did you descend from a pedigree of Peterson watchmakers. Your grandfather, his father. Men who made all the pieces fit together, isn't that funny?"

She pointed out to the water. "I once found a watch in the sand on a beach I used to walk along, far from here. It had your grandfather's stamp on the case, a watch he made. It was nice, it sort of gave him a place in the world."

"And you."

She laughed a nervous laugh and said, "Bobbi, there's no such thing."

She told her she was the kind of person who never found a place. "I'm one of those people who gets tricked by life. I imagined the first snowfall of winter and when it came, it was never as good as I imagined it would be. I went on being tricked."

"You never gave enough."

"Didn't I?"

"Did you ever give anything?"

"I gave what I could."

Gwen stood up. She walked over to Bobbi and touched her braid again. "Look, my sin is this. I had no business marrying your father but I did anyway. I wasn't cut out to have a child, but I did anyway."

"Why didn't you just have an abortion?"

Gwen raised her eyebrows, then smiled at Bobbi with satisfaction. "What a mistake *that* would have been," she said.

There was silence. Then Gwen said, "We should get Pokey to take us out for a little sail."

"I know what it was," Bobbi told her. "What you always thought of as happiness, it was only excitement. Pop never had much excitement to offer."

Gwen seemed to be thinking about this. "There's a wonderful poem by Yeats, didn't I ever read it to you? He's writing about his friends from boyhood and he says, 'Hardly a finish worthy of the start.' It's all about people who threw away their chances, who wasted their promise."

Bobbi cut her off. "You think of me as a girl who'll marry a snowmobile salesman because he has long sideburns like Elvis Presley or something—"

"No," Gwen said. "But anyway, why don't you beat the odds? Why don't you let go of things you can't change, and just go out and make a great ending out of a bad start?"

Bobbi looked at her mother a moment. Then Gwen embraced her and Bobbi pressed against her.

After this Gwen was smiling again, that same wide, clear smile of a child. "You don't have to look so doleful," she said. "And don't worry about me either. Think of it this way: There's not a soul on earth I have to lie to anymore. I don't have to pretend anything."

They said good-bye. Bobbi had already started across the lawn when Gwen called to her, "Your father, give him my, you know, my best."

18

"Think of it," Page had once said to Brad, "the old folks sitting up at night with their radios, staying up long enough to hear the final scores from all over the countryside, not going to sleep until the games are tallied up. That voice summing up all the scores for me. Until I hear that, I don't feel like I can sleep."

Now in late August Brad and Bobbi take a transistor radio with them everywhere they go at night. Brad's time is near, they both know it. And so events taking place in the big leagues are even more important now. After dark on the radio these games being played throughout America are part of some great nocturnal enterprise Brad will soon be part of, an enterprise with the force and tradition to consolidate the entire republic on a summer night.

They walk through the potato fields and picture the ballparks manicured, illuminated by cool, white light, the grass greener than anywhere else on earth. Looking down from another planet these fields are laid out in a constellation that makes stars of Boston, New York City, Philadelphia, Chicago, Baltimore, Milwaukee, Cleveland.

Bobbi can almost imagine herself looking down at Brad from some other planet. She can picture him walking under the bright lights toward the pitcher's mound, his dark hair sticking out below his cap.

Tonight they walked down the Odlin Road, under starlight and a faint sickle of moon, heading for town. They were talking about guilt, the guilt Page felt. Bobbi felt it too. Brad said, "I don't know anyone anymore who doesn't blame himself for something." He said he had always wondered why some people can breeze along anyway and others are destroyed by some pain or regret.

"Maybe it's just that some people don't feel life so deeply as others," Bobbi said. "What I mean is some people don't pull things apart to find what's wrong, what's missing. I want Zoey to feel everything, though, to pull it all apart."

"Even if it tears her up inside?"

"Yes. You just have to try to give your kids faith to offset the disappointment."

"Faith in what?" he asked her.

"Maybe in nothing more complicated than a curveball or another chance. That's enough though, isn't it? I mean faith doesn't ever have much evidence to go on. There's never more than a sliver of proof or it would be too easy."

"And guilt," Brad said. Then he dismissed that. "I don't want to think any more about the guilt."

They wondered if Senator Kennedy was to blame for Chappaquiddick. The world now, it seemed, was consumed with questions of guilt. They both were certain about so little. But with everything that was happening in the world, a lot would be said about these days, they both knew this.

"I want to remember everything exactly as it was," Brad said. "The feeling that everything was possible."

Bobbi thought to herself, Well, of course we'll remember the truth about these days, but then she admitted that, like everyone else, they would amend and delete the truth to make it into whatever they would need to recall. "So much is uncertain," she said.

He asked her what she was thinking about.

"Your brother," she said. "Pop. You."

"Don't worry about me," he said.

The first streetlight was up ahead. It threw an oblong of light on his face. They went down Cedar Street, then turned onto Augusta Avenue. She stopped in front of a large frame house, painted white with three tall white columns in front. The rooms facing the street were lighted dimly. People inside passed slowly by the windows. Outside on the front porch two men stood smoking. They looked uncomfortable in their suits and neckties.

"Do you want to come with me?" Bobbi asked Brad. He was puzzled. He followed her inside anyway. They stood in a dark, murmurous room perfumed by flowers. Bobbi leaned back against the door frame and steadied herself. Brad followed her eyes to the front of the room to a casket sitting on a small wooden stage. She stared at it for the longest time, then said, "I'm going to look in." She started across the room. He followed. He stood next to Bobbi as she leaned over and looked into the casket. A woman approached them.

"Did you know my sister?" she asked.

"No," Bobbi said, "we were passing by and we thought—"

"Oh, well, that's all right. Did you know a poet once wrote a poem for my sister? Would you care to have a copy?"

They saw that she clutched a small stack of printed pages against her chest.

"We'd love to have one," Bobbi said.

Outside, under the fluorescent light of the Red & White Hardware store, they read the poem. It was entitled "For Margaret Horgan." Bobbi began reading it, but then she handed it to Brad and asked if he would read it out loud.

His voice was the only sound on the street: "It was 1927 and a fisherman from the Yarne Islands was out too late hauling bass, mackerel, sturgeon, and his family from poverty when he heard something that had only enchanted him in stories, the pleasant and throaty buzz of an airplane. Things happened so fast, for a moment he lost sight in the brilliant searchlight, as the plane dipped and circled his catch, and fighting through the engine in an accent he didn't know was American a voice screamed, 'France?' And he waved an oar southeast as the plane vanished, leaving only its buzz loitering a moment before it too hesitated into the sea. How could he tell this story, he wondered, which is just what he did next day in the same boat with Margaret, his favorite daughter, who leaned into the sea with a scythe lopping the tops off seaweed to fertilize their garden that had the choicest vegetables in Ireland. Margaret knew about the Irish Sea and her father who worked every day since he was ten, but somehow still managed to cross the world three times, fight in two wars, and read in the original all of the great Greeks and Latins. So she enjoyed the story and asked only those questions which kept him going. Ten years later, seven of her sisters were in Albany, and Margaret was a cleaning woman for the wealthiest family on Long Island who were out one Sunday when the doorbell rang. Margaret answered, and the man standing there told her to say Colonel Lindbergh stopped over. When he was halfway down the path she ran after him and recounted her father's story. "Yes, Yes!" he cried, and he threw his arms around her and called on God five times before he gave a hug for her father and a hug for herself, though from the few pictures we have of Margaret in her twenties this hug was clearly for Lindbergh as well. The years pass and her brogueless grandchildren don't believe her when she tells of the history of this first flight which is found in no book."

When Brad finished reading there was the kind of silence that comes after a bell is struck. Brad said with wonder, "He redirected Lindbergh to Paris, out there fishing in the dark. Can you see him raising his oar toward Paris?"

He didn't have to say anything. She could see that this is what he wished to achieve in his own life, the ability to point the way for people, for his brother and his mother and for her. He wanted it badly, wanted it with a pure hot eagerness.

Later that night she told him why she wanted to go to the funeral home. She had never seen a dead person before, and she wanted to see one so that she could put the experience behind her. "When Pop dies," she told him, "I don't want to have to deal with death too. I don't want death to get between us, but I can't really explain it."

He said he knew what she meant, she didn't have to explain anything.

There was an early frost the morning they buried Page. Two nights later they bundled up Zoey for the trip to Brownville Junction. They met the train at midnight and sat in old, upholstered seats while Maine turned into Canada beneath their feet. Zoey slept in Brad's arms. He looked down at her from time to time, always with the same expression of pleasure and disbelief.

"I remember when she came out of me," Bobbi said. "Her eyes were wide open, and there was this look of surprise on her face. Not surprise that she was here on this planet, but that she was back again so soon. It was as if she had lived another life here."

She talked for a long time about her daughter, how she would wave her hands back and forth when she was an infant. "It was as if she was conducting music."

Brad had note cards in his pocket. The last thing Page had told him was how to pitch to each of the Boston Red Sox batters. He had Brad write it all down. "It must have been hard for him," Brad said, "to think of me pitching against his favorite team."

A conductor passed down the aisle speaking something in French.

"Canada," Bobbi said.

They were both thinking the same thing. They thought of Spenser, and of the other soldiers hiding out here in this vast, safe country where life still went on randomly, out of reach of cities and certain failed beliefs.

On this old train they were riding out the last days of a decade, into a future. They spoke again of Ted Kennedy and Neil Armstrong who were behind them with the summer. They spoke of the war, of how it would eventually end and how it had changed so much around them. The anger and defiance of their generation had brought a new scrutiny upon everything, even love. Some of the mystery had been taken from love, perhaps the myth, and even the honor, too. But they were *free* to love, to do anything.

Neither of them had ever felt so free. The defiance had set everyone free to find or to lose oneself, one's place, one's disillusionment.

Talking of disillusionment, Brad said, "I remember the day my father took me into the city to this little company that made trophies. It was a filthy little brick building in an alley, and we stood at one of the broken windows looking in. These men were working at benches, and they were surrounded by thousands of trophies. There were broken ones all over the floor. The men were stepping on them. Up until then I'd always thought my trophies were special. It was my father's lesson in humility and disillusionment."

They were riding into the future, the old world racketing beneath them. The future. The next war. The bomb. Brad told her that at Princeton he had read this letter from Einstein saying he knew what his formula would mean, but it was too late, he couldn't turn back the knowledge.

"But it means we're all the same now," Bobbi said. "In the future, all of us will be in the same boat. The people in Washington won't be able to order people off to some war, they won't be able to hide from the bombs. The congressmen, the Supreme Court justices, the generals' wives and mistresses will be as vulnerable as the soldiers. Maybe it will make everyone think twice."

She looked down at Zoey sleeping. "By 1990 she'll be about my age, all the problems will be new to her."

"By then," Brad said, "I'll be in my second life, out of baseball." He turned to the window. "I don't want to think about it, not now."

They both wanted things to slow down.

Under moonlight the lakes in Canada were as smooth as glass. Everyone on the train was sleeping. Bobbi woke Brad to tell him how happy she was. "We must never be nostalgic," she said. "Like you said, we have to look forward. They'll say all sorts of things about these days, about how these were the best days. They always say that. But I don't want us to keep looking back. I want the best days always to be ahead of us."

EPILOGUE

People told Bobbi Ann and Brad they would live a charmed life together. But a charmed life is one of the trickiest things in the world to be sure about. Lives become so secure and settled, and then with the arrival of one day's mail or the sudden ring of the telephone, they can be thrown into unspeakable disorder.

Charmed or not, Brad and Bobbi will go on living their lives and changing. And much will depend upon their ability to leave the past behind.

Brad's mother will die of alcoholism at the age of fifty-six. Brad's father will bury her in Westchester County. Then he will buy a sports car and grow his hair long and head to Florida in retirement. Having practiced law for so many years and having relied on facts to build his fortune, he will never learn that facts seldom add up to the truth. Living in Clearwater, Florida, he will often attend spring training baseball games, a gray-haired man in a box seat, telling strangers about his son who played major league baseball. He will buy them beers and brag to them about his son, always omitting the fact that he never once went to see him pitch in the big leagues.

Colonel Ellis will never get any closer to Florida than Atlanta, Georgia. He will reside there and sell real estate and establish himself as a regular customer at the Peach Tree Bar where, for a few minutes on certain afternoons, he will talk as if he had figured out his life and the bartender will pretend he hasn't heard it all before.

Bobbi Ann and Brad will be married before a justice of the peace on Weymouth Street in Cleveland, Ohio, on September 11, 1969, two hours before Brad records his first victory in the big leagues. He will pitch a complete game that afternoon, striking out nine, walking two, and giving up six hits and three runs. He will pitch five seasons with the Indians and then, on the day President Nixon resigns from office in 1974, in the seventh inning of a game against the Kansas City Royals, he will throw a curveball to a right-handed rookie batter from the Dominican Republic. As he releases the ball he will hear a popping sound in his shoulder, and the curve will not break but instead will strike the batter on his temple, knocking him off his feet. The batter will suffer a concussion and will never play baseball again because of blurred vision.

Brad will be placed on the disabled list for fifteen days before his shoulder is completely healed. But in his next pitching appearance he will walk seven men in two innings and will be taken out of the game. He will finish the 1974 season with four straight losses all because of wildness. He will throw balls into the dirt and over the catcher's head. No one will be able to explain this. The Cleveland Indians will send him to their Triple-A minor league team in Elkhart, Indiana, but when his control doesn't return in twelve weeks they will trade him to the Pittsburgh Pirates organization, who will sell him to the Houston Astros before finally in 1976 he drops out of baseball completely. Two years later he will try to make a comeback in the semi-pro Twilight League in Portland, Maine. He will walk the first six batters he faces and then he will leave the field. On his way to the locker room he will give his glove away to a boy in a wheelchair whose father has dressed him in a New York Yankees uniform.

From his earnings as a big league pitcher Brad and Bobbi Ann will buy the farm in Waterboro, though they will rent it to Darcy after her third divorce, choosing instead to settle in the suburbs of Boston in the town of Natick because of the good public school system there. Zoey and Katrina and Michael will eventually go off to college at Plymouth State, Mount Holyoke, and the University of Rhode Island respectively. Zoey will talk about becoming a writer and will fall in love easily and often. Katrina will drift from art history to anthropology and will hang around for a while with a boy from Amherst College who plays soccer and claims to be a Marxist. Michael will major in business administration and will work during the summers in a resort hotel on Martha's Vineyard.

Bobbi Ann and Brad will be the kind of parents who call their kids every couple of weeks to make sure they're all right. They will make a big thing of Christmas together and ski weekends in Vermont, and they will both be sad when the kids start to make other plans. But life will go on. Brad will sell cars for a while, and then skis, and then catamarans, and then he will settle into a teaching and coaching job at a good prep school. Bobbi will take ballet lessons and do volunteer work at the hospital in Wellesley and will canvass her neighborhood in support of a nuclear freeze. She will always think of her husband as a boy at heart, and this will please her. She and Brad will garden together, take up golf, and rent a cottage on Cape Cod for three weeks every August. Sitting out on a porch at night under the stars they will listen to Red Sox games on the radio, and this ritual will remain satisfying to both of them, retaining the restful reassurance of a story being read aloud.

As for the past, they will deal with it in their individual ways. Bobbi will write her mother from time to time suggesting she come visit them. She will put down on paper once that the important thing in life is for parents and children to find a way to pardon each other for their failings and misunderstandings.

Brad will face the past on his own terms, much the way he once faced batters at Veterans Park, with a mixture of determination and wonder. Middle age will depress him from time to time, and he will rely on golf and skiing and jogging to bolster his spirit.

One fall weekend in 1982 he will drive Bobbi and their children to Washington, D.C., and they will stand together before a black granite wall near the Lincoln Memorial, and each of them will run their fingers over the engraved letters of Michael Schaffer's name.

As for Spenser, Brad and Bobbi will never know whether he found happiness beyond baseball, whether or not he went on to live in a house with more than one floor.